Sherouq Elmasry is an art historian, who graduated from Rome, Italy. She currently lives in Dubai with her family, where she works as a self-taught artist and aspiring fiction writer.

Sherouq Elmasry

NARA

AUSTIN MACAULEY PUBLISHERS™
LONDON * CAMBRIDGE * NEW YORK * SHARJAH

Copyright © Sherouq Elmasry 2022

The right of Sherouq Elmasry to be identified as author of this work has been asserted by the author in accordance with Federal Law No. (7) of UAE, Year 2002, Concerning Copyrights and Neighboring Rights.

All rights reserved. No part of this publication may be reproduced, stored in a retrieval system, or transmitted in any form or by any means, electronic, mechanical, photocopying, recording, or otherwise, without the prior permission of the publishers.

Any person who commits any unauthorized act in relation to this publication may be liable to legal prosecution and civil claims for damages.

This is a work of fiction. Names, characters, businesses, places, events, locales, and incidents are either the products of the author's imagination or used in a fictitious manner. Any resemblance to actual persons, living or dead, or actual events is purely coincidental.

The age group that matches the content of the books has been classified according to the age classification system issued by the National Media Council.

ISBN – 9789948817321 – (Paperback)
ISBN – 9789948817338 – (E-Book)

Application Number: MC-10-01-8463245
Age Classification: E

Printer Name: iPrint Global Ltd
Printer Address: Witchford, England

First Published 2022
AUSTIN MACAULEY PUBLISHERS FZE
Sharjah Publishing City
P.O Box [519201]
Sharjah, UAE
www.austinmacauley.ae
+971 655 95 202

I would like to thank my soulmate and husband for profoundly believing in me and in my ability to become a published author. Without his support and motivation, this book would have still been locked away in my drawer.

Special thanks to my dear father who paid attention to my dream of becoming a writer. I also wish to thank my best friend who accompanied me through the development of the story and its characters, and who criticized every chapter to make me a better writer.

I am also grateful to my first readers who gave me a tingle of excitement; without them, fear would still have stopped me from going forward with my writings. Special thanks to my editor who blew life back into the characters and helped me give birth to this book.

Last, I am grateful to my readers, Shaima Demas, Mayada Darwish, and Hebeeba Mourad, for all of their support and time.

Table of Contents

One: A Recurring Dream	9
Two: Mpilo Nsonowa	18
Three: The Blue Water	27
Four: Flight	37
Five: Mark's Time	47
Six: The Healer	60
Seven: The Pick	73
Eight: How Much Time Is Left	82
Nine: Leaked	90
Ten: Answers in the Library	101
Eleven: The Riddle	116
Twelve: White Paper	127
Thirteen: Past Pardons	135
Fourteen: The Seven Blue	150
Fifteen: Last Words	162
Sixteen: The Battle of the Valley	172
Seventeen: The Healer's Choice	180
Eighteen: Departure	186

One: A Recurring Dream

"You know that place between sleep and awake, that place where you still remember dreaming? That's where I'll always love you. That's where I'll be waiting."

— J.M. Barrie, Peter Pan

He visited her again.

She kept having the same dream since she'd moved to Nara last year. A little boy stood on a path between the thick trees of the jungle, engulfed by fog at midnight. Despite the haziness, his deep brown eyes were always clear. He reached out a hand and beckoned her to follow him, then disappeared into the forest. But, her feet were always stuck, firmly rooted to the ground. The boy reappeared and stretched out his arm towards her, but the distance between them grew until she could no longer see his face. She tried to open her mouth and call out for him, but her voice was muffled as the white fog thickened and the little boy vanished.

Rose Peterson awoke in her bed, blinking as the soft morning sunshine snuck in through her open window. Sighing, she pushed herself up against the pillows and looked out of the window at the swaying mahogany and teak trees, wondering yet again of her strange dream. She didn't know what the little boy was trying to show her, but she could see the hope in his eyes. But hope about what?

After months of mystery, Rose finally decided it was time to understand. She decided to tell someone who knew all about dreams, who just might be able to explain it to her. Her eyes glanced at the alarm clock on the bedside table then back to the window, grateful for the spring vacation. Her last year of high school was just about to end.

It had been almost a year since her life had completely shifted. Rose had moved to Nara, a country in West Africa, with her father and stepmother. Her father had a construction company, and Nara was flourishing with new developments. Rose could not deny that she missed her home and life in London, but Nara had been doing her well, especially after losing her mother a couple of years ago. The loss had depressed her, so Rose was grateful for the change of scenery and lifestyle. Yet, she knew it would still take some time until she was back to her old self.

A knock on the door interrupted her thoughts.

"Good morning, love," her father said as he entered the room wearing a white linen shirt and matching pants that deeply contrasted with the dark shadows beneath his eyes. "We're going down to the village for some errands. Angelina needs the post office as well. Do you feel like joining?"

Rose paused for a moment, unenthusiastic about accompanying her stepmother, Angelina, but she remembered whom she needed to see. "Yes, I'll be down in ten minutes."

He nodded and Rose watched him leave the room.

Stepping out of bed, Rose pulled on a simple sleeveless pink dress and stood in front of the mirror to apply sunscreen all over her exposed arms and face. Her usually pale skin was lit up with a light tan and freckles, especially across her high cheekbones. The sun also gave her chestnut hair a bright glow, complementing her hazel eyes.

With a last glance at her reflection, Rose made her way downstairs. The smell of scrambled eggs led her to the kitchen where she found her father sitting at their big oak table with the newspaper glued to his face and Angelina sipping tea out of a porcelain cup. Luba, the housekeeper, smiled at Rose and brought her a plate. Luba was a local of Nara, and a very old woman who used to live by herself at the borders of Nara, since she had escaped the horrors of the civil war twenty years ago. Her mass of white curly hair and colorful wooden accessories always caught Rose's attention.

"Look, Bill! Someone is honoring us with her presence," Angelina said from behind her cup.

Rose could feel her eyes follow her as she kissed her father's cheek. Angelina's green eyes pierced her from behind her fake eyelashes, and then looked back down at her cup. Her silicone body was barely covered in a see-through chiffon dress that flowed with the slightest move.

Half smiling, Rose sat in front of her breakfast plate. She certainly hoped to avoid Angelina as much as possible that day. At first, Angelina's distaste for her troubled Rose, who tried to mend things. But, she quickly realized that Angelina was arrogant and unwilling to change. When Rose tried talking to her father about it, she found out that Bill never saw Angelina's negativity.

It was still puzzling for Rose as to why her father had married Angelina so quickly after her mother's death? Regardless of Angelina's arrogant personality, her outer-shell was alluring. Rose kept hoping that her father had seen something good beyond Angelina's looks.

A small sigh escaped her as her mind started drifting off to the warmth of her mother's embrace. She would do anything to feel Elizabeth's arms around her again and breathe in her light powdery smell.

"You're playing with your food again," Angelina said, popping Rose's nostalgic bubble.

"I'm not hungry," Rose replied.

"Food is good for you, you know," Angelina continued. "You're starting to look like a skeleton."

Glancing at Bill and finding him deeply immersed in the newspapers, Rose looked away from her stepmother and decided to ignore the false, charitable comment. Bill suddenly put down the papers and took off his glasses. "Let's go."

Picking up her backpack, Rose followed them out of the house and into Bill's red Jeep Wrangler. She sat in the backseat and looked out the window as the car bumped its way out the dirt path that led onto the cemented road. Nara's weather was starting to cool these days, with the occasional cold breeze that brought the scent of the Atlantic Sea not far from Rose's house. The village was just a fifteen-minute drive from their house, but it seemed to take longer as Rose tolerated Angelina's constant complaints of how hot it was and how her skin was acting up. Rose tried to block out her voice and found herself once again thinking about the little boy that popped up in her dream. She wondered what Akita would say about it.

Once the car made a stop in front of the crowded street, Rose climbed out the Jeep and took in the smell of monkey fruit and guava that filled the air. She smiled as she watched the local children dressed in their tribal costumes playing around. Nara's people were different than the people in London. Their hospitable smiles and generosity fascinated Rose ever since she had stepped foot in the country and mingled with its locals. Of course, there was the language barrier that sometimes created misunderstandings, but Rose had been doing her best to learn the basics of the Naryan language. Even though her school required all international students to attend Naryan Language classes, it was hard to implement it in reality. She was thankful for Akita who had helped her grasp some of the fundamentals. Being the only local librarian around, Akita had been a friend and confidant to Rose since the moment they met at the beginning of the school year. Rose enjoyed lazy afternoons curled up in her favorite corner and soaking in the translated Naryan books.

Informing Bill that she needed to visit the crafts store and library, Rose slipped away and crossed the crowded road to the other side of the village. She passed a coffee shop, resisting the intense smell of freshly brewed beans, and passed the village's apothecary shed, a place her father warned her about. She was aware of Nara's unusual medical approach, and that always piqued her curiosity. The people who owned the apothecaries were widely known as witch doctors. They were believed to not just heal physical ailments, but also suck the evil spirits out of their patients.

Rose shuddered at the thought as she entered the small crafts shed that displayed all sorts of unusual crafts tools and a collection of handmade festival masks. The scent of clay, raw parchment paper and oils filled her lungs as she picked up some red paint that she had ran out of. It was easy to lose oneself among all the interesting artistic approaches, but she knew it was better to spend all her remaining time with her friend.

Putting her paint in her basket, Rose crossed the dusty street to the adjacent shed that was teemed with books. This was the village library; a small cramped space that held more books than was expected. It was by far her second favorite spot in Nara, after the pond in the forest. Gently, she pushed the door open and was welcomed by the stuffy scent of leather bindings and printed paper. Rose's face beamed upon seeing the librarian.

"*Jambo*, Akita."

Akita stood behind the rather tall wooden desk and smiled.

"*Jambo*, Rose." Her voice was stronger than her appearance. Her body was draped in a worn blue shawl and a black fabric dropped off her shoulders and swept the ground as she walked. Heavy beads dangled and rattled from her massive dark hair. "'ow is you?" Rose loved her accent.

"I'm good." Rose propped herself on the small bamboo chair next to Akita. "Here, I brought you some beads for your wondrous hair collection."

Akita's face brightened up as she accepted them. "I 'ave something for you too." Rose smiled as Akita pulled something small out of her drawer. Rose unwrapped it and gasped as she realized it was a dream-catcher. Did Akita already know about her dreams?

The old woman's eyes studied Rose for a moment. "You 'ave questions?"

She bit her lips a little and nodded. "I have been having a dream... it repeats itself." Rose noticed how Akita frowned for a brief moment before composing her expressions once more. Akita smiled again and gestured for Rose to tell her the dream.

"What do you think it means?" Rose asked when she had finished.

Akita fell into silence, and Rose caught how her eyes lingered on one of the shelves before meeting hers again. "Nara's forest 'as a lot of spirits. Good and bad. Only lucky souls can 'ear dem. You, Rose, is good. Ancestors of past can visit in dreams."

Rose frowned at her words, trying to make sense of it. "So, what you're saying is that the little boy might be my ancestor trying to communicate with me?"

Akita smiled and gently patted Rose's cheek. "Or yo future."

"But... But, what are they trying to tell me?"

"You can only know if you know da past. I tell you story," Akita said and opened Rose's palm. "Der was a *mganga* who lived in da forest..."

Rose watched Akita's withered finger trace the lines in her palm as she told her the myth of the witch doctor that lived deep in the woods. The mganga was very different from everyone so they all feared him. His skin was patched and his hair was so long that some people swore they had seen his locks move like dangling snakes. The people feared him more when they saw how accurate his predications were. It was a power they had never heard of before, and people were naturally terrified of what they could not comprehend. Gathering their finest soldiers, the people of Nara chased the mganga out of the village and into the forest where he became one and whole with the spirits.

Akita met Rose's eyes and smiled, holding both her hands tightly. "Nara is full of secrets."

The images of the witch doctor faded from her thoughts as Rose gradually came back to reality. "But magic doesn't really exist. Except in books, of course... like in *Neverland*." Rose mumbled to herself.

"Now," Akita said, letting go of Rose. "You must be fast. Mark is coming."

Rose frown as she looked around the empty library. "Where-"

Suddenly, the door swung open, and an unmistakable lean figure with short, brown hair stood in the doorway. His narrow blue eyes were fixed on Rose as he leaned against the wooden doorframe, his arms crossed against his chest.

"Knew I'd find you here," Mark Parker said, his thin lips constrained into a smirk.

Rose sighed a little and looked at Akita. "*Asante*."

"You're welcome, Rose." Akita replied, her eyes sharp on Mark.

"Why were you looking for me?" Rose asked, pushing her way past Mark and onto the bustling street.

"Oh, you break my heart with your question," Mark said, walking beside her. "I missed you, love. I don't like that I don't see you every day like I'm used to in school."

Rose gritted her teeth and glanced at him. "Please, Mark. I'm tired of this."

"But, I'm not." Mark stepped in front of her and stopped her tracks. "I'll never get tired of my princess."

"I'm not yours."

"You are always mine, Rose," Mark said, his blue eyes piercing. "And, you are coming with me back to London."

She shifted her weight from one foot to the other and tried to evade his eyes. "No, Mark... I will not."

"Why not? You want to stay here and do what, huh? There aren't any universities around here, you know. You'll come with me for your last term then apply to Richmond."

"I like it here, Mark. I want to finish then see what life throws at me." Rose stepped to the side and passed Mark, knowing she had to get back to the Jeep before her father could get all flustered up. "You can't force me."

"I'll kidnap you, love." He said, keeping up with her hurried pace. Rose despised the tone in his voice.

"And force me to love you?" She stopped and glared up at him. "Mark, you are my friend. Someone I care about for all the things we went through together. And you know I've been through so much already. Don't make it worse, I beg you." A heavy sigh escaped her. "I need my friend."

"I'm offering what's better than a friend."

Rose's eyes softened a little when she noticed how thin his face had become since the last time she saw him. "Mark, you've always been there for me. What happened? You changed suddenly..."

His nostrils flared and his lips pursed at her words. Local children started circling around them and singing in Naryan, cutting off the sudden tension. Rose smiled to one of them, glad for the distraction.

"Hey, Parker!" A deep voice called out above the market's racket. "Wait up."

Turning her head, Rose saw Anthony Marcos making his way over to them, followed by Zane Andile. Mark nodded at his two friends that were known for their diabolical plans, which always ended their day at the local police station.

"You didn't say you were back, man," Anthony said in his thick American accent, hitting Mark on the shoulder in frustration. "Hi, Rose." He nodded towards her, and then his bluish-green eyes squinted at Mark from behind a couple of brown strands that escaped his long bed-head hair. He had a full upper lip that added a pinch of generosity to his edgy features.

"Back?" Rose frowned.

"Yes," Zane answered. "Mark disappeared for a week!"

Her frown deepened as she looked at Mark, knowing well how he grew to be very close friends with his schoolmates, and wondered why he would disappear on them for a week without any notice. Although they did not know each other for long, Anthony was an exchange student from the States and Zane was a local from one of the tribes. They were inseparable. Rose guessed his silence over the past week must have been due to him leaving the country.

Mark brushed a hand through his hair. "Last night. I had things to finish in London." He paused then added. "You know, university papers."

Rose studied him for a brief moment and picked up his twitching eyelid. He was lying. "I've got to go," she said and looked at the three boys. "You guys coming to the gathering at my place this week?"

They all nodded their answer. Rose broke a smile and took a step to leave, but Mark held her hand and pulled her closer to him and away from Anthony and Zane. "Think about my offer. I'm leaving Nara after the gathering."

With a deep breath, Rose broke free from his grasp and hurried away from him. She could almost feel his eyes burning on her as she sped away.

The following day Mark's messages and calls were consistent, and Rose only answered a few of them to avoid his frustration that would probably push him to knock on her door. His persistence was becoming stronger and angrier by the day, and Rose could not help but wonder why he feared leaving without her so much. She knew he dropped everything in London and moved to Nara right after she did. At first, she thought he would not leave his best friend to shift to another country without his support. But, as the days passed, his grip on her had started to suffocate her. He was a brother to her, but apparently she was not a sister to him.

What would her mother say if she was alive? How would she advise Rose about Mark? But, of course, Rose knew she would not be here in Nara if her mother were alive. Life had transported her here for a reason, something Rose was trying to convince herself of.

Everything was not a mere coincidence. Rose was aware that if she allowed herself to look at it from another perspective, she might see that he was meant for her from the beginning. Best friends fell in love all the time, so what if she ended up with him? It happened a lot in many stories, and hers was not so different from them. But, it was not Mark whom she wanted to spend the rest of her life with. Who would it be? She did not know, and maybe she would never know. And, so, she had to tell Mark even if it was going to break his heart.

She pushed open her balcony door and stepped out onto the wooden terrace. The humongous trees swayed their branches against the setting-sun, graceful and enchanting. The wind picked up its pace and blew into her chestnut hair, mesmerizing Rose under the spell of the forest. Spirits of the forest... Rose recalled Akita's words the previous day and felt a chill down her spine. What secrets did Nara have buried among these trees?

A whistle broke through her thoughts. Her eyes frantically surveyed the verdant branches and bushes, suddenly feeling the presence of something different. Rose knew this forest very well. She loved to wander inside to the pond not far from her house, where she always found solace when she was feeling down. The trees were always full of birds singing, and she enjoyed listening to the soothing water. But, something told her it was all changing. Rose shook her head and went back inside her room, blaming Akita's myth for her hallucinations.

Opening her wardrobe, Rose carefully pulled out a blue box tucked amidst her pajamas and sniffed the lid. The smell of her mother's perfume still lingered on the lid, causing her heart to drop a little as the memories crawled back.

Just two weeks before Elizabeth's last breath, Rose had received this box from her. She recalled how her mother had weakly assured Rose to open it whenever she needed her and find her among the memories. After all, memories were the only things the dead left behind.

But, her precious moment was cut off by a shrill of cold laughter emanating from Angelina's room. Rose frowned and followed the sound down the corridor. The door was ajar, so Rose looked through and found Angelina standing in front of a mirror, wearing a familiar green, chiffon dress. Angelina's smile was reflected in the mirror, and it sent a shiver down Rose's spine.

"Come in, Rose," Angelina said, twirling around in the dress. "Come and see."

Rose's frowned as she entered the room. "That's mom's dress."

"Isn't it lovely on me?" Angelina twirled again for Rose to see.

"Why are you wearing it? Where did you get it?"

"I took it from the London house before it was sold."

"You what?" Rose's mouth dropped open. "Take it off. It doesn't belong to you; it belongs to my mother. Take it off!"

"Oh, I know. But I don't think it's of any use to her now, right?" Angelina said and sat at her dressing table. "And, I think I look very graceful in it."

"Oh, really?" Anger started to pump through her veins as thoughts rushed to her mind. Her eyes widened. "Is that why you married my father?"

"What are you talking about, silly child?" Angelina turned to look at Rose with a red lipstick halfway to her overdone lips.

"About you. You envied her, didn't you?"

Angelina raised her eyebrows and lowered them down instantly, as if she knew what Rose's words meant.

"Didn't you?" Rose repeated. "You were jealous of her, of her beauty, and of her fortune. Weren't you? And now, you are trying to take everything she once had."

Angelina did not answer and stood up to look at her reflection in the mirror, checking her makeup and dress. Rose watched her as a satisfied smile appeared on Angelina's face and she twirled one more time.

"You deny it, Rose, but I was her best friend."

"No, you were not," Rose shook her head. "You used her beauty and her popularity so people could also notice you. You lived in her shadow, watching and envying everything she did and had. You became her friend because you were jealous of her. She had everything you never had and wished to have. I bet you jumped up and down when you heard of her passing!"

Angelina suddenly glared at her. "Yes! She had everything I wanted, even the husband I dreamt of! Bill was mine until the day she turned up in high school, looking so elegant, flashy, and extremely rich. Everyone wooed her, but, to my horror, she had her eyes on Bill. My Bill. And, he... he fell under her spell. I was left alone to be his second choice. I was always the second choice. After all of this, you think I won't envy her? Worse, I hated her!"

Such strong emotions around her mother brought tears to Rose's eyes. "My father still chose and married her. You will always be the second choice."

A forceful slap landed on Rose's face, causing her to trip and bump her cheek into the edge of the dressing table. A warm and wet sensation filled her mouth and burned her reddened skin. Blood trickled down from the corner of her lips.

"Your mother was arrogant and selfish. And you are just like her, a fool." Angelina spat the words out of her mouth. "You know why I can't bear you?"

Rose looked up at her with great revolt, trying to hold back the tears as they slid down her aching face.

"Because you look exactly like her. Live evidence to remind me every single, damn day that she once existed! Fortunately, I won't deal with you any longer once you go with Mark. Do hear me? You will move with him, whether you like it or not!"

With that, Angelina straightened herself and smoothed the dress out with her hands, taking another look in the mirror and smiling to herself. "And, besides, that would really help me get out of this god-forsaken hot pit. Off you go! I don't want that blood to stain my lovely dress."

Astounded, Rose picked herself up and walked to the door. But, before stepping out, she turned around to say one last thing. "You will never have her purity of heart. That's why Dad chose her."

Rose ran down the stairs and outside the front door. Darkness had loomed over by then and plunged the forest into inky blackness. Looking ahead, Rose ran towards the pond down the familiar path lit by the brightness of the full moon. She cried aloud as she wiped the blood from her lips. She rushed forward, pushing tree branches out of her way and jumping over giant roots. The moonlight guided her down the misty, moist path as she treaded her way to the pebbled clearing of the pond.

Instantly, Rose sensed the eerie difference. The pond was quiet and still as death. The reflection of the stars and the full moon twinkled on the surface of the water, and the air was heavy and humid. Rose scanned her surroundings, sniffed, and curled up on a big rock that sat at the edge of the water. A sob escaped her.

Rage would push Rose to scream and release all the fire within her, but she wouldn't allow it. She preferred to bury it inside rather than give Angelina the satisfaction of hearing her cries. She knew her father must have arrived home by now, and was probably in the kitchen eating dinner with Angelina. Rose wanted to go and tell him what a fraud Angelina was, and that she was his biggest mistake. But, Angelina had her claws dug deep into him.

Brushing away the last of her tears, Rose kicked off her sandals and was about to dip her toes into the water when the strange feeling intensified. She heard the soft crunch of pebbles from behind her. Someone or something was approaching. She held her breath.

Two: Mpilo Nsonowa

"Are you alright?" A deep voice broke the silence.

Rose gulped and slowly turned, her heart pounding inside her ribcage.

A shadow of a tall, broad man stood at the edge of the trees. Rose thought of running as fast as she could, but her feet refused to move an inch.

"I'm not going to hurt you," he said from the shadows, answering her unspoken thoughts. He had an unusual accent and it made her more anxious.

Rose stood there with fear stapling her to the ground as she waited to see what would happen. The shadowy figure took a small step forward, then back again while Rose waited—her blood gushing with adrenaline. He moved again and finally stepped out into the moonlight, allowing it to illuminate his face.

Rose blinked. To her surprise, a young man with thick, neck-long hair stood in front of her. His strands shielded his face, throwing the rest of his features into mystery. Slowly, he titled his head up a little and locked eyes with a very confused Rose. Regardless of the fact that she could only see half of this stranger, his eyes made her feel calm.

"Who – who are you?" She forced her voice out, trying to keep it from breaking up.

"Mpilo Nsonowa," he replied in his unique accent with a voice that was steady and smooth. "But, you can call me Jack."

His Naryan tongue sounded like it was tinged with an English color. Rose was not certain, but it designated that he was not a fully native Naryan – a stranger like her, perhaps.

"I am sorry," he spoke again when Rose failed to respond. "But, I heard someone crying when I was passing by."

Rose eyed him curiously. Strange that such a strong stranger should have such a soft heart.

"Are you alright?" he asked gently.

Rose replied with a short nod, wondering what he wanted from her.

"Why were you crying? If you don't mind me asking," he said and looked at her with a smile twitching at the corner of his mouth.

It took her a moment to answer, admiring his familiar eyes that were sparkling with life and vitality.

"I'm... I'm hurt." She froze in disbelief at her own words. Why did she say that? She could not speak to a stranger like that. "Why are you here?"

"I was just wondering why you-"

Suddenly Jack stopped and looked away from her. Rose watched him as he took a step backwards and into the shadows again. He seemed to be alarmed.

Something had caught his attention from between the trees behind him, but Rose could not tell what it was.

"I have to go." His tone changed. Rose sensed his alarm and watched him suddenly disappear onto one of the paths of the forest without leaving any sound or footsteps behind.

Staring at where she had seen him swallowed by the darkness, fear crawled back again into her blood. Everything around her seemed menacing and odd, and the mist appeared to have thickened like white dresses wrapping the tree trunks with their vapor. They looked like white ghosts surveying her from the hollow openings of their trunks. Rose ran to the house, through the ghosts of the forest, and dashed to her room. All the while her heart thumped with confusion and anxiety.

In the safety of her room, she plunged herself on her bed and stared out the window, replaying the whole scene inside her mind a million times in hopes of comprehending what just had happened. Never before had she met someone in that part of the forest. She had always considered it her private space.

The image of the young man materialized again inside her head. He had an enigma about him; the way he talked, the way he looked at her through those glinting eyes, and the way he disappeared in a rush raised many questions. Nonetheless, there was something about him that made her feel safe. What an unconventional thing to feel towards a stranger.

Who is Mpilo Nsonowa? Rose asked herself as she wiped the last traces of blood from her lips in the bathroom mirror. Her curiosity triggered her imagination. She wanted to know who he was. Taking in a deep breath, Rose closed her eyes and built his image in her mind, trying to complete the missing details of his face.

"Rose?" Her father's voice at her door knocked her out of her thoughts. She pressed her lips with a tissue and opened the door, preparing herself for a lecture.

"Here."

Bill's exhausted face looked at her, the smell of sweat, cologne, and spices wafted from him. "I asked you several times before not to bicker with Angelina. Please."

"But-"

"Rose, please, there is no need to shake things up when it's finally been stable. I just want life to go on smoothly."

Words escaped her as she stared at her father, and decided to save her own dignity and recall the slap. It hurt her to see how her father dismissed the obvious, but the hurt in his eyes was far more evident. His features were drained and exhausted since the day Elizabeth had passed away. It was clear to her that he was still mourning.

"I love you, dear," Bill said and continued his way to his room down the corridor.

"Me too," she mumbled softly and started getting ready for bed.

Once her head had sunk into the softness of the pillow, her consciousness started to slip away. Deep brown eyes looked at her out of the darkness. In no time, Rose was transported to the realm of dreams. But, her dreams that night did not cease to provoke her.

Rose sprung out of bed the next day. The dream had come to her again, but there was something more about the boy this time; a detail she never had noticed before. There was something red on his chest, like a pendant that sparkled under the moonlight. Her heart skipped a beat as she slipped into a blue, floral dress and made her way downstairs. She needed to go the pond right now for some much-needed meditation. Rose hoped she could take Akita's advice and get in touch with the spirits.

Before leaving, Rose turned into the kitchen and gobbled down some breakfast that Luba had set for her. Luckily, there was no sign of Angelina or Bill around. Suddenly, her eyes caught a car approaching up the driveway from the kitchen window.

Oh no, she thought to herself upon seeing Mark's truck speeding up to their front door.

She quickly swallowed the piece of bread she had been chewing. "Luba, I am not here." The housekeeper squinted outside the window and nodded just as Rose dashed out the kitchen back door before Mark could even park.

She sprinted through the trees, her dress flowing behind her like a pair of wings, and did not stop until she had reached the pond. Sucking in a deep breath, she leaned against the rock and squinted under the sunlight. Guilt gripped at her throat as she took in a couple of more breaths. But, she could not be blamed. Mark had been driving her away from him.

The pond glittered beneath the sun and the trees danced gently to the cool breeze. Fire, Earth, Water, and Wind, the elements of life collaborated together harmonically. Like a team, they played their role perfectly in this vast life. She wondered why people could not be that way as well.

Propping herself up on the rock, she faced the pond and small waterfall ahead of her, and waited for her heartbeat to slow down. There was something else she was waiting for.

From the moment she had opened her eyes that morning she couldn't wait to come here to where she had seen Jack. She did not expect to find him—or perhaps she did. But, only to prove to herself that he had not been a fragment of her imagination.

She had been very upset yesterday, and her mind could have simply imagined Jack. Perhaps she had just imagined him to calm herself and push away her worries. Rose remembered how anxious he had appeared to be. Could it possibly be that this stranger was merely a reflection of her emotions?

The question bothered her immensely. If he were a hallucination, then she would be taking backward steps in her healing progress since her mother's passing. Rose desperately didn't want this to happen, so she decided to prove it otherwise. She carefully climbed down the rock and turned around to face the path that he had disappeared into last night.

Rose froze.

Jack was standing right in front of her.

"You are not crying," he said with a little smile.

Rose's heartbeat made a small flip as she took in his sight. He looked different under the sun. He was wearing a pair of dyed-green shorts that matched with a sleeveless top. His tanned skin complimented his long, deep-ochre hair that waved down in wide curls to his sharp jawbones outlining his face with intelligence. She watched him as he took a few steps towards her; close enough to just allow her curious eyes to discover his face more.

"I apologize if I scared you yesterday," he said, slightly cringing his long neck.

She didn't answer right away, immersed in the duality he presented. He appeared to be a mix of two worlds.

He's got a handsome face, she thought to herself in the few moments before she answered him, *and solid enough to not be a hallucination.* Her eyes continued to explore the young man's profile, completely forgetting to answer him. She took in every detail of his features, and how it was marked by a straight nose that connected thick eyebrows shielding his deep-brown eyes. Rose could not help but stare into them, captivated by both their unique amber streaks and familiarity. Elaborate long eyelashes outlined the beauty of his eyes more, making it almost impossible for her to look away. His physiognomy harmoniously ended with a prompted chin that carried a certain air of determination, adding to the mystery evolving him. Her attention to detail caused her eyes to glimpse a faint trace of a healing scar on his right bicep. She quickly pulled her eyes away from him.

"No harm was done," she said and felt her cheeks flush a little.

His cross-bow-shaped mouth curled up in astonishment, revealing a radiant smile. "Do you mind if I ask why you were crying?"

"I don't know you," she said. "I don't even know your name."

"But I told you my name."

"Well, you gave me two different names... and, your name doesn't tell me anything about you. Except for your name, of course," Rose said, feeling the same sensation of safety she felt when their eyes had met.

"I see," the young man said and nodded his head slowly, a couple of hair strands falling on his forehead. "Ask me what you want to know and I'll answer."

Rose asked the first question that popped in her head. "Why were you in the forest last night?"

"I was taking a night time walk," he replied, and Rose sensed his calm confidence.

"Do you do that often?"

"Yes."

"So, you must live close to here?" she said and watched for any signs of lying, but somehow she knew there was only truth in his deep eyes.

"Closer than you think."

Rose frowned. "How is that so? We are the only ones living around here."

"I do, but my house is very small. I don't think anyone passing by would ever notice it," he said, and looked behind him at the swaying trees, then back at her.

"How come I never saw you before?" she asked as every question raised another, creating a web of questions in her head.

A blank expression covered his face. He seemed to be stirring the question in his mind and choosing his words carefully, but he did not reply. Silence stretched between them, disturbing the calmness. Rose felt the awkwardness and did not push the subject any further.

She jumped to the next question instead. "Why did you leave so quickly yesterday?"

Silence replied.

Her blood rushed as his silence bothered her and provoked her curiosity. She studied his face for a brief moment. "Mpilo or Jack?"

The young man smiled and met her glance from beneath his thick eyebrows, "Jack, after my father."

"Jack," she softly repeated his name. "Very familiar yet so strange."

"Maybe both, Rose," Jack said and leaned against a tree bark, his outfit almost camouflaging with the overgrown moss.

Her lips parted, feeling her heart skip. "How-how... Do you know my name?"

Rose watched him as he opened his mouth slightly, pondering, and then walked the pebbly ground towards her, crossing the distance he had put between them.

"I've known you since the day you arrived..."

"What?" She frowned, looking up at him and took a small step back.

"You came here, by the pond, almost every single day," he continued. "I watched you from behind the trees, wanting to say hello. But, I never had the chance."

She looked into his eyes as he spoke and noticed something different about them. There was a void in his eyes, and it stole the sparkle away, leaving them blunt and pale.

"And you had the chance yesterday?"

"You were crying."

"I do that quite often," she heard herself admit without embarrassment.

"I know," he said softly, his voice almost whispering. "But, yesterday your cries were not the same, and you were bleeding. I had to know what was disturbing you."

"Why?" His concern was very kind, but she tried to remind herself that Jack was a stranger who knew her name. However, his presence brought a beam of unexplained happiness that glowed the world inside her.

Jack's eyes dropped to the ground and stayed quiet.

"Well," she said, realizing she was not going to receive an answer. "I don't know you enough to believe whether what you are saying is true or not."

"You could know me," he said with a hint of shyness. "If you want."

Their eyes met, and Rose was once more reminded of their soothing familiarity. His eyes were not those of a stranger; it was the one reason Rose felt secure around him. She knew that eyes like those do not hurt, even if she stared at them for the rest of her life. Forcing herself to break the eye contact, she turned her gaze away and pondered his words. It felt like the world was bringing some change or adventure into her life. And maybe, he might be the answer to the odd dream she had been having.

Glancing at him again, Rose made up her mind and brought her gaze back to meet his deep brown eyes. "Your accent confuses me," she said and watched as a smile broke on his face. At that very moment, the sparkle came back into his eyes, shining more than the glittering water under the vibrant sun. She could not help but to smile back.

"Because I am half English," he explained as Rose sat on the rock, tucking her legs underneath. Her eyes followed him as he leaned against the rock too, but kept a respectable distance between them. "My father was from London, and my mother was from here."

"Was?" Rose took in a quiet breath.

He thought for a moment and seemed to be weighting his words carefully. "Yes, was," he replied and Rose watched as his features stayed calm.

But, loss was never a comfortable topic. She fidgeted in her place a little and thought about what might have happened to them. Her lips parted, ready to ask the obvious question, but she knew how delicate this subject was.

"My father was an anthropologist. When he was young and at the beginning of his path, he came here to study a certain tribe," he answered her thoughts.

She pushed her hair behind her ear, listening.

"He lived among the people, day and night, gathering knowledge of the ancestors and the ways of rituals. It was something that the people frowned upon; they saw him as someone who was interfering. Then one day a certain woman caught his special attention, and they both knew their fates were entwined." Jack stopped for a moment.

"My parents married after a fierce argument with the leader of the tribe. I'm sure you know how the tribes are here towards unfamiliar blood. Especially when it comes to sacred rituals and marriage. And, my father's interference was not accepted. But, they fought to be together.

"He started to lose hope. But, my mother was there to reassure him a solution would turn up soon…and she was right. The leader finally agreed, but with a price... My father could marry her only if he gave up his research and lived forever in Nara... until his last breath."

"Did your father agree?" Rose held her breath, curious.

"Yes, he did and they got married." He smiled at her.

"What were their names?" She softly asked, careful not to be insensitive.

She watched him as his eyes moved to the water then to the forest.

"Jack and Nandi Casper."

"What happened to them?" She covered her mouth with a hand, regretting her words. "I'm sorry. I didn't mean to-"

"Don't be," he interrupted and turned his body to face her more. "They are dead and gone from this world... at least physically. But, like all others, their spirits are still here and they left a story behind. So, to honor their memory, I tell their story to whoever listens. It's the least I could do for them."

His words sank into her, touching her deeply. She lifted her eyes up and admired his wisdom, realizing that he must have experienced difficulties in life like her.

"And, how many have listened to you?" Her eyes briefly dropped to the scar on his right arm.

"No one," Jack replied and Rose lifted her eyebrows in wonder. "You are the first one to know... Enough about me, what about you?"

"I think you already know," she said and climbed down from her spot.

"Well, the only thing I know is that you cry a lot. And, I can't help but imagine why." Rose caught the softest curious tone in his voice. Her thoughts started to open up as they began to walk abreast, going deeper into the forest. Jack walked beside her silently and she knew he was giving her time to be brave. She folded her arms against the cool breeze. Even though it was the beginning of spring, winter always left a sign of its visit that lasted long enough to delay any other season. Nothing was punctual in Nara.

"My – my..." Rose slowly gulped and took in a deep breath, searching for her courage to show up. But, she did not know from where to start or how to say it. Taking in a deep breath, she spoke the words that haunted her, and kept her captive under their meaning.

"My mother died from cancer a couple of years ago," she said in one breath, feeling the words cut through her veins. The pain was still fresh, and that bothered her. But, she was aware that she had taken a step forward and finally spoke it out. A tear rolled down her cheek as Rose finally found a way out of her own darkness. She quickly brushed it away with the back of her hand.

"That's the reason then?" Jack inquired after a few silent moments.

"For what?" She looked at him, not noticing they were deeper into the forest by then—deeper than she had ever allowed herself to venture. The trees were thicker and bushier, breaking up the direct rays of the afternoon sun and secluding them from the rest of the world.

"Your cries."

Rose bit her lips and nodded.

Jack gave her half a smile, and Rose immediately understood it. His smile told her that she was not alone. It told her that he felt her loss and shared it with her. For the first time in years, the pain loosened its grip on her heart.

From where do I know him? She thought as they made a turn and reached the top of the cliff.

The valley showed itself beneath them, verdant with the continuation of the forest, and trapped between the green mountains. A stream flowed softly below between the trees, and the musical sound of water could be heard.

"I never came here before," she said and breathed in the air filled with the scent of wet grass and blossoming flowers. "It's beautiful."

Jack watched her with a smile, and it caught her eyes. There, at the corner of his lips, was something hiding. A secret. A story. She wondered.

"Do you have any friends, Rose?" he asked.

"Some friends. I trust Akita the most though," she said, pulling her eyes away from him. "And, I used to have a best friend... But, she was a liar," she added when she saw the curious look on Jack's face.

"And, you don't like people lying to you?"

"I hate it," she said bitterly.

He sighed and pocketed his hand. Something he did when he was worried, Rose realized.

"Even, if it was for your own good?"

"What good could there be if people lied to each other," she said, stronger than she had intended to.

"Tell me about the friend," Jack said.

Rose hesitated for a moment. "She used to call herself my friend, but I realized she was a fake when my mother died." Her voice shook, "She didn't stand beside me like best friends should. When she knew I was... not doing well, she stayed away from me. Until now, I don't know why she did that – not that I care – but at least to understand. Her name was Heidi Butterfield."

"I'm sorry," he said softly.

"It's not your fault." She looked at the ground and felt embarrassed at her own exposed feelings.

They stood in silence and watched the beauty of nature. The massive mountains were very high. They looked like they had penetrated the blue sky, clouds circling around the collision point. It was getting late, and the sun would soon reach its destination and sink into the sea. Jack led the way back to the pond while Rose followed with a question in her mind. One that she had asked, but was never given an answer.

"It's getting late," he said the moment they reached the pond. "You have to go home."

"What?" she said, surprised. "Why?"

"Your father wouldn't want you to stay late here," he said and started to scan the forest with his careful eyes.

She was once again surprised by his knowledge of her. Realizing her confused look, he laughed a laugh she had never before heard a match of. A laugh of strength combined with tenderness and humor. There was more to him than she thought.

She nodded in obedience and set off towards her home. He walked behind her through the path until they reached the house. "Will I see you again tomorrow?" he asked, not coming out on the path after her.

She smiled and nodded before he even finished his sentence. He laughed a melodic laugh and left, and the echo of his chuckling subsided into the forest. Within a second, he could not be seen nor heard.

In the house, Rose saw that her dad was not home yet, and Angelina was talking on the phone with one of her friends in London. Her stomach roared with hunger and did not rest until Rose stuffed down some bread and fruits in the kitchen.

"Do you need any help, Luba?" Rose asked, watching her prepare some ingredients for the upcoming gathering.

"Asante," Luba smiled and continued peeling garlic.

Rose smiled back and munched on her fruits just as Angelina entered the kitchen, the phone still pressed to her ear. Rose felt her cheek sting, but she maintained her calm as Angelina glanced at Rose and pulled a bottle of wine from a cupboard.

"Yes, yes, I hear you, Anne. Of course, you need to take care of your son. But, Mark is strong; he'll get through this. Mhmm... All right. I'll see you at the gathering." Angelina ended the call and opened the bottle.

Rose paused, a piece of strawberry halfway to her lips. "What's... what's wrong with Mark?"

Her stepmother jerked her head towards Rose. "Oh, I didn't see you there." She poured the wine into a glass and took a sip. "He is terribly sick. Oh, I wasn't supposed to say."

Rose caught the trace of a menacing smile from behind Angelina's glass. "Is he coming to the gathering?"

"Of course, he will. He won't miss the opportunity to spend time with you, unlike some people." Her eyes sharpened at Rose. "Some even say that a broken heart was the reason behind his sickness."

With that, Rose pushed her chair back and stood up. She could not believe how Angelina was trying to manipulate her, playing with guilt. She returned her sharp glance before going up to her room. Her thoughts wondered if there was any truth behind Angelina's words. She looked forward to the gathering more than she had expected... and a soothing shower.

It was night by the time she stepped out of her shower. She sat on a high, brown armchair in front of the balcony's door to comb her hair. Her mind was immersed in the story Jack had told her about his parents. *What happened to them?* She thought, *I have to ask him again... tomorrow.*

A faint light outside the window caught her attention. She jerked in her seat and drop her brush. Rose searched for it with her eyes in the darkness, but it was gone. The forest was black. After picking up her brush from under the chair, she reached to close the curtains. But, for a second she thought she had seen a pair of eyes. Rose shook her head and pulled the curtains shut.

I must be tired, she thought to herself.

Three: The Blue Water

The next morning Jack was waiting for her in the middle of the forest path. He surprised her when he suddenly appeared between the trees, chuckling at her reaction. He led her again deeper into the forest, going through new paths and passing by different species of trees. Rose decided to trust her new friend. He was kind and respectful. She followed as Jack walked, pushing tree branches out of the way, and glancing behind him to make sure she was keeping up. It was the right time to ask her curious question.

"Jack," she called, and he stopped in his tracks. "There is a question I wanted to ask you."

"How my parents died?"

"Yes," she said and tried to hide her surprise.

Jack beckoned her to come and sit on a huge tree branch that had fallen on the ground. When she sat, Jack continued the unfinished story.

"Before my father came to Nara, there was another man who had loved Nandi. He was crazy about her, but she didn't share his love. He was devastated when she married my father, and he was nowhere to be seen during the wedding. He had disappeared.

"Some said he had gone mad. Some said he'd died in the forest, and others said he was hiding in the woods and planning to take his revenge from the man who took his one love. Many years later, the man reappeared with a distasteful look on his savage face and a sword in his hands. I saw the hunger in his eyes when he came to our house. Unfortunately, my father was not at home, so my mother had to fight off his desires," he paused. She understood what he meant.

"I was only ten at the time, and I didn't know what to do. I ran to call my father, and he saved her just in time."

"What happened to the man?" Rose asked, completely absorbed in the story.

"My father killed him."

Rose winced at the image created in her mind.

"But, of course, what my father did disturbed the tribe. And they revolted against him. The leader was furious at the death of one of his people by the hands of a stranger. He still saw him as an outsider and took every chance to chase him out, and that was his chance to get rid of him forever. He sentenced him to death."

Rose gasped as Jack took a deep breath and continued. "Fortunately, they didn't get the satisfaction of killing him. My father died of malaria a few days after the accident. I remember running in the village and searching for a doctor, but no one was willing to help us."

"And your mother, what happened to her?"

"She died six months after my father's death. The pain was too strong for her."

Rose felt her heart squeeze with pity. "What did you do?" Her voice shook. She felt a heavy lump gather in her throat and she resisted the tears, but to no avail.

Jack noticed the change of her voice and bent down in front of her, leveling with her eyes. "I ran away."

Her eyes met his, and she fell into silence. A feeling stirred within her heart.

"Come tomorrow," she mumbled softly. "My father is throwing a party for some friends and family. I'd rather be here with you." She instantly felt her cheeks redden and broke their eye contact. "If you're free."

Rose heard Jack took a deep breath. He straightened up and scanned the forest before meeting her eyes again with a smile. "I'll be there, if you want me there."

The next morning, Rose woke up at the early bells announcing the first comers. With a little push of excitement, she got up to dress for the day. The house started to fill with people and caterers, and cars filled the front of the house. Downstairs, Anne Parker arrived, followed by Maggie Carter and Jennifer Hale, and they gathered in the terrace. Rose heard their excited voices over the magnificent view of the forest and the purity of the air. She peeked through the curtains at the women below and saw Anne standing with Angelina and talking on the phone.

Her thoughts flew to Mark and she scanned the parked vehicles for his car, but it was not in sight. Rose wished she would not bump into him today, only to avoid confronting him. However, Angelina's words the other day stayed in her mind. Worry started to grow inside her chest as she checked her reflection in the mirror before making her way downstairs. Her knee-high, peach dress matched her lips and the high-heels gave her an elegant posture. She untied her hair, letting it hang in waves to the middle of her back, and kept her face without makeup.

A local band played a mix of traditional Naryan music and some other international classical ones. Hired caterers, carrying plates and silverware, bustled in and out of the kitchen. Although, it was a little too much for the amount of invited people, but Angelina loved the extravaganza and the attention she received. The only advantage Rose enjoyed was how Angelina was forced to put on a loving face towards her stepdaughter.

Family and friends, who Rose had not seen for a year, talked to her and asked about her health. She was happy to see them, feeling that they had last met only yesterday. Rose wanted to greet them back and ask about them too, but her mind was back in the forest. *Where is Jack?*

She excused herself and retreated to the terrace where Anne was still on the phone looking very upset.

"Mark, honey," Anne continued her call. "Everything is done with the agent, so don't worry about it and come down here. Yes... yes, sold to a lovely couple from Spain. Okay... good. Love you, dear." Anne ended the call and opened her arms when she saw Rose.

"Oh, look at you! My little Rose is blooming," she said and took Rose in a tight hug.

Rose hugged her back tightly. Anne was her favorite among her mother's friends and cousins, and she was very loyal to Elizabeth. Rose remembered when Anne called every day to ask about her. She wished that it were Anne who her father had married; it would have made things simpler. Anne got divorced from her selfish husband a long time ago, and she would have found a great husband in Bill. Mark would have become her legal brother, saving him all the torture he went through by Rose's denial.

"I miss you, Anne," Rose said, holding on to her.

"I miss you more, love," she said and released her to look at her. "You look more like your mother every time I see you. How are you, dear? Is everything alright with you here?"

"Yes. Things are getting better."

"Really! I am pleased to hear that." Anne smiled warmly, holding Rose's hands tightly. "Now, Mark is on his way, and he can't wait to see you... I am sure you can't as well."

"Yes," she said and escaped Anne's friendly eyes. "Yes, I can't."

Angelina took Anne away and went over to their friends. Rose exhaled heavily, trying to push out the guilt filling her. But, her guilt was immediately set aside once she realized that Mark and Jack would meet. Panicking a little, Rose made her way outside and to the opening of the path.

It was dark in the forest. The sky was cloudy and the sun could not find a way around them to cast its light, causing everything below to be in shadows. It was the perfect weather for an outdoor party. A movement from behind a nearby tree caught her attention.

"Jack?" she whispered.

There was another movement and a crack of twigs before Jack appeared from behind the tree, wearing a short-sleeved black shirt.

"Sorry I'm late," he said and went over to her.

"Where were you? I thought you were going to stand me up," she said and noticed something different about him.

"I would never stand you up," he said and frowned when he found her staring at him. "What's the matter?"

"Your arm," she said. "What happened to your arm?"

"Nothing," he said hastily and pulled his sleeve over his carelessly wrapped right arm.

"What do you mean nothing?" She pushed away his hands to see his arm for herself. "Who did this to you?" she asked, her eyes widened when she saw the cloth covered in blood. He pulled his black sleeve lower and did not open his mouth.

She looked into his eyes and he stared back. A thin line of a frown crossed his forehead. Jack eluded her gaze and faced the ground, pocketing his hands.

"Don't worry," he told her. She opened her mouth to argue, but Jack stopped her. "Your guests are waiting."

She turned on her heels and they walked together from under the trees. A lot of her questions were answered by silence from Jack, and it annoyed her. Sometimes she felt he didn't trust her with the answer. *I have to confront him later*, she decided as they made their way to the drinks table.

"What would you like?" she asked him.

"A glass of water would be nice," he said without looking at the drinks available. Rose noticed the water jar was empty and told Jack she would go and get him some from the kitchen.

"Come with me," she said.

"No, Rose. I'll wait for you here."

"Alone?"

"I won't be when you come back," he smiled.

She softly smiled back and went into the kitchen cramped with all sorts of food and drinks. She felt a stare burning into her back as she poured the water.

"Looking good, princess," Mark's voice came from behind her.

A small sigh escaped her as she turned to face him. The exhaustion in his eyes was more evident than the last time she had seen him in the village.

"I can't say the same about you," she replied back, and then bit her lips. "Are you alright?"

Mark's forehead creased a little with confusion. "Yeah, who told you otherwise? But, my heart isn't doing well, you know. Cause I may be waiting for an answer from the most beautiful girl in Nara."

"Mark," she said, wishing she could wipe the devious smile from his face.

"Come on, you won't regret it."

Unable to handle this at the moment, especially the fact that his skin was paler than before, Rose took a step towards the door, but Mark blocked her with his arm.

"Let me pass." She looked directly into his eyes and her heart dropped a little. "Mark, you're not okay. I can see it."

He smirked a little, disregarding her comment, and tapped his cheek for a kiss. "If you want to pass, you got to give me something."

"Anne!" Rose called from over his arm when she saw her coming towards them from the terrace.

"What is going on in here?" Anne said.

"Please, Anne, can you tell Mark to move. He is stopping me from passing and serving my guests."

"Oh, you mean the handsome young man with the black shirt?" Anne said.

Mark dropped his arm absentmindedly and stared at Rose, waiting for her answer. Rose switched her weight from one leg to the other, regretting her choice of the high-heels, and regarded Mark's expression. Anne's words sank slowly into his mind.

Before Mark could open his mouth, Rose hurried out the kitchen and found Jack.

"*Asante*," he said and took the water from her, gulping it down all at once. "Are you alright?" he asked.

She faltered. *Should I tell him now?* She asked herself and stared down at her glass.

"Yeah, I am fine." She paused; he will know it anytime soon. "Well, there is just a friend of-"

"Rose!" Mark called, hurrying towards them and stopping beside her.

Jack stood up taller than Mark, and his expression hardened when he saw Rose's look to Mark. The two men stared at each other, and Rose saw the building of contempt on Mark's lined mouth. Electricity between the two men was felt even before either of them spoke a word to the other.

Rose fidgeted between them and cleared her throat. "Mark, this is Jack," she introduced, "Jack, this is Mark Parker."

Jack stretched out his hand and Mark shook it spitefully, disclosing his impudence.

"I need a word with you," Mark told her the moment he broke the handshake. She gave Mark a sharp look, but he nudged her elbow and ushered her away.

"I will be right back, Jack," she said and saw a small frown of worry crease his forehead.

Mark took her to the side of the house, making sure to keep away from any observers.

"Who is he?" he asked, disclosing any space between them.

"Excuse me?" Rose blinked up at him. "Mark, he is a friend."

He smirked more. "A friend? Really. Have you seen the way he looks at you?"

Rose bit her lips. "He is my friend. I'm allowed to make friends other than you." A cold breeze blew from the depth of the forest and sent an unpleasant prickle down her spine, giving her goose bumps; the forest was warning her. She glanced at the swaying trees then back at Mark again. "I have to go." She pressed a palm to his chest, pushing him a little a way, and paused when she felt his bones underneath her fingers. "You're getting thinner, Mark."

Mark pressed her hand against his heart, and stopped her from moving. "You're mine."

"Mark, please, I'm not in the mood for-"

"When will you ever be in the mood?" He interrupted her, pulling her closer to his body. "What is it that you don't see in me, huh?"

"Let me go, Mark, please." She felt his face inches away from her, his hot breath tingling her skin.

"You know that I love you, but you don't seem to appreciate it!"

"You are not giving me the liberty to make my own choice!"

"Does it have something to do with him?"

"With whom?"

"With that friend of yours, and-"

"Jack has nothing to do with that!"

"Then what can I do to change your mind!" He grabbed her waist, pinning her to him.

Rose tried to move, but Mark held her so close that she could not look anywhere else except at his furious, pleading eyes. "Leave me to make-"

A kiss forced itself on her lips and smothered her words. She tried to push Mark away, but he was stronger than her. She wanted to scream out loud, but the kiss was too hard against her lips.

Suddenly Mark was pulled away from her and a bone breaking punch hit his face, causing him to fall flat to the ground.

Jack took Rose's hand and ran into the darkening forest before anyone could come to investigate. As tears flowed from her shocked eyes, she ran with him deep into the dark. Her high heels kept sinking into the ground as she ran and her ankles burned with pain, but she couldn't think of anything else other than what had happened back there and how her lips burned.

Without any notice, she was lifted off of her feet and was carried effortlessly by Jack as he continued running. Rose wasn't aware of what was happening, and her eyes were full of tears so everything appeared to be a blur.

After what seemed to be seconds, Jack put her down on a wooden chair, pillowed with animal skin. The wooden floor she stared at was strange to her and the chair was surprisingly comfy, but she did not dare to lift her eyes and meet Jack's. She did not care to know where she was, all the mattered that she was away from Mark.

Rose was silent for a few minutes, having cried all the tears possible, and she gaped at the floor while Jack sat opposite her, looking grave and solemn. They sat like that for what felt like an hour until Jack gathered himself to speak.

"Are you better?" he said in a croaked voice and she nodded without lifting her head. "Do you want to talk about it?"

She heaved her head up and looked to her right, trying to elude his gaze. She froze dead in her seat and her mouth dropped open at what she was viewing. No words in her mind could explain her shock. She was not in a house as she thought, but in a tree. Rubbing her eyes to make sure she was not daydreaming, she gasped at the scenery. Space stretched in front of her until it reached the mountains ahead, and a dark, green carpet of trees relinquished under the radiance of the moonlight. The massive mountains' silhouettes were erased by the crawling mist at their peeks, causing them to appear like silver rocks.

Rose stood up slowly and took a step forward, realizing the floor she had been staring at was a wooden platform plunged neatly between two huge branches of a tree. When she looked down from its edge, her head spun fast and she lost her balance. Jack caught her just in time before she slipped.

They were high up in a tree and on the edge of a cliff with no solid ground beneath them. Rose gulped and tried to catch her breath, realizing what she was looking at. The cliff, where they walked to the first time they met, and the valley below were seen from a different angle. It was breathtaking and extraordinary. Such places existed only in fairytales and movies, but here she was.

She took her time admiring the view and saw the water falling from the pond shine silver against the moonlight, and felt the air blow lightly in her face. She fell in love with the place, but she still didn't understand what this odd house was.

She turned around to face Jack's anxious face and searched for her voice. When she found it, she asked in a whisper, "Where are we?"

"My house," Jack said after a deep breath.

"You live in a tree house?"

"Not everyone can have a comfortable place to live," he said and ushered her away from the edge of the platform. "I thought you might like it."

"Are you joking?" she said, forgetting her pain. "I am in love with it already. And I envy you being able to wake up every morning to look at such a place."

"It is beautiful."

Turning to look at the view and admiring it more, a question slipped into her mind and demanded an answer immediately. "How did we get up here?" She looked up at him and saw a hint of discomfort in Jack's eyes.

He took a profound breath and started to explain. "I possess something which allows me to," he paused, considering his words carefully, "ride the wind." Rose frowned in confusion. "Fly, in other words."

Rose stared at Jack blankly for a few moments. "What?"

Without having second thoughts, Jack stood up, ran and jumped off the platform into the emptiness. Rose screamed and went over to look below when Jack soared up into the air in front of her and touched back down silently.

She stared at Jack, wide eyed, and tried to let her mind digest what she had just seen. Was her mind playing tricks on her? Was she going mad? Her legs shivered and she sat back in the chair. Jack looked at her, waiting to hear what she had to say.

"What you did right now, did it really happen?" she whispered, trying to force her lost voice out of her mouth.

Jack nodded and sat down opposite her. "I was going to tell you," he started and looked deep into her eyes.

"And what stopped you?" She asked, having found her voice and the courage to use it.

"I didn't find the right time, but I was going to tell you."

"Tell me what exactly?" she stammered, completely baffled. Rose watched him as he stood up and went over to the edge. It was very obvious that what he was about to say was hard to explain.

"When the chief of the tribe knew about my father's sudden death, they were furious. They didn't get the chance to take revenge by their own hands, so they decided to kill anyone who had his blood running in their veins... me."

Rose gasped in horror and disbelief. Slowly, she stood up and went to his side. When their eyes met, secrets shined back from behind his eyes and her mind wondered.

"That's why you ran away?" she whispered.

"Yes." He sighed. "When I was ten years old, they came looking for me, but I had already escaped at night into the forest. For the past ten years, they never stopped hunting me. And, they won't... not until they finish me off."

A tear rolled down Rose's cheek. How could a person live when they knew that death was hunting them down?

"That's why I live in a tree house," he continued. "They can't find me up here. It is the only place where I can hide."

"Why can't they find you up here?"

"It's one of the things that I can't understand myself." He folded his arms. "I have seen them look up at the tree, but they always turn around and leave. As if there is no house built between its branches."

"That explains a lot," she said, remembering the alarmed look on his face the first night she had seen him. "But, I still don't understand how… what you can do… happened."

"On that day, when I ran away, I found an unfamiliar bag of water among my possessions. It was the only drinkable water I had with me and my throat was burning with thirst, so I drank it. Just by its taste I knew it was not normal. And what's more, the water never runs out. The bag always refills even after ten years."

"Why didn't you tell me before?" Rose frowned, still trying to understand.

"What would you have done if a stranger came up to you and revealed something as impossible as this?"

She considered it for a moment, but she already knew what she would have done. "I'd have gotten scared," she admitted without meeting his eyes. "And ran away."

"And we wouldn't have known each other," he added.

They lapsed into silence, and Rose pondered about how her days without him would have been, dark as before, or darker than the shadows of the solid mountains. But now it appeared that not only she lived in darkness, Jack lived it too. Only now they had each other to hold on to.

Rose wasn't able to imagine how many mysteries and secrets lay within him. How could it be that a single, wild, young man held so much between his bare hands? And Rose felt there was still more to come.

"Are you scared?" Rose broke the silence.

"That they'll catch me?"

"Yeah."

"No. After ten years of successfully fleeing, I think I have become a master at it."

"And are you going to live the rest of your life like this? Hiding?" She blurted, recognizing the seriousness of the problem. To Rose's annoyance, he folded his arms and didn't reply. "Was that why you always left quickly when we first met?" She pulled out one of her unanswered queries. "Were they in the forest looking for you?"

He nodded slowly.

"But, I didn't see anyone there after you left."

"That's because I had already left."

"Which tribe is it?"

"It doesn't matter which one." He looked away from her.

She didn't press on the point and continued using her opportunity to ask him her questions. "How did you feel the first time you tried the... Umm..."

"The flying," he finished her sentence. He smiled and thought for a moment, scratching his chin. "It was like riding on freedom itself."

Rose shivered at his description. "Was that any help to your problem with the tribe?"

"Yes, it was a massive help. As I have figured out, the Water is some sort of magical substance and it could give abilities to whoever needs it. I found myself faster and lighter than the Kal – tribe, I mean, and much quicker." He looked anxious. Rose noticed he was about to say the tribe's name, but he had gulped it back quickly. "It's the reason for my survival."

Rose stared out into the open moonlit sky, lost in thought. It was a very strange night for her, and she had to wait until her mind grasped the odd facts. Life was unexpected.

"You have to go back. They'll get worried if you're late," Jack said, interrupting her thoughts as he stood up. "Come on, there is something I want you to experience."

"What is it?" she inquired, surprised.

"I am not going to tell you."

"Why?"

"You'll see," he said, a smile forming on his moonlit face. He offered her his hand and helped her walk to the edge.

"Jack, what are you going to do?" She started to panic.

"Don't worry," he assured her. "You'll thank me afterwards."

"Jack, no!" she cried as he swiftly picked her up and soared into the night's cool air. It was like a shot of overwhelming ecstasy. It rushed through her blood with extreme velocity that she felt her veins about to explode. The breeze blew on the back of her neck and played with her dress's hem. Even though she was between his strong arms, Rose tasted what it was like to have no boundaries, and, surprisingly, she wanted to drink more of the feeling.

It didn't take him five seconds to touch the ground of the forest below and put Rose down. She stood for a moment, paralyzed, and tried to regain her balance.

"Amazing, isn't it?" Jack asked, watching her closely.

She nodded. Her voice seemed to have stayed behind in the tree house. "Are you ok?"

She nodded again.

"Are you dizzy?" he said, worriedly.

She shook her head. "Unbelievable," she finally said.

Jack exhaled with relief. "I knew you would like it."

They started to make their way through the dark path and towards the house. Jack kept scanning the trees with his eyes, sometimes stopping to listen to a sound unheard by Rose, all the way through the forest. Now she knew what he was looking out for, and started to open her ears wider for any sounds, but nothing was caught by her untrained ears.

"I never lied to you," Jack said, focusing on her. Rose was taken aback by his sudden statement. "I am not like your friend who lied to you."

"I know you're not," she said, realizing what he was referring to, "but your silence confused me."

"You thought I didn't trust you." He pushed a tree branch out of their way and stood at the end of the path where the dimly lit house came into view.

"I was suspicious," she replied and stepped out of the path. "It was the only reasonable explanation I could think of."

"It's better to stay silent than lie to you."

"And, are you still going to stay silent?"

"It depends," he said and pocketed his hands.

"What about your arm?" She pointed at his wounded arm that she had seen in the morning.

"I didn't see them coming."

"They attacked you…"

"It's nothing to worry about," he said in his soothing voice. "Rose, go inside, it's getting cold. And you look like you need some sleep."

Still mesmerized by what she had been through, she turned around towards the house.

"Take care, Rose," Jack said after her, standing under the trees.

"You take care." She smiled feebly back at him. "Don't let them catch you."

"Don't let anyone hurt you again," he said with half a smile and left.

Four: Flight

By the time Rose was back home, the last of her family's local friends were saying goodbye. After she made sure neither Mark nor Angelina were in sight, she quickly tiptoed through the terrace doors and up to her room. Her heart and mind were racing. She threw off her muddied heels and stood in front of the mirror. Something was different about her; vitality and excitement brought a flush to her cheeks and sparkle to her eyes.

A knock vibrated on her door and Anne's voice came from behind it. She took in a deep breath, pushing away the memory of Mark's unwelcome kiss, and opened the door.

"Anne?" she said. "You're still here?"

"Ah, Rose! Where did you go?" Anne hurried towards her. "Are you OK?"

"Yes, Anne. I am fine. I thought you left."

"No, dear. Mark and I decided to stay for the week," Anne announced to Rose's horror. "Just to recover from our travels. You know, we went back to London after we sold our house here. University starts soon."

"I see..."

"A few days here won't hurt," Anne said, obviously having no knowledge of her son's recent action. "And, besides, his left eye is horrible. He said he got into a racket with someone, but he refuses to tell me what happened. Do you know anything about this?"

Rose parted her lips and paused for a moment before answering. "N-no... I don't. Actually, Anne, Mark hasn't been looking well recently. Is something wrong?"

Anne smiled nervously and shook her head. "Oh, no, he is just love-stricken."

Rose tried to keep her smile soft and polite as Anne talked a little more, fighting the heaviness in her eyes. Once Anne retreated back to her room, Rose immediately changed and slipped under the covers in hopes to get a peaceful slumber.

There were screams. Women's screams filled her head as they searched for their children among the huge flames eating away at their houses. She looked around at the devastation and saw people running, trying to escape the fire and fight through a fierce rainy storm. There were other people with arrows and swords, fighting. The faces were a blur, as if she was looking through a window on a rainy night. Only one face was clear, and she was able to recognize it. Jack was on his knees, head held low, and chains tied to his legs and hands. He looked up at her when he noticed her arrival and smiled victoriously. She was about to smile back when suddenly a sword stabbed him in his heart. A bright light covered the scene, and then there was nothing but darkness.

Rose woke up from the nightmare in the middle of the night, soaked in sweat. Her heart was beating frantically, and she could not breathe fast enough for the oxygen to enter her brain. She sat for a couple of minutes until everything in her body settled, and then she crawled from beneath the covers. The smell of ashes still filled her nose and the screams echoed faintly in her ears. Checking to see that it was only a dream, she stood up to peek from behind her window curtains and found everything to be normal. There was no fire or storm, and there was definitely no Jack tied in chains with a sword– she could not think about it. The scene was too heartbreaking to recall.

Trying to tell herself it was only a dream, she reclined back in bed and closed her eyes. But, she was afraid to sleep. What if it came to her again like the other dream? It would be torture. At dawn, when the sun was resurrected from the depth of the sea, Rose finally fell asleep.

A headache followed her throughout the next morning as she nibbled on an apple slice at the kitchen table. With everything she'd learned, Rose started to believe her dreams were not to be ignored. As Akita had said, only the lucky souls were able to hear the spirits of the forest. Her worries grew, and she needed to know if Jack was safe or not. Her heart started beating with a new wave of emotions.

But, before that there was something she knew she must do.

"I need to go to the village," she spoke her thoughts, then checked who was in the room. Bill and Mark were sitting at the kitchen table with her. "Dad, can you drop me?"

"Me too," Mark chipped in casually, as if nothing had happened between them.

"Alright, then Mark can take you," Bill replied, much to Rose's annoyance.

"No, I ain't driving." He paused. "Terrible hangover."

Rose surveyed him for a moment, and caught his eye twitching. Lying again. Her blood shot to her brain, but she remained calm.

Bill ended up dropping them both to the village.

"Don't follow me," she said to Mark and hurried towards the library. Rose had decided that the best way to punish Mark for his unwelcome advances was to ignore him. He never listened anyway.

"Akita, I want to ask you a question," Rose said once she entered the library. "Is there any tribe around the area that starts with the letters K, A, and L?"

Akita looked at her with a frown and Rose realized that she had used too much English for her to understand. Rose went over to the desk and picked up a pencil and a piece of paper. Akita came next to her and bent low over what Rose was trying to explain. On the piece of paper Rose wrote the letters Kal with a blank after them and gave the pencil to Akita to fill it with the rest of the missing letters. Akita looked at Rose and an expression masked her withered face, but then she smiled, taking off the mask, and shook her head.

"I know no tribe in that Abc," Akita said and looked at Rose directly in the eyes. "But, like I say, Rose. Nara 'as spirits, danger. Be careful. Very."

Rose felt the warning flags in Akita's words, and her worry grew more.

"Well, do you know of any tribes that live in the forest? Maybe near the waterfall?"

Akita was silent once again. Then she said, "Is there something you want to say to me Rose?"

Though she shared everything with Akita and trusted her fully, Rose wasn't ready to share this secret yet. She had promised Jack not to tell anyone, as this might actually risk his safety. Thinking about him made her feel worried once more, and she suddenly wanted to leave to go see him.

Gathering herself, she shook her head and dashed out the library. Mark was waiting outside talking on the phone. He ended the call once he saw Rose approaching him.

"Done?" He asked her and coughed a little.

"Yes," she said and sent a furtive glance at him as his breathing shook a little. Mark called Bill who took them back home.

Once they were back, Rose hurried towards the forest. She had to find Jack.

"Rose!" Mark called her when she was about to enter the path. "Where do you think you're going?" She did not stop to look back and stepped into the path under the trees. "Your father said you are not to go in there today," he yelled. "He said to stay with your guests."

"Oh, really?" she replied without stopping. "Watch me go." She broke into a run and was out of Mark's sight in a minute. She was sure he did not have the guts to follow her. Maybe it was because he was weaker and ill these days. But, she was also certain that there was a new burning rage inside him that rumbled deep down.

By the pond, she waited for Jack and wondered how he was going to come, flying or walking? If it were her, she would fly everywhere. The feeling she had experienced the previous day was something beyond freedom, and that was only when Jack was carrying her. So, how would it feel if she were the one on the wind's back?

"You woke up late," Jack said, walking out from between the shadows of the trees. When the sun hit his face, Rose noticed a fresh cut beside his right eye.

"What happened?" she frowned a little, worried he was hurt but also relieved he was alive. Maybe the dream was just a dream.

"Don't worry," he assured her. "I think you have to get used to it. I always try to escape without getting wounded, but sometimes my luck abandons me."

"What do they attack with?"

"Why do you ask such a question?" he asked, raising his brow.

"I just want to know." She shrugged.

"Curiosity?"

"Maybe."

He nodded. "Alright." He smiled at her and thought for a moment. "Well, let's put it this way, they don't use any machinery; you would have heard it. They use anything else that doesn't produce a sound."

"Anything else?" she echoed. "Arrows and swords?"

Jack nodded slowly and she flinched at the images in her mind.

"Why didn't you come flying?"

"It's better to stay low all the time."

Rose bit her lips gently and looked up at him. "I want you to teach me."

Jack stared at her, somehow unsurprised. "I knew this would happen."

"Please, Jack. You don't know what that'll mean to me," she said and watched him as he paced in front of her, looking worried.

"Yes, I do, Rose," he argued and looked at her apologetically, "But, I am afraid I can't let you."

"Why not?"

"It's dangerous and not as easy as you think. It took me years to have total control."

"That's why I want you to teach me how to do it," she said. "Please, Jack."

"What if you fall? What if anything bad happened to you? How am I to live without..." he said and left the sentence hanging in the air. Rose looked into his deep eyes, then away as she blushed.

"Nothing is going to happen," she said softly. "I won't allow it to... Will you teach me?"

Jack stopped in his tracks and gazed into her eyes as he gently touched her cheek with a finger. Rose's heart made a small flip.

"How can I say no to you?"

Rose's cheek reddened under his finger and smiled at him.

"Because I'm your friend?"

His lips broke into a soft smile, a little torn, and retrieved his hand away from her. "My best one... the only one."

And before Rose could reply to him, he moved with unbelievable speed and carried her. A shriek escaped Rose as they shot into the air. When Jack put her down on solid ground, she found herself in the tree house once again. The extraordinary view witnessed from above had a different feeling under the afternoon golden sun. Rose turned away from the view and took a moment to admire the perfection of the tiny dwelling.

Iroko and mahogany woods were neatly cut and smoothed out into a straight platform and a firm roof. Two shelves lined both sides of the con-caved structure that made the whole house appear as if it was hugged by the thick tree branches. A curtain acted as a door to a caved-in room at the far end of the area, which Rose judged to be where he slept. Tree veins crawled around the pitched wood and over the surface of the house, and wove a silk-like green robe around it, camouflaging it to appear as part of the enormous extended tree branches.

A sheathed sword hung beside one of the shelves and a bow and a bunch of arrows laid on top of the other one. Rose cringed at the sight of them and pulled her eyes away from the devices that were designed to kill.

"You built this place?" Rose asked, and sat in one of the bamboo chairs in the middle of the area, still looking around.

"Yes, a long time ago."

"You must have been so young to build a place like this. As you have told me that you've been living here for ten years, then you must have been-"

"Eleven years old."

"So, you're twenty-one now, I presume."

He answered with a small nod, his mouth twitching into a smile and his eyes shining bright. Rose looked away and felt her cheeks get warmer against the cool air. Jack stood up and took only two wide steps to reach the end of the platform, and reached inside his pockets, pulling out an old, ragged bag made out of animal skin.

"Is that...?"

"Are you ready?" He undid the straw that roped the palm-sized bag and held it out for Rose. "It's the Water I had with me that day," he answered her confused look. "If you really want it and you are sure of your decision, just take a sip."

Rose hesitated. With this tiny bag and this ridiculously small amount of water, her wildest dream was knocking at the door. There were opportunities, but some of them escaped the rules of normalcy, and this 'water' did. If she took a gulp, she would be breaking the rules, except she knew that anything with Jack was possible. It might be a risk, but Jack was there, guarding and protecting her.

"You changed your mind fast." Rose looked at him.

"Something I don't usually do, but I know how much it means to you."

She smiled and took a sip out of the bag. The water tasted very weird. It was like a mixture of sea and fresh water, but it was not clear and had a hint of blue color when the sun touched its surface. A tremble started at her toes and ended at her erected hair tips the moment her lips had touched the water. It didn't last more than a second and left Rose's heart pounding heavily.

Energy filled her blood and demanded to be released. She wanted to run as fast as she could and jump off the platform, but she was scared. Jack, knowing exactly what she was feeling from his own experience, started to assist her.

"First lesson," he said and lifted himself a few inches in the air, "control your emotions. Don't let fear or excitement overrule you."

Rose nodded, understanding exactly what he was indicating to. The two feelings were strong, causing her not to know what she was supposed to do, walk or jump, run or fly. As a result, she was frozen to the spot.

"Now, very slowly push yourself upwards," Jack instructed her as she made her first try, but nothing happened. She was still on the ground. "Rose, look at me."

She lifted her head and looked into his eyes obediently.

"Reach deep within yourself," he said. "Forget everything and concentrate on what you are trying to do. Now, close your eyes."

She did as he told her.

"Take a deep breath and feel everything around you... What do you feel most?"

"The wind," she said as the breeze picked up its pace.

"Concentrate on it. This is what you want to control. The wind from now on will be under your command. Focus, Rose."

She tried to do so, focusing and closing her eyes.

"Now you are riding the wind's back." Jack held her hand, still in the air himself. She opened her eyes quickly and found herself leveling with him. She had made it; she was hovering in midair. Rose casted her eyes around and found the view extraordinary. The sea was seen from way up here along with the dark blue line of its depth that met with the serene sky. Flying was different; it broke the rules of gravity and went against everything she was taught to accept.

She looked up and admired the vast emptiness above her.

Without thinking, she pushed herself upwards and sped into the air. Exotic happiness filled her, she felt like a caged bird that was set free, stretching its wings for the first time.

"Rose, slow down." She heard Jack call after her.

"I don't know how!"

"Straighten yourself up. Remember you're the one who is in control."

She stopped abruptly. *I need to practice this*, she thought to herself; *this is not easy.*

"Try to turn around," Jack said, resting behind her. She controlled her balance and her body position with the flow of the wind until she was able to turn and face him.

"You're a fast learner." He beamed.

"That's because you are a good teacher," she said, trying to stay still. A bird fluttered past Rose's head, and she could have sworn that the bird looked at her with disbelief. Well, Rose couldn't blame it; she had after all broke the rules of physics.

Jack ushered her back down to the tree house, where he showed her how to rein all her energy and land without hurting herself. When she touched back down, everything in her body settled and relaxed. Rose went over to the nearest chair and sat down, heavily, still not believing what she had been able to do.

"Are you dizzy?" he asked and sat down as well.

"No. I am fine," Rose assured him. "I just can't believe it. If anyone overheard us talking about it or saw us at it, they'll reckon we went mad. I mean … it's too much to believe!"

Jack smiled then his face turned solemn. "Rose, don't let anyone see you when you are flying. It's even better if you keep your feet on the ground all the time when I am not with you. Ok?" There was a disturbing hint of worry in his voice.

"Why?"

"Please, Rose," he said. "Don't let me be worried about you. You are still new to the whole experience and any mistake could get you hurt. So, promise me that you'll keep your feet firmly on the ground until you master it."

"Fine. I promise," she said reluctantly.

"Thank you," Jack said, relieved, and held out an apple for her to regain back some of her lost energy.

They spent the day on the ground, and walked within the familiar places of the forest. Rose explored him more, and felt closer to him with every passing second. Throughout it all, she noticed how Jack never brought up Mark.

"Jack?"

"You want to ask something, right?"

"Um… yes. How did you know?"

"From the way you say my name." He smiled. "There is a certain tone you use when you come to ask a question. It's full of curiosity."

"Am I that obvious?"

"No, not always." He shook his head, and she saw him fight a smile. He suddenly stopped with a deadpan expression on his face. A cold break disrupted the bushes and rattled against the tree leaves. There was something among the trees around them, threatening.

Something soared beside Rose's head, almost brushing her right ear, and hit the tree trunk behind her with a thud. She jerked her head and found a silver feathered arrow stuck deeply into the wood.

"Rose!" Jack pulled her down, crouching over her to protect her from the now shooting arrows, and they ran deeper into the trees. Rose ran as fast as she could and didn't dare to look behind, lest of the horrors she might see. She heard their footsteps so close behind her and felt the heat of their anger pervading the air.

"Rose, set your mind to get ready for flying!" Jack said as they ran for their lives.

"What? I won't know how while running!" She panicked as the end of the cliff come into view in front of her.

The arrows frequency increased as they ran, and their silver color made them look like shooting bullets.

"Yes, you'll know!" he said, running towards the cliff's edge. "Lesson number two! Unleash every atom of energy within you and let the wind do the rest!"

Rose was scared. Frightened. They were so close to the edge and she was supposed to jump off it and rise into the air, but she did not yet master lesson number one; fear overruled her. She looked at Jack and he looked back at her, taking hold of her hand.

"Never let go," he said and both of them jumped into the wind's open arms, holding them. They soared high up, higher than she had gone during her first try, and into the low clouds. Jack wrapped his arms around her, and pulled her into the protection of his body. Rose could hear his heart beat louder than hers; hiding her face against his neck as a couple of arrows followed them up before they ceased.

After a while, Jack led the way back down and landed in the tree house, a serious look still on his face. Rose was not able to stand on her wobbly feet and dropped into the chair, trying to catch her breath.

"Are you hurt?" Jack asked and stepped over to where she was sitting. She shook her head. "I am so sorry. It was out of my hands."

"How could you?" She met his eyes, her body shaking a little.

Jack frowned and sat down.

"How could you live like this, Jack?" Worry was evident in her shocked eyes. "You live every moment of your life in fear…No, you can't continue like that…you have to put an end to it."

He stood up and looked at the setting sun with contemplation. She watched Jack as he took a deep breath and pocketed his hands. The courage and braveness in his eyes evoked her admiration of him more than ever.

"I can't fight alone," he said after a few moments of thought. "If there was something to be done, it would be to kill the chief…but, I am weak by myself – the time will come very soon." He mumbled the last few words to himself.

Rose was about to ask him what he meant when the sound of hurried footsteps interrupted her.

In a swift movement, Jack grabbed his sword and unsheathed it. He walked to the edge of the platform and peeked down, sword clutched tightly behind his back, and he let out a breath of relief.

The moment he replaced the sword back to its place, someone jumped into the house, causing Rose to lurch with fright in her chair. A young lady was standing in front of them. Her heavy black hair and dark skin contrasted with her sharp, bright, clear, green eyes, and her gracious figure was adorned with wooden accessories and leopard skin. Rose guessed she belonged to a tribe and the animal skin was a sign of her brevity.

"Jack! Are you all right?" The young lady said and grabbed him into her arms. "They were so close this time!"

"Did anyone see you?" He released himself from her strong hug.

"No, they left from another route."

"Good," he said and breathed deeply. "Come, there is someone I want you to meet." He walked over to where Rose was sitting with a confused smile.

"Lilly," he said, referring to the young lady who looked at Rose with a frown. "I would like you to meet Rose. Rose, this is Lilly; my sister."

Rose felt immediately relieved.

Lilly looked from Rose to Jack and squinted her eyes. "I never knew you had a friend," she said in the same mixed accent as Jack's, though hers was slightly more Naryan.

"Well, now you know," he said quietly.

"Sorry, but Jack never told me that he has a beautiful friend like you," she said and smiled at Rose with cordial eyes. She stretched her right hand, which was wrapped with a coarse cloth, and Rose shook it, holding Lilly's firm handshake.

Rose smiled back, her voice had escaped her again.

"How did you two meet?" she said, and started to open the small cupboards and search the shelves. She got out three cups and a bag full of dark brown powder.

"Not far from here," Jack said and looked at Rose, who was staring back at him uncertainly. "By the pond." He continued. The smell of brewed coffee filled the air, and Rose watched Lilly from her seat as she poured it into the cups.

"I know you are confused," Jack said to Rose, who hadn't uttered a word since Lilly had come. "I couldn't speak about her. She is undercover. She was able to live with the tribe because of her resemblance to my mother. The tribe accepted her to live with them and they thought she wouldn't be able to contact me after I ran away. But, she's been a great help to me, filling me with their news."

"I see," she finally said, however, she was a little disappointed that Jack had not confided her with it. She watched Lilly as she gave her the cup of coffee.

"Is there anything new you can tell me?" Jack asked his sister.

Lilly fell silent for a moment. "They are up to something big, Jack," she said. "They won't give up until they get your head so, you have to start doing something. Stop it before it's too late."

"It's not time yet," he said, avoiding eye contact with either of them.

Rose frowned at Jack, not understanding his meaning. Lilly looked at him sharply and was about to negotiate more on the subject, but stopped when she found Jack giving her a reproachful look.

"Why don't you, Lilly, read Rose's cup," he said, breaking the silence.

"How can someone read a cup?" Rose asked as Lilly took Rose's finished cup and started looking inside it, rotating it left and right. Jack lit up some electric lamps that were hanging from the ceiling so Lilly would be able to see the many different patterns at the bottom of the cup.

"Not anyone can read or see what's inside," Lilly said and drew a smile, which carried something with it, like the one Jack smiled sometimes. "Only the gifted ones can see what lies within the patterns of life—."

Lilly broke off mid-sentence and her eyes widened with horror at the cup. "Jack!" she said in an alarmed voice. "Take Rose back to her house immediately!"

"What is it?" He jumped up from his seat.

"They are after her!" she said. Lilly and Jack looked at each other for a couple of seconds, as if they were communicating non-verbally.

"What's going on?" Rose asked when she saw the stern look on Jack's face. "Why are they after me?"

Without any second thoughts, Jack took hold of Rose and shot through the night's air. When they had set foot on solid, she found herself back in her house and in her own balcony.

"I am so sorry, Rose," Jack said in a croaked voice. "I should've been more careful."

"Why are they after me?" Rose asked him again and leaned on the wooden rails of the balcony for support, trying to catch her breath.

"So they could get to me," he said.

"What do you mean by that?"

"They're trying to take advantage of our friendship," he said, his eyes shining beneath the moonlight.

"Was that what Lilly saw in the cup?"

He nodded.

"What are we going to do?" she said and felt a tear escape from her eye.

"You are not going to do anything," he said, looking at her falling tear. "You will stay here, Rose, safely with your family... Promise me, Rose. Promise me that you won't set foot in the forest until-"

"Until?"

"Until I sort things out."

Silence.

"I need your promise," he told her.

"I promise," Rose nodded slowly, a deep sadness inside her. It felt like she was about to suddenly lose all the wonderful new things she had gained.

Jack hovered in midair, ready to take off, and stared at her for a few moments, as if he was taking in her sight. Before Rose could utter a word, he shot into the blackness of the night with extreme power that she felt the rails vibrate under her hand.

Five: Mark's Time

The next three days had passed without any news from Jack. Rose was not able to go and search for him in the forest, and he did not come to assure her that things were all right... or that he was fine. Instead, Rose spent her days worrying about him and trying to answer her thoughts. Jack had a sister whom he had never spoken of before, and she lived with the mysterious tribe which was hunting her brother down. And now, they were after Rose. Was that really what Lilly had seen in Rose's cup? Was it even real? Could the future be predicted or was it a presumption? There were no rational answers to her provoking thoughts.

Life had turned upside down in a moment. Since the day she had met Jack, everything in her life felt better. She had learned how to overcome fear and discover the impossible. Rose believed that fate and destiny were involved in every aspect of life; that was how everything worked. She was destined to meet Jack and everything that happened since then was built upon it. Where would her fate take her? And how about Jack? Thinking about him worried her; he was the one struggling with a harsh life.

Sometimes dreams came to Rose in colors, other times they were brief visions, and rarely there was nothing at all. That night her dream was different. There were no colors nor phantasms, but eerie darkness. Along with the blackness was a soft and calm voice, yet it was commanding. The unknown voice was repeating the same words, forming a command. 'Mend what was fractured for the time is near to rise...'

Rose was awakened by a dreadful scream that pierced her ears. She sprang out of bed in shock and raced out of the room into the dark corridor. Looking for the source of the shrill, Rose spotted a couple of figures standing by Mark's room. She moved slowly towards the dark figures that were standing around someone, and her heart started to skip faster when she noticed Angelina in her nightgown and a strange plump man who looked from the village. When she went closer, she was surprised to see Anne standing between Angelina and the man and crying heavily.

"Calm down, Mrs. Parker," the man said in a perfect English accent.

"What's happening?" Rose asked, looking panic-stricken.

Anne looked at Rose, her face crumbled with misery, and threw herself in Rose's arms.

Before Anne could utter anything other than the unstoppable sobs, the man spoke.

"It's time," he said, ashen-faced.

"Who are you? And what are you talking about?" Rose demanded, feeling that she was about to hear something dreadful.

"I am Dr. Liu," he said. Although he had an English accent, his appearance stated otherwise. "Mark's doctor."

"Is Mark all right?"

The doctor looked down at the floor, escaping her terrified eyes, and shook his head. "I am sorry, but Mark is not doing well."

"What do you mean he's not doing well?" she asked, looking around the three of them. "Can someone answer me?"

"Mark is-" The doctor started.

"I will tell you," Anne interrupted between sobs. "When Mark was a baby, he was diagnosed with a severe lung disease... The doctors thought he wouldn't make it past his early months, but he survived. Then, they said his life was limited and he wouldn't last for long..." She paused and drew in a long breath. "I have stayed up nights for years and took care of him. I was determined to give him the best temporarily life. When he got older, it was time to tell him. Oh, I can't forget the way he looked that day! He was twelve years old, almost a young man, but he cried like a baby." Anne stopped and took Rose in her arms. "He was so attached to you," she continued. "I saw the way he looked at you and I understood why he had changed. He loved you, Rose – but, he wasn't able to tell you about his illness because –" Anne sobbed more in Rose's arms.

"His health was stable for more than a year now," Dr. Liu said, "and I thought that this was a good sign, indicating a possibility of being cured. But, it came back."

"I want to see him," Rose said and released herself from Anne's grip.

"I advise you," the doctor said before she turned the doorknob, "to not let him speak a lot. Let him save his breath."

She entered the cold room, slowly and soundlessly. The only light in the room was coming from the bedside lamp beside Mark who was lying immobile in bed, almost like a lifeless body. Rose went by his side and looked at his pale face that was once alive and bright. His lips were pale blue and the area around his closed eyes was grey. The sound of his shallow, rapid breathing filled the room as his ribs went up and down with every breath his lungs fought to make.

Suddenly, she felt responsible for his sufferings. Tears raced down from her eyes like a rushing waterfall as she walked closer to Mark and reached for his hand. She was appalled at its icy cold touch, and he woke up at the sense of her warm hand against his.

"I'm sorry," she said and sobbed quietly, dropping herself in the chair that had been drawn beside his bed.

"Now you care," Mark said, barely speaking. "I have to be weak to win your kindness…Well, here I am... waiting... to die."

"Don't say that," she said and held his hand tightly. "I always cared about you, Mark."

"You never loved me…" he said and tried to draw in a breath.

"Shush. Don't waist your breath on false words," she said.

"It's not the disease…" Mark said and looked at her feebly. "I'm exhausted and out of breath... pursuing something that could never be reached."

The door opened and the doctor came in, fiddling with his case and mumbling under his breath. He beckoned to Rose to come out into the balcony.

"I believe you are a close friend of Mark," he said.

"More than a friend actually," she said. "A sister."

"Yes, that is why I have to tell you," he said and clutched his hands. "Mark's condition has become worse than it's ever been."

She felt her heart drop.

"What's that supposed to mean?"

"There is a tumor in his lungs."

Rose stared horridly at the doctor, then turned her head and looked at Mark through the glass door. "Lung cancer?" she heard her quivering voice say.

"I am sorry, Ms. Peterson – isn't it?" he said.

"Rose," she said absentmindedly, still looking at Mark. "When does he start treatment?"

"I am afraid it's too late. However, there are some changes in his medication. We'll have to wait and see their reaction."

"Shouldn't he be taken back to London to get the best treatment?" she said as tears refilled her eyes. "There might be a possibility..."

"I am sorry, Ms. Peterson," Dr. Liu said, "but the only possibility that Mark has is for tumor to disappear by itself. And as that's unlikely to happen, it'll be a miracle if it did. As for taking him back to London, it's best to keep him here. The plane's pressure would not be a pleasant journey and it could harm his respiratory process."

"How many days?" she said, not believing that they were talking about Mark Parker.

"Two weeks," he said and made his way to re-enter the room. "Who knows? It could be more or less. But, this must be kept between you and I. Mrs. Rodger does not know of the development that happened in her son's lung."

Dr. Liu left Rose to process and went to check on Mark. "How is your chest pain?" the doctor said.

"Durable," Mark replied in a whisper.

"Then we'll hold back on the Morphine. And by tomorrow the rest of the medication will arrive from London. It's better for you to sleep now. Goodnight, Mr. Parker. After you, Rose." Dr. Liu had walked to the door and opened it for her.

"No," she said and sat in the chair by Mark. "I'll stay until he sleeps."

"Very well then. Goodnight, Ms. Peterson. I'll come back tomorrow afternoon." He closed the door behind him.

Mark opened his mouth to speak, but she hushed him and held his hands until he went to sleep. At dawn, when Mark's breathing was slow and steady, she went back to her room and tried to sleep. But, her eyes would not close and her brain refused to rest. It was hard to believe.

The sky rumbled outside her window. Her thoughts immediately flew to Jack and she prayed he was safe. The sound of gushing rain and thunder chased away any sleep, causing her to end up in the kitchen. She hoped a warm drink would calm her racing mind.

She heard footsteps coming down the stairs. "Dad, you're up early."

Bill entered the kitchen dressed in a robe.

"Make me one with you," he said as he watched her make some tea.

When she had set the cup in front of him and sat down, her dad asked. "Are you all right?"

She lightly shook her head. "Mark..."

He let out a sigh and nodded, "I did not know either..."

They both sipped their warm drink in silence, before Bill spoke again. "So, what about him?"

"About who?" Rose asked, confused.

"That young man. Jack." Bill looked at her with concern in his lined face.

"Um…yes?" She took a sip to hide her anxiousness.

"He seems to be a nice fellow."

"We are not going to have this kind of talk, Dad," Rose said.

"You misunderstood me. I just wanted to know if it was true what he did to Mark."

"Do you know what Mark did then?"

"Yes, I do – and thank Jack for me for defending you," he replied.

Rose was taken aback. "Did you say anything to Mark?"

"I definitely did," he said. "I threatened him. Told him that if he touches you one more time, I'll strangle him to death."

Her mouth twitched a little. "Maybe when he gets better..." Her heart sank. "It's hard to be the second choice. Unrequited love."

"Don't feel guilty."

Rose was a little surprised at her father's words. "I know... I forgive him."

"Forgiving like your mother," he said and looked at Rose with nostalgia in his eyes and reached out to touch her face. "I can see your mother in you whenever I look at you. Especially your eyes... sometimes I feel that she is looking right at me." The broken heart was still evident in his fatherly eyes, and the wrinkles in his face made him look older than he already was. "She loved you very much," he said. His eyes turned red and were ready to cry, but there were no tears left to shed.

"I know," she said and squeezed his hands warmly.

The sky cracked and vibrated the kitchen windows, startling Rose and causing her to almost drop her mug. Bill pushed his chair back to leave.

"Dad, wait," she said before he went out of the kitchen. "How did you feel when you chose Mum instead of Angelina?"

Bill's expression was unreadable and he stared at the ground. "A little selfish," he replied at last. "I hated myself for breaking her heart, but my love for your mother was greater."

"That's why you chose her after..."

"Yes, yes," he said. "I had to make amends."

"Second choice," Rose said, remembering Angelina's heated words.

"Yes," Bill said slowly.

"Do they always have to... change when they know that they are second?"

"Not always, but yes. Something gets fractured and it stays with them forever," Bill said softly and went out of the kitchen, leaving Rose at the table.

She reached for an apple and started to cut it into slices. Lost in her thoughts, the knife slipped and cut through the skin on her finger. Frowning, she wrapped the wound with a cloth, and went back to her room to try to sleep just as the clouds started clearing up.

Well after noon, Rose woke up again with a ringing in her ears. The voice had whispered in her dream again... 'Mend what was fractured for the time is near to rise...' These words followed her around as she went to Mark's room and found Anne plunged in the armchair next to him, almost as pale as her son. After Rose had convinced Anne to go and rest, she sat down and touched Mark's cheek lightly, wishing she could take his pain away. Every painful word she had said to him and every ungrateful look she had given him, spat back at her and she wanted to take them all back. She had never felt so disgusted with herself.

He smiled, barely twitching the right corner of his lips, when he opened his eyes and found her in front of him.

"How are you feeling?" she said.

He gave her a small nod. "You know about the tumor?"

"Y-Yes," she said, feeling her eyes fill. "Why didn't you tell me?"

"You never gave me a chance."

"You could have took-"

"I can't run away from it," he interrupted. "It gets closer with every passing second... It doesn't matter if I was ill or not... We all die at the end. Now or later."

"Mark, no!" Rose shook her head, terrified by his breathless speech. "Don't say that again..."

"So you really do care, don't you?"

"Of course, I do! You were the closest person to me and you know that. You were my best friend. You were my big, protective brother and I loved you for always standing by my side and never letting go of my hand." She dabbed the sweat on his forehead with a piece of cold wet cloth. "And when my mother was gone, you were the one who pulled me back on my feet. After all of that, you think that you don't hold a piece of my heart? But, when you started to think of me in a different way than I thought of you, I had to run away."

"Why?"

"Because I wanted to keep you in my memory as my friend and brother, nothing more."

"That's when you started hating me, then?" Mark asked, weakness conquering his voice.

"I never hated you, Mark. The reason for my actions was because of my anger at how you were making me choose. Like the rest of them, you are not giving me the chance to make my own decisions."

"I did not want-" he took a deep breath before continuing, "to put you in that position."

"Maybe you did not realize what you were making me choose between. I was to be your girlfriend or else you would not be my friend anymore."

He took in a deep breath. "I... did not want... to lose you."

A small relieved sigh escaped her. "You never will, Mark, as long as you're honest with me."

But before he could take a breath to reply, a spell of heavy coughing trapped his breathing. His whole body crumbled into a ball as his face went paler and his lips darkened to a deep shade of purple until blood spluttered on the bedcover.

"Someone help!" Rose cried out of the door. "Call the doctor!"

The coughing stopped instantly as it had started and Mark raised his head up very slowly. He did not utter a word and his eyes started to close. She froze for a moment and felt him slip away into unconsciousness. She hurried over to the bed and pressed her hand against his chest, feeling his weak heartbeats and shallow breaths his lungs fought to make.

Dr. Lui dashed into the room and with one look at Mark, he quickly set up a mask and oxygen tube. Mark's lungs made a deep, loud grunt as it drew the oxygen through the mask.

"You've got to take him to a hospital!" Rose declared and tears of fear fell from her eyes. She tried not to look at the bloodstained bedcover.

"We can't, Ms. Peterson. And the nearest hospital in Nara is too far away from here. I'm afraid he wouldn't be able to make it through the bumpy streets of Nara," the doctor said, taking out a bag full of long needles. "So, if you would please step outside and calm down until I finish giving him his injections. Unless you don't mind the sight of needles."

"Fine," she said, feeling her stomach turn. She left Mark's room and returned to her own, entering her bathroom. The bloodied cloths she'd seen reminded her to change her own bandage. Rose unwrapped her finger, and her heart dropped. She blinked several times and looked quizzically at her finger.

There was only a soft pink line where the cut was supposed to be, and it looked as if it was a week old. But, it was just this morning. Did she dream that she had cut her finger?

A soft knock brought her out of her puzzlement. The sight of Jack standing in her balcony was like taking a much needed deep breath. She hurried towards him and threw herself into his arms, for once letting her emotions take control over her. Once she felt his strong arms lock around her, her tears came rolling down and staining his shirt.

He did not speak for a while and stood there holding her in his arms. She could feel him cautiously placing his cheek lightly against her head.

"He's dying," she mumbled against the crook of his neck.

"What happened?" he asked, and she felt his arms stiffen around her.

"I don't know... I did not know anything... at all..."

"Calm down, Rose, and tell me what happened to him," he said, trying to comfort her.

"Mark has lung cancer, Jack," Rose said. She released herself and looked at him, her eyes sparkling with tears. "He's saying his goodbyes."

"How do you know?" He looked distressed.

"From his doctor. He said that it would be a miracle if he survived after the coming two weeks!"

"How can I help?"

"I think I'm the one who is supposed to help him," she said, thoughtfully. "That's what the voice said, I assume."

"Hm?" Jack frowned.

"I had a dream the night before I found out about Mark," she explained, recalling the words she had heard during her sleep. "It was very weird. Oh, I don't know. It could be nothing important."

"Dreams are important," he said, the frown still on his face. "They can be messages from the spirits, a key to an answer or to something we have lost. Everything has a purpose and dreams do as well...and we won't understand them except if we look and listen carefully to what they are trying to deliver."

"Even in a bad situation you are good with words." She half smiled, drying her tears with the back of her hands. "Alright then, I'll tell you."

"Pliable," he teased her.

"No, I am not. You are relentless, that's all..." She sniffed. "In the dream – well it wasn't really a dream – it was just darkness and someone repeating a sentence. It was very short, like an order. The voice was saying, 'Mend what was fractured for the time is near to rise.'"

When she had finished, Jack stared at her with a deadpan expression on his face and clenched his teeth.

"Do you know what it means?"

"I am not certain," he said. "I could be mistaken..."

"Tell me your thoughts," she said. "I want to help Mark, please. If the dream is uncovering a way to help him survive or a medicine that would do the trick-"

"I can't tell you."

"What?" She frowned in confusion. "Jack, I know that you don't like Mark, but you've got to help me."

"It's nothing personal," he said. "If I could help him, then I would do so. But, things have changed, Rose. It's not like before."

"Jack, you're scaring me," she said and looked at him apprehensively.

"Don't be," he whispered and pulled out a long necklace with a large red bead from underneath his shirt. "Here, I want you to keep this." Jack fastened the necklace around her neck.

Rose stared at the red bead, images from the dream of the little boy rushed into her head.

"My mother gave it to me before I escaped." He smiled a little. "She said it would protect me from harm and danger, and I want you to have it... " He paused for a moment, "to let you know that I'll always be there with you and for you."

Rose hesitated for she knew what he meant. By giving her the necklace, he was certain that she would never forget him if anything went wrong, which could easily happen. Whatever destiny held for them, it could be brutal.

"You can tell me what's disturbing you," she said, noticing the sorrow in his eyes.

"I wish I could, but I can't," Jack said.

"But, Jack, how am I-"

"I am afraid I can't give you the answer to that question."

"I thought you meant it when you said you'll always be there," Rose said, her view getting obscured from the tears that were filling her eyes.

"Of course I'll always be there for you, Rose. I would die for you," he said strongly. "But, I don't have the answer to your dream. You are the one who holds the answer to it in your hand. You, Rose, and not anyone else."

After Jack left, Rose felt the pit of her stomach getting heavy, but the weight on her shoulders was even more unbearable as the days passed by. She did not figure out what her dream was trying to tell her, and wondered if the healed cut on her finger had anything to do with it. Her worries swayed between Jack and Mark, feeling a large desire to burst into tears. But, she kept it together for everyone's sake.

A few days later, Rose entered Mark's room to find several of their schoolmates visiting. Anthony, Zane, and two other young men stood around his bed, or what seemed like his deathbed. Mark slowly turned his head and looked at Rose, a weak smile on his face.

"Rose..." He said to her.

"Hello, boys," she said, nodding to their friends and went to sit by Mark's side.

"Ay, she is a princess," said the shortest one of them all.

"Shut your mouth, Paul," Zane snapped at him. "Don't mind him, Rose."

"He's just saying, she is a real beauty," a dark-haired Julio said in an Italian accent.

"Could you all stay away from her," Mark said in a whisper. "Or I'll stick a…"

"Got it, mate," Anthony chuckled lightly then fell quiet as he watched his best friend suck in a painful breath. "Is it worse than before?"

"Nah, same." Mark's blue-lips smirked, but he reached out for the oxygen mask beside him and placed it on his mouth.

"Are you ok?" Rose asked, worriedly.

He nodded.

"Do you want me to call the doctor and tell him to come now, instead of at night?"

He shook his head and pulled the mask off his face. Anthony cleared his voice and said, "By the way, Mark... Heidi wants to see you."

A small sting ringed inside Rose's chest as she heard the name.

Mark paused for a moment and closed his eyes. "Where – is – she?"

"Downstairs," Anthony said calmly, but could not stop himself from beaming at Mark's effort to show how irritated he was.

"Why, Anthony? How could you?" Mark hissed.

"Told you he'd take it like that," Zane told Anthony.

"I knew you'd say that, Mark," Anthony said, his face suddenly wiped out of any expression. "But, she insisted on coming when she heard that we were, and I just couldn't tell her not to come... Sorry, mate, but I believe she has every right to see you."

Before Mark opened his mouth, the door opened and all of them jerked their heads towards it. Luba appeared in the doorway, carrying a wooden tray full of glasses filled with chilled drinks. Rose breathed out with relief as Luba passed the drinks around the boys. She had thought Luba was someone else.

"Who's the mental here that told her?" Mark asked when Luba exited the room and closed the door behind her.

"I did," Julio said, shrugging casually. "What? I thought she must know."

"You should have asked Anthony before opening your big mouth!"

"Mark. Give her a break, will you?" Anthony said. "The girl's been in love with you since, I don't know, middle school maybe. You should have seen her face. She was terrified as if she'd seen a ghost."

"Wait a minute," Rose said before Mark could open his mouth to reply. "Are you talking about Heidi…Heidi Butterfield?"

Anthony looked over at her and said, "Rose, it's-"

"Excuse me," Rose said without looking at Anthony, and stamped furiously out of the room.

How was she going to act? After all of these years, how could she dare to show up here? On her way to her room, Rose looked down from the rails of the stairs and found a body with a mass of familiar, blonde hair sitting with its back to the stairs. Heidi Butterfield held her face in her hands; her shoulders were shaking.

Anger and fury filled her blood at the sight of the unwelcome visitor. Fighting the urge to go down and kick her out of her house, Rose proceeded to her room and slammed the door with all her might.

"Someone is very angry."

She jerked when she saw Jack standing in her room. "Goodness, Jack, you scared me. But, good timing." She let out a breath and smiled up at Jack.

"Are you ok?" he asked and touched her cheek lightly before retrieving his hand.

Rose noticed there was something different about him, something sad. His eyes were desolated and he looked haggard, but he managed to pull her favorite smile. "No, it's not," she said, her voice subduing. "I still did not find the meaning to the dream, and there is an unexpected and undesired person downstairs."

"Let me guess, the friend that had lied to you?" he asked.

"How did you know?"

"Well, I have seen an army of young men and a single girl enter the house earlier. And from the way you described the 'undesired' visitor, I could tell it's her."

"Yes, it's her," Rose said and folded her hand tightly.

"Ignore her," Jack said, putting a red rose in her hair, which he had picked up on his way to her. "Act as if she's not here."

"That's what I was going to do anyway, but I am not able to let it go just like that... you don't know what she said after I left."

"Can I know?" Jack asked, carefully. "It's up to you."

"After I quietly left school and packed my bags, she said that – that I died," Rose answered, tears swarming in her eyes. "Whenever anyone asked what happened to Rose Peterson, she told them that and made a scene out of it!"

"But, why did she say that?" he asked with a frown.

"I don't know…I really don't."

"And Mark is still friends with her? Even after what she had said about you…?"

"That's what I really don't understand," Rose said, shaking her head. "Since when was she close with Mark? I know she hated him when he used to come around to play with me."

"Did he play with her as well?"

"Well, no. He only played with me."

"Maybe that's the reason then," Jack said and squinted at the setting sun.

"You mean she was jealous?"

"Probably." He shrugged. "Can you think of someone who had done the same?"

"Angelina!" Rose said, realizing what might have pushed her ex-best friend to spread the terrible rumor. "Heidi loved Mark, but he was not giving her any attention back. But, that's just unfair. I didn't do anything to her to make her say that!"

"Jealousy can push people beyond their limits."

"But, we were children..." Rose frowned slightly. "Mark did what... he did, because he was intimidated by you. His love is strong but... controlling."

Jack fell silent for a few moments before speaking. "You have to let it go, Rose. You have to focus on finding the answer. Concentrate or you won't find it. Don't let anything distract you."

"Well, how am I supposed to do that? I just can't find an answer in eight words that I heard in a dream," she said, playing with Jack's necklace that never parted her chest.

"I believe you can," he said and gave her the favorite smile. Her heart skipped a little faster. "Do you think it's fine if I checked on Mark?"

"Yes, of course," she said.

"Meet me downstairs in one minute," Jack said.

"What?" Rose frowned, but Jack had already zoomed out the balcony door and over the house. She ran out the room and into the corridor, puzzled. The doorbell rang and she heard Angelina answering it.

"Good evening." Bill's voice was heard from downstairs and Rose guessed that he must have just arrived. She went down to greet him and froze when she saw Jack standing next to Bill on the porch.

"Oh, there she is," Bill said, talking to Jack and pointing at her. "Rose, Jack here came to see Mark. Take him to Mark's room. I am sure he would be delighted to see Jack."

Rose looked from Bill to Jack, and then nodded to Bill. Jack passed Bill and followed her upstairs.

"I had to make a proper visit," he whispered as they climbed the stairs and walked along the corridor. "I was lucky to find your father getting out of his car."

"Did he see you flying over the house?"

"No, I landed a few meters into the forest. But, it would have been a close one if I hadn't seen him in the darkness."

"Take care next time," she said and stood in front of Mark's door, the sound of laughter filled the room. Rose was sure Heidi was inside because she had not seen her when she was downstairs. Her eyes met Jack's as she reached for the knob.

"What's wrong?" he asked in a hushed tone.

"You are truly different from any other person I have ever known. You forgive, Jack, and that's something people usually don't do."

"Is that bad?"

"No, it gives you freedom, Jack Casper."

Jack broke a smile as she pushed open the door and peeked into the room.

"Mark," she said and tried not to look at Heidi, who was sitting in the chair Rose usually sat in beside Mark. "You have a visitor." Rose noticed the suspiciously raised eyebrow on Anthony's face and Zane's curious stare at Jack as he entered the room. "He asked to see you," Rose added when she saw Mark's glare.

"What an honor." Mark breathed out and turned his face away from Jack. "But, I am afraid I don't need your pity, so don't bother to waste your time."

Rose cleared her throat. What was she thinking?

"Can you excuse your friends for a minute?" Jack asked.

"You can say whatever you want in front of them. There is nothing to hide," Mark said, still looking the other way.

"Is there a problem, Mark?" Anthony asked and slowly stood up from his seat. He scrutinized Jack closely, maintaining a neutral expression that evoked his brooding eyes. Jack slowly turned his head and looked sharply at this stranger, but did not speak. Anthony was indeed as big as Jack, and tough, but he could not ignore the power in Jack's eyes.

Feeling the sudden acceleration of cold tension in the room, Mark gave a light nod to Anthony who signaled for the boys to get out of the room. With another glance at Jack, he exited the room. Rose felt Heidi look at her as she went out before Anthony, but she did not dare to look back.

"I came here," Jack began when Rose had closed the door behind Anthony, "not to give you my pity, although I was planning to. However, I would like to tell you a few words... You are a good man, Mark."

Mark returned a bleak stare, and Rose could almost detect the sarcasm in his lined lips.

"If you were not a good man, then none of your friends would be standing by your side, not even your best-friend Rose," Jack continued. "Not even the one whom you thought was your enemy, a great misunderstanding." He paused and walked to the window, looking at the starless night.

"What are you trying to say?" Mark asked, perplexed by Jack's speech.

"People change, Mark. They change in how they feel and how they look at situations as they discover certain things in life…they look at it from a different perspective, and they forgive," Jack said, turned around at the last word and winked to Rose.

"Who are you to lecture me?" Mark exclaimed, but his voice ended up in a croaked whisper.

"Calm down. I'm only saying I hope you get better soon," Jack said and made his way to the door.

"Oh, don't count on it – it's too late already. Can't you see? I am dying," Mark said gallantly.

"No, I will. And, you'll see that it's never too late to hope,"

Jack said before getting out of the room. "It's never too late," he repeated and looked straight into Rose's eyes, sending her a message that she did not catch.

"What are you two playing at?" Mark asked the moment Jack had closed the door behind him.

"No, Mark. I did not know what he was going to say," Rose said and sat beside Mark on the bed. She was surprised by Jack's speech more than Mark was. His speech and words were very strong and powerful that throughout it she just wanted to watch him and let his words sink into her.

"Who does he think he is? Talking like that..." Mark complained, however, Rose felt that he was affected by it too. "I am sorry, Rose," Mark said, changing the subject.

"For?"

"Heidi's arrival. I didn't know that she'd come, and I know that you are angry that she's here."

"I know it's not your fault," she said. "But, I want to know why she is here. Is what Anthony said about her true? That she's in love with you."

"Yes." Mark mussed, his hands started trembling a little. "Unfortunately." Rose broke a small smile and held his hands. "That makes sense."

Another coughing episode claimed Mark's ability to breathe, and having some practice by then, Rose was able to assist him through it until his shivering body calmed down, and he fell asleep.

Rose walked out of the room and met the doctor in the corridor, muttering something underneath his breath. He was always muttering, she realized. She told him what had happened to Mark and he gave her a nod and went inside the room. When she reached the bottom of the stairs, she found that his friends had not yet left. They were all gathered around weeping Heidi, who was sitting with her hands covering her face.

"He's going to be all right," Julio said to Heidi, trying to comfort her.

"You shouldn't have come," Anthony said, standing behind her chair and looking extremely worried. They all stopped trying to calm Heidi down when they saw Rose.

"Mark is asleep. Try not to disturb him," she said. "And, he is going to be well, don't worry. I – I assure you of that..."

They all gave her a nod and a smile back except for Heidi, who was staring at her with fire in her eyes. Rose stared directly back at her, and the fire in Heidi's eyes went out immediately. She seemed to be afraid of Rose and covered her face again, pretending to be weeping. Rose did not understand what had happened, but all she knew that power had suddenly filled her at that moment. She felt stronger.

They did not linger around for long, and each one returned to their homes, promising to return in the morning to check on their friend. Once they were out of sight, everything collapsed back on Rose's shoulders. Every part of her felt heavy and she dragged herself to bed. But, the good-night sleep she had hoped for was disturbed by Mark's choked shouts for painkillers. Listening to him, she hugged herself and cried silently until she finally drifted off to sleep.

Six: The Healer

Jack's 'proper visits' increased since his pep talk to Mark, and since Bill had cordially welcomed him in. He lessened his usual visits through her balcony and came through the front door. Rose did not care how he made his entrance as long as he was there with her for a longer time. Bill did not complain nor comment on Jack's frequent presence, and Jack always made sure to leave before he arrived from work.

With everything going on, Anne did not notice Jack around, and even if she had known that Jack was the reason behind Mark's blackened eye, which had left a small mark behind, she would not judge him. Angelina, on the other hand, was not very hospitable towards the situation. Whenever she would answer the front door, Angelina greeted Jack with a disgusted look from head to toe. She looked at him as if he was a contagious virus that must be fought immediately; however, Jack's decency won over her hostility. He would wait outside the door until Rose came and gave him the permission to enter.

They were all waiting for it to happen, and Rose felt more responsible for every painful breath Mark took. His friend's occupied themselves and wandered in and out the house as they pleased after they had checked on Mark. Rose envied their freedom to wander off whenever they desired. She watched Heidi as she stepped into the path between the trees and picked up some wild flowers. Her blood boiled. Her territory was being intruded and touched by unworthy people, her territory that she could no longer visit.

"You promised me," Jack said, standing beside her on the balcony.

She wondered if he could feel the heat of her boiling blood through her skin. "If I only had the chance to release myself a little, to ease the stress away, I would not be standing here looking desperate," Rose said and looked at him pleadingly.

"No, don't even think about it," he said, understanding her tone. "Everything's better with your feet on the ground."

"Stapled to the ground more like it," she mumbled.

"I am sorry, Rose, but this is for your safety."

"I know." She lightly nodded and stared at the trees. "How is Lilly?"

"Don't worry about her. She's been doing this for the past ten years and was never caught."

"Why didn't you tell me about her?" she asked and cranked her head towards him.

"I couldn't risk talking about her and uncovering her role if anyone overheard us," he whispered. "And I didn't lie to you."

"I know that," she said, a little annoyed. "But, you are keeping secrets from me. And I wonder how many more there are that you still did not tell me about."

Jack fell silent and avoided meeting her eyes.

A sigh escaped her. "Is there any news about the you-don't-want-to-say-its-name tribe?"

"No."

"At least tell me the name."

"No."

"Then tell me your theory about my dream," she said, giving in to his stubbornness. "I still could not find the slightest coherent meaning to it."

"I told you I am not sure myself," he said softly, but his voice held something heavier.

"What is it that you are not sure of?" She turned around and locked him with her eyes. He sighed. "Is it that hard for you to trust me?" she whispered.

"It's not about that," he said, torn. "It is never about trust. How could you even think like that? I would trust you with my life, Rose."

She tried not to smile, but to no avail. "Considering the circumstances I'm in, I would have argued with you until I squeezed out any answer from you. However, I need to concentrate on finding the mysterious unknown something that could save Mark." She tried to keep her smile, but it resisted lingering on her lips.

"You will."

"What if I don't?" She felt a lump forming in her throat.

"Why are you dealing with this as if it's your own fault?" he said. "Rose, don't blame yourself for something you haven't done."

She bit her lips slightly and turned her face away from him. "I am not blaming myself, it's just... I feel it's my responsibility to cure him. Like it's my mission." She mumbled the last word. "I don't know how that could be. It's absurd..."

Jack reached out for her chin and gently turned her head to meet her eyes. "You don't have to understand everything in life. There are some things better to accept than understand. I don't understand half of my life, but I accept what it offers."

Staring into his warm eyes, Rose took a while to reply as she tried to calm her racing heart. "I don't understand the dream, so how am I supposed to find the hidden message?"

"But you can change what might happen in the future. You have a choice."

"A choice in what, Jack? My life is full of decisions made by other people, decisions that are supposed to be made by me. Life sometimes doesn't leave you the chance to make your own choices." She felt tears roll down her cheeks as a suffocating feeling grabbed at her heart. It was frightening and demanding, and all she wanted was to let the wind carry her away from the heaviness in her heart. Her eyes closed as the wind rushed through her hair and felt her feet lift up from the ground. In a matter of seconds, she was hovering and about to sore with a blasting energy.

"No, Rose!"

His alarmed voice caught her off balance and she hit the balcony floor with a loud thud. He crouched beside her. "Are you hurt?"

"My knees," she said in a pained tone and panted as she tried to calm her racing heart.

"You could've got caught, Rose." His tone was a little strong.

"I can't handle this anymore, Jack. It's too much!" she said and tears rolled down her eyes. "Too much thinking, too much stress. I just wanted to clear my mind from everything and to stop thinking for a moment. I thought a little wouldn't harm..."

"I am sorry, Rose. I know you are going through a bad time, but that doesn't give you the reason to put yourself in danger."

"I don't want to lose anyone again," she said and brushed the non-stopping tears with her hands. "I don't want to go through it again… I don't want to see it again – Death. No, I don't. I can't. You don't know what happens to me after it – dark days and frozen nightmares... They whisper in my ears... I won't be able to sleep for days."

Jack was frozen by her words. He looked at her for a moment, searching for the right words to calm her, but there were none except to share with her the silence. Pain throbbed at Rose's knee and she felt a wet sensation crawl down her skin, but she ignored it.

"I know you can do it." He spoke in his soothing voice and held her between his arms as they both sat on the balcony floor.

"That's what I really hate!" she said and cried harder. "How can you put so much faith in me when I don't have a clue what to do? I am just standing there and watching him slip away from life when I am supposed to be-"

She stopped abruptly when something had caught her attention. The wound on her knee was oozing thick blood that ran down her legs and on the balcony floor. It was neither the slit's depth nor the amount of gushing blood that caught her eyes, but the way the slit was moving. She watched with panic as it began to shrink and heal itself, sucking with it the blood back into the veins. The slit kept on getting smaller and smaller until it completely vanished, leaving no pain, no trace, and no blood behind.

Rose and Jack stared in silence for a couple of seconds at her healed knee. She wanted to look at him and ask him to rationalize what had just happen, but she couldn't take her eyes off her knee. Suddenly, a flashback rushed through her head; a flashback of her cutting her finger on a rainy night.

"Jack," she said, looking at her hand. "I know the answer."

"Go quickly," he said, his tone was steady but bleak. He helped her get out of her panicking state and onto her feet. "I am sure you know what to do. Now go before it's late."

With shaking legs, Rose hurried into the room and tried not to fall down as her legs gave way under her. It was too much to believe, too impossible to be logically applied, but it was the only way to do it. She would ask Jack to explain it later, but right now she accepted whom she was and was going to save her best friend. She was going to accomplish her mission.

When she entered Mark's room, there was a heavy silence; Mark's breathing could not be heard. His bed was empty and half of the covers were pulled to the other side and down the bed. Her heart pounded in her chest as she went over to the other side of the bed.

"Mark!" she screamed when she saw him lying on the floor with his face against it. His hand was stretched out in front of him in an odd angle that had been trying to reach the oxygen mask. But, he had failed to reach it in time. She quickly knelt beside him and turned him on his back. His face was strikingly white and his chest was not rising nor falling with any breath.

Anne came rushing in when she heard Rose scream. The color in her face disappeared and her eyes widened with horror when she saw her son looking like a ghost on the floor. "My son!" Anne wailed and dropped beside him.

"Go!" Rose said and pushed her to get up. "Call the doctor! Hurry!"

Rose held his freezing hands and looked at his sullen face. The answer was with her, but how to use it, she didn't know. She moved her hand and pressed it against his heart; the place where she knew his pain was carried, the pain that was partly caused by her. She could still sense the soft beating of the suffering heart, and they may be the last ones she would ever feel if she couldn't save him. Time was crucial.

Gradually, she started to feel light and dizzy. Her heart beat quickened and her whole body felt as if it was at tremendous physical work. *I am mending what was broken...* The room started to spin, all its colors blending together. *I am mending what was broken...* She felt very weak and her eyelids were heavy with sleep... *I am mending what was broken...* Rose tried to fight back, but fatigue won her over into its black abyss.

***

The darkness was eerie, cold, and silent. Nothing could be heard except the inhale and exhale of her breathing and nothing could be seen except the endless blackness ahead of her.

"Am I dead?" she asked.

No one replied. Rose started to walk blindly forwards, hoping to find something to lighten up the unknown place. But, the blackness prevented her from finding anything. Adrenalin rushed into her heart and raced around her body. How was she going to get out of this place? She panicked and ran right, left, backwards, and forwards, but there seemed to be no hope. She was trapped. Giving up, she collapsed to the cold floor, or to what she thought to be a floor, and panted. *There must be a way out...*

"Help!" She thought she had yelled, but to her horror, her voice was not heard even by her own ears. She clapped her hands together but no sound was produced. She was trapped in a place where actions had no reactions. Jack, Bill, Mark, and Anne came to her thoughts and she wondered where they were. Were they here with her and she was unable to see them? Thinking about them made her panic even more. What if she was trapped here for the rest of her life? She wouldn't be able to see Jack again nor look into his deep and warm eyes. She wouldn't be able to spend a day in the forest under its warm sun, unlike this place. She would miss her father and miss Mark's humor and annoyance. She had to get back to them, to the people she loved, and back to the sun and light. She tried to remember what she was doing before coming here, but her brain could not recall a thing.

Suddenly a faint light glowed at the end of what seemed to be long a tunnel. It sent hope to Rose and she ran towards it, ready to find her way out. The light stood waiting for her as she ran through the tunnel, stretching her hand in front of her. But, as she got nearer, screams started to fill her ears. Many different screams and cries that were pleading for the same thing—help.

She was almost there when the light started to take the form of a wooden door, her bedroom door. When she stood in front of the familiar door and reached for the doorknob, she heard her own yell pleading for help from between all the screams. It came the last and silenced the rest, reviving back the loud silence of the darkness. She turned the knob and swung the door open.

***

"Bill, she opened her eyes," a voice said from somewhere beside her.

"Oh, finally." Bill's voice was so close to her ears. "Rose, do you hear me?"

"What happened?" Rose asked and bolted straight up in her bed. There was something tight around her head and hands, and they were annoyingly pressured.

"Easy, easy," said Dr. Liu, who was standing by the bed. "Lay back down if you please, Ms. Rose. You definitely do not want to go through another day while you are unconscious."

"What?" Rose asked and looked at the doctor, waiting for him to explain more and did not lay back.

"You have been unconscious for the past twenty-four hours," Bill replied instead, sitting on the bed next to her. "You fell and hit your head against the bed in Mark's room. That is what Anne told me."

"I fell?" Rose felt her head and realized that it was a bandage that wrapped it. However, she was not feeling any pain. Perhaps she was a little weary, but there was a great deal of energy and strength stored within her that was ready to explode out.

"Don't you remember?" Bill looked more worried. She slowly shook her head.

"Of course she won't be able to remember," said the doctor. "She fell pretty hard on her head."

"Are you sure that I fell?" She looked at her right hand that was also wrapped, and wondered if she had broken her wrist as well.

"Of course," the doctor replied. "It was just clumsiness that made you trip over Mark's bed and hit your head when you were hurrying to call Mrs. Rodger. There is nothing to worry about, I assure you."

"No offence, doctor, but I have to take her to a hospital to get her checked on properly," Bill said. "To lessen my worries. The local hospital—"

"No." A clear voice said from the far shadowed corner of the room. Jack, his face twisted in distress, came into sight and stood beside Bill. When Rose locked eyes with Jack, a picture leaked into her memory. She tried to avoid the impossible thought, but through his eyes truth stared back at her. She had done something beyond reality and reason, but she refused to think of that now.

"Excuse me, young man?" Bill frowned deeply.

"I apologize, sir, but you must not take Rose there," Jack said.

"And why is that?"

"The hospital is very far from here. It's on the other side of those mountains," Jack reasoned. "And it's badly equipped-"

"Yes, it is indeed," interrupted the doctor. "I was there a few days ago, and I could not bear the stench of rotting-"

"That is not true, doctor," Bill said and stood up from the bed. "I have personally visited it on several occasions and found nothing of the sort. On the contrary, it was very clean and advanced."

The doctor and Jack stood silently.

"I will have Rose checked at Krag Hospital first thing in the morning," Bill said strongly.

"But-" Jack said.

"Dad, I'm fine-"

"Very well then, Mr. Peterson," said the doctor, interrupting both Jack and Rose, and made a brief apprehensive glance at Jack. "Give me some time to prepare her with some treatments for the long road. If all of you could kindly step out of the room please."

Bill bent over to Rose, kissed her forehead, and walked triumphantly out of the room. Angelina, who had been very quiet in her seat, followed him. Before Bill could close the door behind him, he stood at the doorway and looked at Jack, waiting for him to follow as well. Understanding the hard and worried expression on Bill's face, Jack winked to Rose and made his way out of the door.

Dr. Liu opened his leather briefcase and pulled out some papers. He sat in the seat opposite the bed, put on a pair of glasses that rested on his crooked nose, and started to read the papers.

Question after question and thought after thought twirled in her mind like an angry storm while she rested her head against the bed and stared at the white ceiling above. What felt like an hour might have passed without a word uttered from both of them. The doctor's eyes were fixed on the bundle of papers through his slightly askew glasses, but his eyes seemed to be far away.

"Where is Anne?" she asked, breaking the silence.

"With Mark," he replied without taking his eyes off the papers.

"Err... and where is Mark?"

"In his room, of course. Where else could he be?"

She gulped as the image of Mark lying on the ground crept to her. She did not want to think of what had happened afterwards, and feared the answer of her following question. "How is he?"

"Asleep as usual," he replied. "Good for your fast thinking that saved him."

"W-what did I do?"

"You placed the mask over his mouth. If you were a second late..." he trailed of in mid-sentence, and she was grateful he did so.

"I don't remember putting the mask-"

"Then what do you remember?" he asked, jerking his head away from the papers and focusing all his attention on her, as if she had suddenly become very interesting.

"A bright light," she said and looked at her bandaged hand, lost in thought. She moved it in all directions but did not feel any pain. Her hand was not broken as she had thought. "And there was a scent-" she stopped, realizing who she almost uncovered a secret to. "Are we done here?"

He gazed at her with suspicious eyes that seemed to be able to see straight through her. "Yes. We are," he said and looked at her wrapped hand. "I'll just take off your bandages."

"Aren't I suppose to keep the wound covered?" she asked and feared if he would not find any trace of a cut where he believed there was one before.

"Your father was exaggerating; it's only a scratch," he replied and unwrapped the bandage on her head. "You can manage the one around your hand." With unexplained hurry, Dr. Liu packed his papers, sealed his case with a loud click, and went out of the door without another word.

Once he was out of the room, Rose jumped out of bed and hurried to the balcony. She looked at the peach-colored clouds caused by the setting sun, and searched for Jack among them, and then among the trees. *He has to explain!* She thought to herself before he suddenly jumped into the balcony.

The worried expression on his face was enough to make her heart race violently, and see it reflected on her own face. She opened her mouth to ask what was it, but he interrupted her and said, "I'll explain everything now. Take hold of my hand." He held her hand and ushered her to the house's roof.

"I thought I was not allowed to be doing that, remember?" she asked. She tried to enjoy the non-gravity moment, but Jack's distress was her distress, making her feel heavy in the air.

"Don't worry. No harm will touch you," he said, anxiousness choking his voice.

"How come? You said that they might try to catch me," she said as they landed gently on the wooden roof.

"I know, but-"

"But?" she echoed. "Were you lying to me then?"

"No, Rose," he said. "I never lied to you. I just never told you the rest of my story."

"Jack," she said and took in a deep breath, "tell me everything. I am tired of trying to get you to tell me what is happening. And, don't tell me that there is nothing going on because I feel there is something happening... please just tell me."

He looked at her, and his eyebrows came together in agony. In his deep eyes there was something unexplainable. Regret? Guilt? Jack pulled his eyes away from her confused face and composed his lips into a straight, thin line. She watched him for some time as he contemplated his thoughts.

"I am very sorry if I have caused you any worry or pain," he said, picking his word with extreme caution. "But, I was trying to keep you safe. I will tell you everything now because it's time for you to know the rest of the story. Please understand..."

"I will," she assured him and went to sit beside him on the edge of the roof's platform. "But, first, let me ask you the one question I badly want answered. What did I do to save Mark?"

"You healed him," he slowly answered and watched her face twist with confusion then back to normal again. Rose gulped the information in.

"You mean that I posses..." she said, unable to name it.

"Healing powers," he finished her sentence.

The statement shook her.

"You knew this from before?" she said, forcing her voice out.

"No, just when you told me about the dream you had," he said.

"So, why didn't you tell me before now?"

"I was not sure if I was right or not."

"Is that why you scared me and made me fall?"

"Yes," he replied and closed his eyes as if he was being tortured by the guilt that followed his action.

"You could have just told me, even if you were in doubt," she said but her voiced quieted when she saw his tormented face. However, she knew that she would not have believed him if he had said such an idea.

"Do you think you would have found the answer had you not seen what your body was capable of doing when injured?"

"Maybe not..."

"And, besides, I was not allowed to tell you... I'd be breaking the rules if I did."

"Rules? What rules?"

He took a deep breath and clenched his jaws. "The Rules of the Blue Water."

She frowned at him, knowing there was more to come than her possessing healing abilities.

"The Water that I gave you to drink," he explained. "The one that made you and I able to fly. It was Lilly who put it in my bag ten years ago. My mom told her to put the Water in my bag before I left. Lilly only acted so according to my mother's orders, but Nandi had made Lilly sip a little out of it before she put it in my bag.

"I went mad the first time I experienced the flying, and I believed that I had lost my mind. It was not normal. But, when I knew that Lilly could do the same, I was relieved and was able to gather myself again. During the years I have found out that it was not only flying what the Water was able to offer, it gave several other powers and protections. It protects your dwelling, that's why the enemy can't see or attack my tree house, or why you're safe at home. It also protects itself from the wrong hands, wherever it is there is always an invisible shield around it." He paused for a moment before continuing. "And according to your personality, it gives another power. Like you, Rose, it gave you the power of healing the weak."

Jack reached for her wrapped hand and uncovered it. Underneath it there was a mark. A circular symbol or emblem was engraved in her palm right under her thumb. She touched the slightly red-skinned circle with shaking fingers and did not feel any bumpiness; it was smoothly engraved in her skin.

"That is the symbol of the healer," he answered her confused look.

"What about you?" she asked, trying to decipher the impossibility of what was happening.

He opened his right palm in front of her, where there was a trace of a previous deep cut. But when she looked closer, she saw three red-skinned lines of the emblem parallel to each other, giving the image of strong bars. "I have no idea what they mean. I never used it before, but I will someday..."

"And what about the cut? I did recognize it from before, and I wondered what could have caused it. But, I never thought it would be hiding a symbol."

"If I tell you now, you won't understand. Not before the end of the story. The Blue Water," he continued, "gave me other abilities for I am the leader of the army."

"Army!" Rose lurched.

"Army of the Blue Water," he said quietly. "The Blue Water had chosen me to be the leader of its army, and my mission is to build one and fight the Kalano."

"The what?" she said as the last ray of light rushed back home to the setting sun, leaving the moon to take its place.

"The tribe's name," he replied.

"Why are you supposed to fight them with an entire army?"

"Because it's not only my blood that they want, although they'll be quite satisfied with it. However, they want the Blue Water and they won't be able to get it unless they kill me first. I don't know if you have noticed it or not, but the weather is not the same. It's supposed to be summer by now, but it's still cold. Things are constantly changing around us as we speak. It's not only in Nara, but all around the world. War and hatred are spreading like venom. Everything happening is because of their existence..."

"Jack, you lost me here," she said. "How could a small tribe be the cause of-"

"They are not a small tribe nor are they normal people. I am not even sure if they are human beings in the first place. But, what I am sure of is that they possess massive dark powers, dark powers that can't be imagined in your worst nightmares. And, if they are left to grow in size and number, they'll soon control the world and cover it in shadow."

Rose gulped and stared at Jack, frightened. "Why do they want the Water if they already have great powers?"

"Only the bearers of the Blue Water can defeat them. Its powers are far greater than the Kalano and they will never settle if there is something out there that is able to destroy them. They are always hungry for more power..."

"Who told you about all of this?"

"The people of Nara," he said and stood up, scanning the top of the trees as he did so. She feared it when he did that, for now she knew exactly what he was looking out for. "If you sit with the old Naryans and let them open their hearts to you, you will hear all sorts of stories, legends of great warriors and myths of hooded creatures. They say that there was once an old man who had lived thousands of years ago, and he was known as the most powerful human being. Some said that he was from another race and others said that he came from another planet, but then he was known to be the sorcerer. All people feared him for he was able to do extraordinary things. Flying was one of them. But, being feared by people shook him deeply. He hated not having friends and not being able to talk to people for they fled once he walked the streets. So, he locked himself in a cave on top of the tallest mountain and was never seen for several years after.

"Just then, the Kalano had started to re-awaken from their long sleep. When the people noticed the threat that lay ahead, they went screaming for the sorcerer to help them. The old man heard the yells and came down from his cave and fought against evil. They said that the sorcerer had performed unbelievable powers that day and the Kalano were crushed for hundreds of years after. The old and wise sorcerer became their hero; however, no hero stayed alive forever no matter what powers he had. He was mortal like any other less powerful human. So before he died, he had transferred all his powers into a small amount of water that came from a river that he had found on top of the mountain where he used to live. The Water turned to a bluish color when his powers dwelled in it and that's where it got its name; the Blue Water.

"He had left the Water to his son who had then left it to his own son until it had passed through generations. The Water activates only when evil is at rise..."

Rose stayed silent as the images of the old sorcerer faded from her mind, and she tried to digest the story. Akita's warning ringed in her ears, and Rose realized that there were indeed many dangerous spirits around. She stayed quiet until Jack came and sat beside her again.

"But this is just a myth, right?" Rose asked, her voice shaking.

"That's what the people say, but it's history. Nara's history. If it was just another story from the many that Nara has, then where did the Water come from?"

"D-did you find an army then?"

"No," he said and half smiled. "That's one of the reasons that pushes the Kalano to kill me as fast as possible. If they catch me before I can build an army and gather followers, it will be easier for them to defeat me and take the Water…" Jack looked at his cut that partially disfigured his symbol and tightened his fist around it.

Noticing his throbbing vein in his neck, she took his hand into hers and held it tightly. "Aren't you going to tell me about the cut?"

"Oh, it's just something stupid."

"I still want to know."

Jack sighed then told her, "When I knew about my role in life, I was scared and I rejected it. I didn't and don't want this to be my life. I was young, and I couldn't quite understand what was going on. I wanted to be normal, like the beautiful girl by the pond. I didn't approach you before because I was sure that you'd be scared of me as much I was scared of myself and of my own fate," he said with a small smile. "And, even though I never used the power of the symbol, it showed up anyway to remind me of what I was destined for. So, I tried to cut out the symbol, but was not able to... the scar never seemed to go away."

"That's what you think," Rose said and let go of his hand. He looked at his palm and found no trace of the scar. His symbol showed clearer than ever. He met eyes, and seemed lost in them for a moment.

"I'm in, Jack," she said without second thoughts.

Jack stared silently at her, his jaws clenched and his eyes bleak. She stared back and did not shake. She had made her decision.

"Don't even consider it," he said.

"Then why did you give me the Water?" she asked.

Jack dropped his head, "I thought that it was the leader's duty to choose who could be in the army, but I was wrong. It's the Water that made its pick. The Water has amazing powers, and the ability to protect itself. Lilly told me that the day you met her." He paused then said, "But, I should have never given in and given you the Water."

Rose felt more certain after hearing that the Water had chosen her. She finally felt like everything in her life was making sense. Moving to Nara, her dreams, and meeting Jack. This was where she was meant to be.

"Jack, the Water chose me, so I will fight the Kalano, as well." She wrapped her hand around his. "I won't leave you to do this alone, Jack."

"Let's not talk about this right now," he said and stood up. "I don't have an army in the first place."

"We'll figure it out together," she said and stood up too.

"It's not time yet."

"You said the same thing to Lilly, remember? What are you waiting for?"

He looked at her, took a deep breath, and folded his arms.

"There is still something you haven't told me."

"We are incomplete," he said and turned away. "We've got to be more than just three. How much I don't know, but there must be several main powers to be able to build an army."

"We could-"

"No, Rose." His tone was sharp. "You can't take any part in this. I only told you everything because I couldn't bear hiding anything from you. Don't think that I didn't see the disappointment in your eyes. I knew you were unhappy because you thought I didn't trust you, and I hated feeling your doubt. I tried to keep everything away from you to keep you safe – because... because..."

Jack turned to look at Rose and said, "*Nakupenda.*"

Rose paused in her spot. *He loves me?* She thought, momentarily swept up higher than even a tree house.

Jack rushed on, "I never wanted my life to be like this, and I would give up my powers if I could." He took in a deep breath. "I was worried sick when you were unconscious for the whole day..."

Rose stared into his eyes, her heart fluttering inside her heaving chest, and took a step closer to him. "I knew there was more to you than the wild, young man who lived in a tree." She paused and felt her face flush as Jack's eyes softened, his hair falling over his cheeks. Tentatively, she lightly touched his cheek and pushed back his hair strands. "The brave, gentle, and heroic Jack Casper..." He closed his eyes at her touch for a moment before meeting her eyes again.

She wanted to say more but was so overwhelmed with everything she had learned today. Rose was swept up in emotions and events, and still processing everything. In one day, everything was turning around. She belonged, she was loved, and she had healed her best friend.

A roar of a car's engine brought them back to the world below. Bill's car drove down the driveway and out of sight. They had lost track of time, but there was still so much to say. Jack must have felt it too, for he stood up and dropped her back down to her balcony.

"I'll check on you again tomorrow," he said. "Relax tonight... *mpenzi wangu.*" He kissed her hand and flew off, leaving Rose stare out at the sunset behind him and replaying how he had called her his love.

Back in her room, she twirled around and danced in the mirror. She was loved by none other than the wonderful Jack Casper. Why hadn't she said it back, she wondered. She would soon, at the perfect moment, just like he had. Rose relaxed on her bed, drifting off with a smile on her face, certain she would have no more nightmares.

***

The next morning, Rose woke up feeling ravenous. She bounced down the steps to eat a large breakfast, and Bill was so impressed that he decided she didn't need to go to the hospital anymore.

Then, she went to check on Mark, her step light. In his room, Anne was sitting in the armchair beside Mark who was sound asleep; his breathing was quiet and steady. Anne looked at her very carefully then gave her a feeble smile.

"How is he?" Rose asked the moment she reached her.

"He's been asleep for the past two days," she whispered. "Only wakes up to eat then goes back to sleep. But, at least, he is still alive. How is your head?"

"Oh, it's fine. Dr. Liu had said it was something small, and I feel better already."

"He's a great doctor," Anne said. "He left me these medicines for Mark and explained what I should do before he travelled this week to London." She handed Rose the doctor's prescription note. A familiar medicine was scribbled there. It took Rose a second to remember it, until she realized it was a sleeping pill, she used to take herself long ago. She frowned, unsure why Dr. Liu would prescribe this.

Rose heard Anne's stomach growl. "Why don't you go downstairs and have some breakfast? I'll watch over Mark." Anne nodded and left the room, looking a bit relieved and like she needed to not only eat but sleep as well.

Alone, Rose took a good look at Mark's face. There was color in his skin, his smooth light-brown hair was scattered around his face, his eyelids were peacefully shut, his eyebrows were not frowning in pain but resting, his lips were full and pink, and one corner of his mouth was slightly curled up in a smile – he was dreaming. Tears of joy filled her eyes as she leaned down and planted a soft kiss on his forehead. She was thankful that Jack had made her find the answer just in the right time to save Mark. She was proud of her power.

Seven: The Pick

Over the course of the week, Mark stayed asleep due to his strong medication. Anthony and Zane were more worried about their friend's constant comatose state. But, now Mark had started to regain his awareness after the pill's effect had worn off.

Rose lingered around Mark, waiting for the best opportunity to tell him what he had to know; however, she was afraid. She knew very well that it would not be easy to tell him such a mythical story, let alone telling him to believe it. She had told Jack about the sleeping pills the doctor had prescribed him and they both had tried to come up with a reason, but they couldn't find any. However, the doctor had kind of done them a favor by doing so; no one suspected that Mark had healed, and it gave Rose and Jack more time to think of a way to tell Mark.

Her opportunity arose when Angelina and Anne decided to go to the village for some groceries and a change of scenery. Jack distracted Mark's friends downstairs as Rose hurried to Mark's room, where she found him sitting on the bed in bewilderment.

"How are you feeling, Mark?" she asked and stood at the end of the bed. She smiled once she looked into his eyes and found them sparkling with life.

"I don't know," he replied, shaking his head slowly.

"Do you feel well or tired?"

"I am feeling f-fine," he said and frowned in concentration. "But, no. I am supposed to be sick – I am sick. Then, I am not well. I think."

"No, you are not."

"You mean I am not well, right?"

"No. I meant that you are not tired," she slowly replied and watched him stare at her incoherently. "You are not sick anymore, Mark."

"Come again?" he stared at her.

"You are not sick anymore," she repeated, this time slower.

"How?" He frowned.

"Before I tell you how, let me ask you to do something," she said, came beside him, and stretched her hand in front of him. "Take my hand and try to get out of bed."

"What?" he said, raising one eyebrow. "Are you serious? You know I can't."

"Just do it," she interrupted and grabbed his hand, but he drew it back from her.

"Rose, no. I am not strong-"

"Yes, you are. Take my hand," she said and waited for him this time to take hold of her hand. "Trust me, Mark."

He looked at her, but he slowly raised his hand and held hers as she helped him to stand up. Even though his muscles were stiff and his bones ached, he took a few steps until he reached the balcony window. Rose opened it and stepped outside, ushering him out. With an expression that could not be read, he stood out into the balcony and held the rails for balance.

"Take a deep breath," she told him. "Come on, just take one," she added when he looked at her uncertainly.

Mark closed his eyes and inhaled a profound breath, without it turning into a cough that ended with spluttered blood. His head spun from the sudden increase of oxygen in his lungs. When he opened his eyes again, he looked at Rose with a blank expression and took in another breath. But then, his expression changed and a wide, excited smile broke across his face as he took in one deep breath after the other.

"Rose," he said and raised his head towards the sky, breathing in deeply and fast. "Rose, I don't feel any pain – I can breathe, Rose, without the pain... no pain – seriously, Rose. Can you see me breath? I am not joking. Hear my breathing... there is no pain."

"Yes, Mark," she said, smiling widely. "I can hear you."

"Then the new treatment has worked, right?" he said. "Dr. Liu is a genius!"

"No, Mark, it is not the treatment. Actually, the treatment never worked."

"What?" he said, and the smile disappeared. "Of course it's the new treatment. Dr. Liu-"

"Dr. Liu had prescribed you with sleeping pills," she interrupted. "You've been swallowing sleeping pills for the past week."

"What?" He raised his eyebrows at her and slowed down his breathing. "Sleeping pills? Why would he give me sleeping pills?"

"I don't know," she said. "We asked ourselves the same question, but we ended up at nothing."

"We involving mum?"

"No. It's just Jack and I who know about the pills."

"But, didn't anyone notice that I was oversleeping?"

"I don't think so," she paused, "everyone probably thought that it was normal for you to sleep that much considering the condition you were in last week."

"What happened last week?"

"You don't remember, do you?"

Mark shook his head

"You were reaching for the mask, but..." she said, uncertain how to say it exactly.

"But?" he echoed. "Did I reach it?"

She shook her head and lowered it down.

"Then how," he said, frowning with puzzlement. "How am I still...?"

"I healed you, Mark," she blurted out.

He stared at her for a moment. "What?"

"Mark, listen. I know what I am about to say will sound crazy, but please hear me out," she said moving them inside.

"I am sure you remember the gathering at my place," she said once they were inside and out of earshot from the danger in the forest. Mark went over to the dressing table and looked deeply at his own reflection, touching his pink lips and his reddened cheek. "On that day, I discovered something about Jack." She continued, talking to him through his reflection. "Jack has powers, supernatural powers..." She told him the whole story, and he listened while he stared at his reflection with utter bewilderment.

"So, basically, Jack is the leader of an unformed army, and he has powers like me." She finished and waited for Mark to hear what he had to say.

"Are you out of your mind!" He jerked his head towards her. "This is insane!"

"Look, I know that this sounds mad, but you have to believe me."

"Prove it then," he said, challengingly. "Prove that people can fly!"

Without another word or thought, she stepped back and lifted herself, ever so lightly, into the air. Mark's mouth dropped open, and he gawped at the space between her and the floor.

"How on earth did you do that!" he said, taking a step back as fear masked his face.

"I already told you," she said, touching back down silently. "Jack and I have something that allows us to do that."

"I knew that there was something wrong with him the first time I saw him."

"That's not all that I can do," she said, pretending as if he had not said anything. "I can heal people."

"Rose, on that day I was supposed to be dead!" he said and walked to sit down on the edge of the bed, his face pale.

"No, you were almost dead," she said. "There was still life in you-"

"Look, look," he interrupted. "This does not explain how you healed me."

Starting to lose her patience, she went over to the dressing table and searched in the drawers for something sharp. She found a pair of scissors and separated the blades, so that their sharp edges were more reachable.

"What are you doing?" he asked worriedly and crossed over the room to her.

"Giving you proof," she said and held one blade tightly in her hand. She winced as she felt the cold steel cut through her flesh, and blood oozed from between her closed fingers to the floor.

"Are you mental!" He snatched the scissors from her hands.

"Watch," she said and opened her blood-covered palm. Just like what had happened with her knee, the blood on her hand was sucked back into the diminishing slit until it was completely closed without any traces left behind. "Is that enough for you to believe?"

His mouth dropped in disbelief. Rose could tell his mind was racing to process everything, and she could not blame him. A shadow moved outside the window, catching their attention. Mark gasped with wide eyes at where Jack had passed. He tried to gather his courage to open his mouth and protest, but not a word could come out. Not believing nor understanding anything, he went over to his bed, slid under the cover and closed his eyes. It was better to leave him now so his mind could catch up with everything she had told him.

Rose opened the balcony window again and flew up to the roof, where Jack was waiting for her with a small impressed smile. Her eyebrow rose in question.

"You're graceful at it," he replied to her questioning look. "You fly like you've been doing it for years."

"Well." She smiled back. "That's because a very talented teacher taught me."

He smiled, but looked down not really accepting the compliment.

"You were born to do this, Jack," she said and pulled his chin up again. "You were born to lead. I can see it in your eyes and I can even hear it in your laugh. This is you, Jack. Don't try to run away from who you are."

She paused, looking at the driveway. "Isn't that Dr. Liu? He came back to check on Mark!"

"He can't know that Mark has healed," Jack said. "We must not be exposed."

"What are we going to say to them?"

"I don't know," he said and huffed, irritated at his lack of plans.

"Then Mark has to play ill until we find a solution," she blurted out of nowhere. Rose was shocked at her own idea, but she quickly realized it was the only thing that would help them get by in the meantime.

Before Jack could reply, they saw the doctor park his car, and Lilly stepped out of the passenger seat. At first they barely recognized her because she was dressed in normal clothes, rather than the traditional skins she wore before. The pair started walking to the front door.

"This is not right," he said in a low and worried voice that caused her heart to skip. "Rose, go into the house and speak to Mark. When the doorbell rings, answer it. Don't worry, it will be us."

She nodded and half ran and half flew into the house, reaching Mark's room in a matter of seconds. What had brought Lilly here? Would she betray her own brother? Rose was so worried and scared if such a thing might happen. She looked to Mark who was shocked to see her fly into his room through the open balcony doors.

"Mark, the things that I told you a while ago about the healing and everything, do you remember?"

"So it wasn't a dream," Mark mumbled.

"No, now everything that you learned must not be known by anybody, OK? This is very important, Mark, and it means our safety, everybody's safety," she said in one breath.

"Fine," he said.

"Promise me, Mark," she said with urgency.

"I promise!" Mark said, annoyed at being forced into this.

Downstairs, the doorbell rang and Rose rushed to open it.

"*Jambo*, Rose," Lilly said and took her in a tight hug. "I missed you. It's been long since the last time I saw you." She rushed into the house like she was running away from something.

"Good afternoon, Ms. Peterson," the doctor said with a smile and stepped in. "How are you feeling?" he added and joined Lilly in the living room. Rose smiled as calmly as she could.

"Rose," Jack said, stepping in after the doctor. He winked at her, informing her to act along with him.

"I'm fine," Rose said walking them into the living room. "Please, doctor, have a seat. You must be tired from your journey. You too, L-Lilly."

"Oh, yes. You are right," the doctor said, sitting down and sinking into the sofa with a loud sigh. "However, my journey this time was not tedious for I happen to have this beautiful young lady as my company in the car. She is a sweet girl. You are very lucky to have her as your friend, Ms. Peterson."

"No, I am the one who is lucky to have her as my best friend," Lilly said with a dazzling smile that showed perfect white teeth, like her brother. "It's too bad that we don't see each other more often. But, today I got fired from the shop I work at in the village, and Rose is the first person I have to share this happy news with. Right, Rose?"

"O-of course," she said and felt her face redden; she was never good at lying. "It's great to hear about you getting fired. Finally." Her heart started pounding, knowing very well Lilly would not risk her life by coming here, only if something terrible had happened.

"Well, it seemed like it was a job you disliked," the doctor said, falling into the trap. "No one could succeed in anything unless they have passion for what they are doing, even if it seemed impossible. With a little belief and trust in one's self, and with those who are around to help, our dreams can come true." He looked at the three of them, then back to Lilly. "I wish that you find your passion."

The kitchen door opened and Luba came from behind it, holding a tray full of steaming hot tea. Rose frowned as she put down the tray and served everyone with tea. When did she arrive today? Rose asked herself, accepting the cup. Luba was supposed to be enjoying her day off today. With her warm and grandmotherly smile, Luba returned to the kitchen and closed the door behind her.

A curious question was burning on Rose's tongue. "How did you get here, Lilly? Did you not say that your car is broken?"

"Yes, it is," she lied easily, "But, I have missed you so much, and I wanted you to be the first to hear the news. I couldn't wait for my car to be fixed, so I decided to take a taxi. But, as you know, sometimes it's hard to find an empty taxi at the village stop, so I started walking. Luckily, Dr. Liu offered me a ride and we found that we had the same destination."

"Today is my lucky day," the doctor said and took a sip from his tea. "Anyway, I was hoping to catch Mrs. Rodger before she went out. But, as it seems that she has already left, I might take the chance to check on Mr. Parker."

Instantly, Rose's eyes stole a brief glance over to Jack. From behind where the doctor was sitting, Jack signalled her to tell the doctor to wait.

"I have to wake him up and get him prepared to see you," she said in one nervous breath. "Excuse me." She ran up the stairs, taking two steps at a time, and reached the top when she heard Jack excuse himself as well. Where was he going? Rose panicked from within.

She found Mark sitting on the unmade bed with his knees bent in front of him and his head resting against the wooden back of the bed. He turned his head slowly, looked at her with blank eyes, and then straightened it back again without saying anything. Rose came closer to him and opened her mouth to speak, but a knock at the balcony door cut her out; it was Jack.

"I thought you'd left," she said. She watched him as he crossed the room and closed the door without producing a sound. He signalled to both of them to speak in whispers lest they be heard by the doctor. But, of course, Mark ignored him and his entrance, and continued staring at the wall.

"Mark." Jack tried to grab his attention. "I know what I am about to ask from you now may be hard and brutal, but it's very important for everyone's safety..."

Mark did not move or even blink and he sat still as a statue.

"Very well. Not for everyone's, but for Rose's safety?"

"What do you want?" he snapped out of his immobile state and looked at Rose instead. "You made me promise not to say anything, not even to my mother. What more do you want!"

"Your help," Rose whispered.

Mark snorted. "Isn't he helping you enough?"

It was more of a declaration than a question, Rose realized, and it frightened her.

"No," Jack said when he saw Rose's opened mouth, but no words were coming out. "I am not enough. She needs you too."

Rose was still surprised by how easily he could read her mind, and by his growing knowledge in that aspect of her yielding emotions.

Mark looked from Rose to Jack and back again, his mouth slightly open with hesitation. "Fine," he said, a little edgy. "How can I help you?"

Jack signalled for Rose to explain her plan.

"There is something else that I have to ask you to do, Mark," she said and stepped closer to him. "Everyone thinks that you are still sick. So, if anyone came in now and saw the color of your face, our secret will be exposed and put everyone in danger."

"Get straight to the point," Mark said.

"You have to act sick for a few more days," she blurted out with a sigh, removing its heaviness from her chest. "Until we figure out what to do."

"What?" Mark blinked.

"Mark, please," she said and sat beside him. "Dr. Liu is downstairs, and he wants to come up and check on you. What will you say when he finds there is nothing wrong with you anymore? How will you explain it? And if you did, do you think he'll believe you?"

He opened his mouth to argue, but stopped when he saw the confused frown on Rose's face.

"What is that?" she asked, standing up and looking at Mark's forehead. There was light coming from the area between his eyes. It was so bright that it lightened the dim room.

Mark sprang from the bed and stood in front of the mirror and examined his face. "What is it?" he asked, a little frightened from the looks on Jack and Rose's faces, and how they stared at him.

"There is light coming from your forehead. Can't you see it?" Rose pointed.

"No, Rose. I can't see anything. There is nothing!"

"Jack," she said, turning to face Jack and found a hint of comprehension between his frown. "You can see it, right?"

"Yes," he said and squeezed his eyes shut, as if this was a terrible sign.

"What does it mean?"

"It's the Pick," he said. He walked to the window, and did his usual scan on the forest. "The Water always chooses who will enter."

"What is he talking about?" Mark asked, still looking at his face. "Could somebody please tell me what is going on here?"

"You mean that-"

"Yes," Jack interrupted her. "A new choice is made."

The blinding light suddenly disappeared form Mark's forehead, leaving the room dimmer than before. The message was sent.

"I am sorry," Jack said, turning to look at confused Mark. "You are one of us now."

"Translate what the freak just said." Mark ordered.

"You are now one of the Blue Water army," she said, trying very hard to restrain her rising temper and excitement. "And, don't let me remind you that the person you are ignorantly calling a freak is the one who saved your life. He gave me the ability to do so. And, without him you would not be standing here in front of us. You would not be standing here and judging the person whom you owe your life to." She had lost her patience with Mark's ill judgment towards people he barely knew and his profound jealousy.

"Rose, we must hurry," Jack said, cutting their tense eye contact. "The doctor is waiting."

She looked at Mark who yielded.

"Fine," he said, arduously. "I'll do what you want me to do. But, on one condition. I need to talk to you after the doctor leaves."

She nodded and Jack left through the window. She ruffled his silk-like hair, making it appear badly groomed. She wetted his face and the hem of his V-neck shirt with the soaked cloth to fake sweat. Mark made brief glances at her while she prepared him for the act, but she did not have the courage to meet his eyes. Rose was ashamed of what she was making him do. She remembered the pale, white, suffocating, and dying Mark, contrasted so deeply with the red cheeked Mark that was sitting in front of her now. To make the situation more agonizing, she felt guilty that Mark had been chosen to fight in a war when he had only just healed. And he didn't even know yet.

Once she was done, Rose went back downstairs to the doctor and let him go up to check on Mark. Leaving Lilly downstairs, Jack and Rose followed the doctor to Mark to make sure he would stick to their plan. Rose knew that Jack was restraining himself from asking Lilly what had happened to bring her here.

The doctor did his usual checkup routine, measuring Mark's blood pressure and temperature. He pulled out a small light and shined it into Mark's bloodshot eyes. At first she was very impressed with his acting abilities, until a single tear gathered at the tips of his eyelashes that changed her thoughts completely. Before it could roll down his cheeks, Mark quickly brushed it away and continued staring ahead.

He was not acting after all, and his tears were not fake. It was the first time Rose saw him shed a tear, and it tore her insides. She always knew him as a flagrant young man who spoke his mind clear and loud. He never lost hope and pursued the girl he loved. He had lived a life battling a monster inside him that had tried to steal his health and life away. She could not see him so upset, even after winning the battle and gaining his freedom. Her guilt came to her again and whispered a solution into her ears.

"What do you feel now?" the doctor said, noticing his teary eyes.

"Pain," Mark said with a blank expression. The meaning behind the word, the terrible and brutal meaning, hit her body like a sharp razor. Jack gave her hand a squeeze and she returned one back. She knew what she had to do.

The doctor prescribed him some more sleeping pills and promised to return at night to give him some injections. Rose was puzzled at how easily he fell for their act. Jack offered to walk the doctor to his car, leaving Rose and Mark for their promised talk. Once the door was shut behind them, Rose went closer and sat in the chair by the bed.

"Don't do this," she whispered. "Forget everything I told you today." She paused when she found that Mark was still motionless and appeared to be not listening. With a deep breath she continued, "Leave, Mark."

"Leave?" He echoed without moving anything except for his lips.

"Yes. Leave."

"Why?"

"You just got your life back," she said. "Go and live again. Travel, see new places, meet new people, and make new friends. Take advantage of your second chance. Don't waste it."

"You think I am wasting my life being around you?" He met her eyes. "I'd prefer living my life with you. But, that's impossible as I have figured out – but, no. I am not leaving."

"No, you have to," she said, almost pleading. "Leave if you love me."

"That's the point," he said and jumped out of bed. "I love you, so how on earth am I supposed to leave you? ... You don't understand."

"Then explain."

She stood beside him. Even though Mark's mind was difficult to change, she had to give it a try. This war was never meant to be his burden nor duty, and it was unfair. He did not even spend a day to enjoy his healthy body without hearing what was suddenly thrown at him. By the look on his face and the agony in his voice, she woke up to see the mistake, and she was going to fix it.

Mark spoke. "You stole my heart from the first time I saw you." He looked at her and continued, "Young, stupid love – you can call it. Then I knew I was sick and most probably dying before I turned twenty. You, Rose, were the first thing that came into my mind. I was afraid to leave you after your mother's death – I couldn't leave you. I couldn't find the courage to tell you what was wrong with me either, so I decided not to tell you at all. Telling you would have made things worse for me. I accepted it at first, but with time I saw what I was going to miss. I realized I had to be with you before it was too late..." He paused for a moment and took in a deep breath. "Losing you was my biggest fear... still is."

His words sunk deep in her heart and she gently pulled him into her arms. "I'm so sorry." The lump in her throat chocked her words.

"I know," Mark mumbled against her neck and took in her scent, his arms tightening around her waist a little. Instead of pulling away, like she would have done in the past, Rose stood there for a few moments longer and held her best friend. But, before Mark can relish in her embrace, Rose gently pushed him away and met his eyes. She could not bear the look on his face. The gallant young man suddenly was transformed into a forlorn, deserted man too young for his despair.

Softly, she cupped his face between her palms and planted a small kiss to his cheekbone. "Leave, please. I am begging you," she said at last and left the room, drying her tears on her sleeves. The image of him sitting there with those tired eyes haunted her as she ran down the stairs.

At the end of the stairs, Rose almost bumped into Jack and Lilly. Their faces were disturbed.

"What happened?" she asked, tired of the continuous problems that did not allow them to rest for a second without worrying.

"They have figured it out," Jack said in a low voice. "Lilly is on the run."

"What do you mean-"

"The Kalano discovered that Lilly is an active member of the Blue Water Army, and that she has connections with me." He rushed.

"But, how did they know?" she asked, panicking.

"Every time a member is added they feel it," Lilly said. "I don't know how they do, but I think that is why they are after you too, Rose."

"You have been a member for ten years now. How could they just figure it out now?" Jack turned to his sister.

"Ten years back they were nothing except an ordinary tribe with little stories and myth surrounding them. Once they started getting stronger-"

The sound of an engine interrupted Lilly. Jack looked out of the window, then he and Lilly rushed out through the terrace doors. Seconds later, Angelina and Anne entered the house.

Eight: How Much Time Is Left

Young women had disappeared from the village this morning, Rose learned from Anne and Angelina upon their return from the village. Rose frowned at the news, and knew something dark was behind it. It was the perfect opportunity to convince Anne to leave.

"Anne, Dr. Liu checked on Mark and said he might make it through this time," Rose told her once she had taken her aside and far from Angelina's curious ears. Anne's face brightened for the first time since the gathering. "Yes, I think you should take him back to London... put him in a hospital there."

"I was thinking the same thing," Anne said. "But, Dr. Liu will never agree. He believes it's too risky."

"Then, don't tell him," Rose said.

"But, I have to."

"No, Anne, you don't. The doctor doesn't want to take the risk because he feels that Mark is in his responsibility. But, what if taking that risk is better than keeping him here? And, if Mark now is fit to ride a plane, why not seize the opportunity to put him under care at home?"

"I take Mark back without consulting his doctor first?" Anne said and brought her eyebrows together, considering the idea.

"Yes, because if we ask him, he'll definitely refuse." Rose nodded her head and waited anxiously. "Well, I was only suggesting it. If you want the doctor to…"

"No, no. I guess you are right." Anne nodded. "It might be a risk, of course, but it's definitely worth it."

"But, don't tell Mark yet. Book the tickets and arrange everything, and then tell him. That way he won't be able to protest."

"Yes, good point," Anne said. She withdrew her phone from her pocket and dialed a number. "I better contact the airlines now."

If everything worked out as she had planned, Mark would be getting on a plane tomorrow without letting the doctor know or anyone else that he had healed. As for Anne, Rose hoped that Mark would know how to deal with her when they got back to London... at least they would be far away from what was happening here. With the tickets booked for the day after, Rose made sure to inform Anne to keep their little plan a secret from everyone, especially from Angelina. But, her momentary relief did not last long as she suddenly realized what she had done... and what she must tell Jack.

She found Jack and Lilly sitting silently on the roof, watching out for any unusual sound or movement. Even though she tried not to disturb the silence, Jack sensed her presence and quickly came over when he saw the look on her face.

"Rose, what is it?" he asked, and signaled Lilly to leave them alone for the moment. Lilly hesitated a little, but left when he gave her a sharp look. "Come sit," Jack said and guided her to the edge of the roof, where they sat overlooking the dark and deserted driveway.

After a few silent moments, she took a profound breath and looked into his concerned eyes, and told him the conversation that had passed between her and Anne.

"It was a sane thing to do," Jack said when he found a hint of sadness in her voice. "It's not the fate that I would like to choose, that anyone would like to choose..."

"I am so sorry," she said.

Jack looked at her, perplexed.

"Mark is one of the main powers," she explained. "And, asking him to leave means that I have caused the Army to be incomplete."

"It's already incomplete," he said. "Don't ever be sorry for giving him another chance... not everyone gets such chances."

He reached out and took her hand, his touch gentle.

"You helped him see the importance of a second chance... and I hope he takes your advice."

A feeble smile curved at the corner of her lips, carrying relief.

But there were still a million questions running through her mind. From where she stood, they were in a terrifying position. The enemy was getting stronger day by day and knew about the Blue Water Army's rise. But, were they, the Blue Water Army, really rising? Were they getting any stronger? How many main powers should there be and how were they going to discover them?

How much time is left? Rose asked herself. She shuddered at her thoughts and tried to push them out of her mind. But, for how long could she control her rising curiosity? She knew that there would be a time when all of her questions would be answered. Not only answered, but materially seen in front of her. Time played a huge role in life, and she must be patient. *How much time is left!*

"You remind me of my mother," Jack said, as his smile broke through the tension. Rose met his eyes, a little surprised. "She always had that same look you just had. A look of total... mystification. I think that's how my father used to describe it."

She smiled softly and absentmindedly threaded her fingers through his. His eyes glanced down at their entwined hands, and he cautiously brought her hand up to his lips and planted a warm kiss inside her palm, right over her emblem. She felt her cheeks change color and hid her face behind her hair locks.

"He's late," he mumbled, breaking through their intimate moment. "The doctor was supposed to be back here by now."

"Yes, but what are we going to tell him this time? Mark won't be able to put on another act," she said, suddenly aware of what might happen.

"No," Jack shook his head. "Don't allow him to see Mark. Tell him that he left or is sleeping, anything that'll prevent him from going upstairs... and I need to go back to the tree house to check of its safety, then I'll come to take Lilly. She needs a place to sleep."

"No, Jack. I think they'll be after her because they know that she'd come to you. Look, don't take her tonight and let her stay here with me. My bed is big enough for two."

Jack folded his arms tentatively.

"We'll be fine," she reassured him. "We are two tough girls, and I believe we can take care of ourselves... and, besides, you haven't told me what is Lilly's power."

"Storm."

She raised her eyebrows. "Sounds impressive." She tried to imagine how strong and fierce a storm would be when it was produced by a little aggressive personality. "How come I did not get something like that? Something more dynamic?"

"You should be proud of your power, you know. At least you know what yours does, unlike me," he said and Rose noticed him clench his right fist. "I must go. Will you be fine?"

She nodded slowly.

"Are you sure about Lilly staying with you?"

"Yes." She gave him a smile. "Stop worrying. Remember who we are; tough girls."

"I just don't want to cause you any problem with Angelina."

"Don't worry about that," she said confidently.

"Thank you." He smiled a little. "I'll see you in the morning."

With that, Jack stood up and soared with accelerating speed into the sunset sky, not knowing where the protective shield around her house extended. Just as Jack was almost halfway to the tree house, he halted in midair and looked down at the forest. Something was glowing from deep within the forest. There were spots of red light hovering under almost every tree.

Rose squinted her eyes, trying to identify the odd lights, but then everything happened so quickly. She cringed back with mingled confusion and horror as the spots of light surged into the air and aimed at Jack like glowing bullets. Rose stared as he darted across the sky, missing them in nick of time before any could hit him. But, more sprang from the depth of the forest.

Only then did she realize what the shooting lights were. A throng of ignited arrows had besieged Jack and was obstructing him from reaching the tree house. They were shot continuously one after the other, creating an impenetrable wall of fire.

Rose wanted to scream, but her voice had abandoned her. As her heart raced frantically, she jumped off the rooftop and landed on the ground. She had to stop whoever was trying to shoot him down, but something held her back and nailed her to the ground. Someone was restraining her from going to help Jack. She tried to free herself, but the grasp was too strong.

Jack soared up into the sky and the arrows raced after him, until he was gulped by the thick clouds away from sight. However, the arrows did not stop and persisted to shoot where Jack had disappeared.

NO! STOP IT! She wanted to yell and tried to push her feet off the ground and fly after Jack, but the unknown hands were determined not to let go. Without glimpsing behind her, she blindly kicked and struggled to free her hands, but to no avail. Her breathing was loud in her ears. She looked up at the sky and found no sign of Jack. Then, he reappeared from between the clouds and descended towards the ground... and the arrows had stopped.

Rose gasped when she realized that a single, burning arrow had achieved its target and pierced Jack's bare chest. *No!* She screamed from within. *Please, no!* She tried again to fly to him, but her state of terror froze all her limbs, and the hands did not loosen their grip.

"Concentrate!" A voice ordered from right behind her. Jack was falling, head first, from thousands of feet in the air and would soon crash to the ground. Rose winced and fought to release her arms, willing to do anything to get him back safely.

"Concentrate on him, Rose!" The voice came again, and the clench on her arms became tighter. "You can do what you can from afar. Just concentrate!"

Whether it was by instinct or not, an aura arose within her when she noticed what she was supposed to do. A strong and dominant sensation filled her, shaking her body as she focused all her attention on Jack. Another single arrow was shot from the depth of the forest and stabbed him directly beside its friend.

No! A force so powerful burst from within her, and she tried to wrap it around Jack's falling body that would soon be gulped by the trees. She started to feel a little dizzy as her energy was drawn from her, however, she did not take her eyes off Jack. Even though the intense heat from the arrows had made her breathing hard and her vision blurry, she saw what happened. Before Jack's frozen body could brush the treetops, he was revived and soared with amazing speed into the sky. The arrows started to fire again, but they were too late. Jack had already flown so high to the point where the angry clouds became his guards again. But, this time they shielded him.

Rose's shaking knees surrendered, and she fell to the ground, feeling the hands loosen their grip a little. A sudden, cool wind rushed through her hair, helping her breathing and drying her sweat away. As her eye vision refocused, she saw what the wind was doing. The strong wind disturbed the tree branches and made them dance fiercely in every direction, revealing anything between them, and the bushes were laid down to the ground in an unsuccessful attempt to fight back. She was not sure of what she had seen, but there were hurried movements between the trees, as if people were trying to run away from the storm.

When her head had stopped from spinning and she had regained enough energy, Rose stood up with the support from the unknown hands and twirled around on the spot.

"Dr. Liu!" Rose was utterly gobsmacked.

Dr. Liu was standing right in front her with a sullen face, panting and dabbing the prickling sweat on his sleeve.

"What are you doing here? I don't under-"

"Quickly! Get inside!" he interrupted Rose and pulled her by the arm, ushering her back to the house. "You too, Lilly! Come now, hurry!"

Rose glimpsed behind her as she hastened towards the house and saw Lilly rush over to them, looking extremely anxious. Rose then understood where the sudden strong storm must have come from.

"Who are you?" Rose demanded.

"I'll explain everything once both of you are safely inside," he said, and took the girls back into the house and closed the double-glass doors.

Rose glimpsed anxiously at the kitchen door and found it closed; fortunately, Anne and Angelina did not hear nor see anything for the kitchen window overlooked the driveway and not the forest. And luckily for her that her voice had abandoned her when she had wanted to scream, or else Anne and Angelina would have seen everything.

"Who are you?" Lilly seized the doctor by the collar and set a small blade against his throat. "Answer me."

The doctor did not show any signs of fear or means of force, he only signaled to keep her voice down. Automatically, Rose landed her eyes on his right hand to check for any peculiar sign, but there was nothing there. She saw Lilly do the same.

"I will gladly tell you once we are out of earshot," he said and eyed the stairs, indicating where to go in order for him to speak. Lilly pulled him up the stairs and Rose followed. The doctor, still held as a prisoner under Lilly's strong hands, pointed at Rose's room and they all got inside.

"Now speak!" Lilly ordered and cornered him. "Who are you?"

"I am here to help."

"In what exactly?" Rose stood beside Lilly for protection.

"In all of what you are blindly going through... and the fate that you will soon meet; the war."

"How do you know about the war?" Rose asked.

"Every Naryan knows about the war, Rose," Lilly replied instead. "But, only in stories. The question is how did he know it was us?"

"Yes, Lilly." The doctor raised his eyebrows in approval. "Every civilian in Nara knows about it. It's written in books and in documents. It's part of our history, only obvious to those who dig deep... How I have found out it was you, lot, I am afraid I cannot give an answer to that."

"Then how are you going to fully explain yourself if you are not going to tell us how you have found out about us?" Rose pressed.

"I am a Protector."

Lilly and Rose exchanged looks and said in union, "A what?"

"A Protector of the Blue Water," he explained. "My job is to protect and help you find the right path. I've been keeping an eye on all of you for many years now, especially you, Lilly, as well as your brother."

"Are we supposed to believe this rubbish!" Lilly twirled the blade between her fingers. "And, not suspect you to be a spy from the Kalano?"

"Nonsense!" He snapped. "I am not a spy from the Kalano."

"Give me a reason not to be suspicious!" Lilly hissed through gritted teeth.

"My intentions are perfectly pure, Lilly," he said in a lower voice after he had composed his temper. "Please listen to what I've got to say then you can decide whether I am trustworthy or not.

"There is a Protector for every main power in the army. Our job is to help you find your way to power and fill you with important information about your opponent, which in this case are the Kalano. *Niago Siathe* in the Naryan tongue, which means the Dark Army."

"If what you are saying is right, then whose protector are you?" Rose asked.

"I am Mark's protector."

"Since when?" Rose was taken back, however, she had suspected that the doctor knew that there was something going on. But, she never thought that he would be somehow involved.

"Since his infancy," he said, a little proud. "I was working at a hospital in Fleet Street when Mrs. Rodger came in with Mark between her hands. He was only a baby when she bound me to be his doctor. I did not understand why she had picked me out of all the other more experienced doctors, but I guess that is how fate works, letting me be beside Mark and take care of him. Only after a while, I felt that I was taking care of something much bigger than a helpless child. I knew it was important to take care of Mark... for it might help someday.

"However, Mark's condition was unstable. He got tired very quickly and became better even quicker. And, on the days his health allowed him to step outside under the sun, he spent all his time playing with you, Rose. I saw you when you were just seven years of age. And when I saw you, I knew it was time, time for history to repeat itself."

Lilly looked like she was doing some serious thinking, however, she did not put off her guard.

"If what you are s-saying is... true and you are the Protector of Mark, why didn't you heal him yourself?" Rose frowned.

"I don't have the ability to do that," he said, a little relieved that he might have convinced one of them. "In fact, I don't have the ability to do anything unusual. I am an ordinary person, and a doctor."

"Was it a coincidence that Mark got ill during his visit here?" Rose remembered her guilt.

"No," he said and looked at her with a hint of touching sympathy. "I was expecting his lungs to re-attack anytime soon, and when he consulted me whether it was fine for him to travel, I told him that it was better for his health... It was meant to happen here, Rose, because if it had not, then you would have never found out what was your gift. I apologize if my words have disturbed you."

Rose was relieved. "The sleeping pills?"

"I think that had given you sometime to put things together, had it not?"

She slowly nodded.

"Who is my Protector, our Protector?" Lilly said, and lowered her hand a bit.

"Yours, Lilly, I am afraid has left us in an attempt to keep you and your brother protected..."

"My mother?" Lilly said in a quiet whisper.

He nodded. "Nandi Casper, daughter of Jabu and Kaya."

Lilly looked at him for a few silent moments, proving the topic's sensitivity, then she dropped her hands and slid the blade back in her pocket.

"And mine?" Rose asked.

"Your Protector is still active. But, I am not allowed to say anything further. When the time is right, your Protector will reveal themselves to you."

All the faces that Rose knew flashed in front of her eyes. Someone was watching over her to help and guide her. But, who? Rose looked around and thought, *Are they watching now?*

"Now, ladies. Both of you need a good night's sleep," he said, interrupting her thoughts, and started walking towards the door. "I am sure it has been a long, long and exhausting day. And, I need to leave before anyone can sense that I am still here. Take care both of you. Time is running out."

"Wait," Rose said and ran after him through the door. "What about Mark?"

"What about him?" he said, making his way towards the door.

"You are his Protector," she said, trying not to make the slightest sound as she hurried after him. "Aren't you supposed to stay?"

"I am afraid I have to leave." He faced her just as he was reaching for the doorknob. "And, one more thing, do not stop Mark."

Rose opened her mouth to ask what he meant, but he had already dived into the darkness of the driveway.

"What was Dr. Liu doing upstairs again, did he check on Mark?" Angelina asked, coming from the kitchen, and stopped at the front door.

Once more Rose opened her mouth to reply, but all the reasonable replies had slipped out of her mind. How was she supposed to answer? Should she say that she had just witnessed a hundred flaming arrows shoot at Jack, or that Jack was nearly killed and she had saved his life? Why not say that she had just found out the doctor's secret identity? As if Angelina would believe her.

"Dr. Liu forgot some important papers in Mark's room," Lilly said from the top of the stairs. "He came back to reclaim them."

"And you are...?" Angelina asked, startled by Lilly's appearance.

"This is my friend, Lilly," Rose replied this time and made her way up the stairs. "And, she is staying over."

"Excuse me! What the-"

"I said she is staying over, and as long as she likes!" Rose snapped, interrupting Angelina's objection.

Her stepmother stared back at her, but did not dare open her mouth again, for there was fire in Rose's eyes that looked as if it might burn anything she laid them upon.

"What is happening to this family? Everyone is going mad," Angelina mumbled as she hurried back to the kitchen.

Rose and Lilly walked to Rose's room and took Dr. Liu's advice to retire for the night. When they had made themselves comfortable in their sleeping position and switched off the lights, Rose whispered in the darkness, "Lilly?"

"Hmm?" Lilly said.

"Are you sure you don't want to sleep on a bed?"

"Yes, Rose," Lilly said from where she was laying on the floor. "I have lived all my life under the fierce sun and slept on dry and rough ground. So, sleeping on a carpet is almost like heaven. Now, please go to sleep."

Rose was silent for a moment, but she couldn't bear her provoking thoughts. "Lilly?"

"Don't worry about him, Rose." Lilly answered her unspoken thoughts; however, Rose was sure it was evident in her voice. "Jack is strong, stronger than you think. And, he is very fast. Don't forget, Rose, he is the leader of the Blue Water Army, and a leader is not to be underestimated. However, he will always need our help... He needed yours today."

"I thought for a second that I had..." Rose was not able to continue her sentence and left it hanging in the darkness. She shivered at the memory that leaked into her drowsy head.

"Me too," Lilly joined her fear. "You were very brave..."

Without further talk about what had happened, Rose and Lilly drifted off and slept. They were brave enough to sleep and close their eyes when danger was lurking behind the intense shadows of the forest.

Nine: Leaked

"Good morning," Rose said the following day when she found Lilly in the balcony.

"Sawubona," Lilly replied, her eyes distant.

"Thank you for allowing me to stay," Lilly said. "I did not want to trouble you, but Jack insisted that I should stay."

"Don't mention it, Lilly," Rose said.

"And thank you for standing up for me when your stepmother did not want me to stay," Lilly continued.

"No. Thanks to you." Rose pointed. "You saved me twice from being speechless. You can come up with a reasonable story very quickly. You're talented."

"You mean I'm talented in telling lies," Lilly said and a radiant smile broke her stiff expression.

"No, that is not what I meant at all."

"I know what you meant." Lilly smiled. "Well, living with people who want to kill my brother has developed my imagination... I was in one of the searching troops, and every time they went out to look for him, I had to come up with a reason to stop myself from joining..."

Rose smiled half-heartedly. She knew that it must not have been easy for her. "Did you know about your mother before what happened yesterday?" Rose asked carefully.

Lilly's face did not convey any signs of disturbance and sustained her green eyes from exposing any. "No," Lilly said. "She never told me anything about it... at least not directly. But, she used to tell us the stories about the Kalano when putting us to bed over and over again until we memorized every word."

A cry emanated from inside the house. They both froze.

"Anne..." Rose mumbled and ran to Mark's room. Her heart jolted when she saw Mark fully dressed and walking about the room, tossing clothes into two huge luggage bags.

Anne was standing with her hand over her mouth.

"B-but?" Anne stuttered.

"Mum," Mark said and stopped stuffing clothes in one of the suitcases. "I already told you that it was a false alarm, like last time. So if you please, help me finish packing. We have a plane to catch."

"You're leaving now?" Rose said, and both of them looked at her, just noticing her presence.

"Do you know about this?" Anne asked, looking at Rose.

"Rose has nothing to do with it," Mark said and came over to his mother, who had broken into a confused hysteria. "It's just like I have told you. It's one of those attacks and it has passed... so, now I am pretty much able to ride a plane and go back home."

"I have booked two seats on tomorrow's flight," Anne said, sobbing in her son's chest. "So, I could take you to continue your treatment there..."

"No, Mum," Mark said and looked over at Rose. "I am done with doctors."

Rose's eyes widened in shock. *Are you going to tell her? Oh, please don't!*

"Of course, you must see a doctor!" Anne protested.

"No, I won't. I really don't see the point of living anymore. If my fate is to die now then I will not fight back. So hurry, Mum, we have to leave in five minutes. I'll put my suitcase in the car."

He heaved the suitcase up with extreme effort and hauled it out of the door. It was obvious that he was still weak, not to mention that he had become extra skinny that his backbones showed through his light shirt as he bent to pick up the suitcase. Rose followed him out into the corridor and Anne started to pack her belongings, an expression of disbelief still on her face.

"What are you doing?" Rose asked him.

"I'm doing exactly what you told me to do." He descended the staircase, his bag banging behind him at every step, and opened the front door. "Leaving."

"Are you serious?" Rose asked, relieved.

"Do I look like I am joking? Huh, do I!" he said as he went over to the rented car. "I reconsidered your opinion about using my second chance to live, and I think you are right. I must leave and live my life to the utmost. Enjoy every bit of it while I still can."

She eyed him closely as he struggled to put the suitcase into the car's boot, and she noticed how he eluded her eyes. "You saw what happened last night." He stopped stuffing the suitcase into the car at her words. "You saw what happened to Jack, didn't you?"

"Yes." Mark's lips thinned and he ran a hand through his hair. "I am not a coward!" he snapped underneath his breath. "If that is what you are thinking then you are wrong!"

"I did not say anything about cowardliness," she said, defensive. "I asked you to leave."

He headed back to the front door and called for Anne to speed up, then came back to face Rose, his irritating smile spread on his mouth. "I am sure he will be upset after I leave," he said. "He wouldn't want to lose a member of his army, would he? In fact, I hope that when I leave he'll get really helpless and eventually have to surrender. Then this would all be over."

"Now, how you are thinking is cowardice," Rose said, composing her rage. "If your motive for leaving is because you are too scared to face the fact that I am in love with someone other than you, then you are a coward, Mark Parker. Love is greater than this. Love is pure."

He stared at her then kicked the car door with anger. "Why did you save me?"

"Because I did not want to lose you."

He sighed and contemplated the ground for a moment.

"You doubted that, didn't you?" she said and tilted up his chin to look into his eyes.

He pulled her hand gently away and let go of it before he answered. "I thought... I thought you only did so to use me."

"Mark! How could you ever think like that?" She snapped. "Oh my goodness, you are such an idiot to think that was the reason!"

"Then come with me," Mark said hurriedly and took a step closer to her. "Rose, come back with me."

"You know I can't, Mark... My purpose is here."

"Rose, can't you see what you are putting yourself into?" He wrapped his hands around her shoulders. "Wake up, Rose. This is not a game that you can restart if things ended badly. This is a war, Rose, and I really don't know what might happen if you don't gather a proper army. Look at you. You are still young, Rose, and naive. How could you tell if you are making the right choices?"

"It's a matter of saving lives-"

"It's a matter of death!"

Rose stared at him and released herself from his hold, not shaken nor affected by his words; however, they were annoyingly true.

She lowered her voice upon seeing Anne make her way towards them. "I have made my decision, and I am not turning back."

"Come on, Mum," Mark said and helped a confused Anne into the front seat. Without looking at Rose, Mark opened the door and jumped in the driver's seat. She watched as he fiddled with the keys and revived the engine. For just the tinniest moment she wanted him to stop the engine and tell her that he was not leaving. That her brother had changed his mind and will stay with her in this savage world.

Mark gripped the driving wheel tensely until his knuckles turned white. "I have nothing more to say."

"Neither do I," she said, her hands shaking a little. Mark stomped on the gas pedal and took off at high speed down the driveway. She stared after him and couldn't help but think, *I hope to see you again.*

Rose returned back inside the house and followed the smell of freshly brewed coffee to the kitchen, trying not to think about the fact that maybe that was the last time she would ever lay eyes on Mark.

Lilly had prepared some coffee and picked out some fruits from the fridge. "Sit."

Rose took her seat and ate, grateful for the burst of energy. She knew she needed to eat constantly from now on since her power sucks the energy out of her body. "I'm worried about Mark."

"Why?" Lilly said as she measured the amount of coffee with her eyes. "He left. You don't have to worry anymore."

"I know, but what if they attacked him," she whispered. "He is pretty powerless."

"Don't worry. Nothing will happen to him," Lilly said with confidence, pouring the hot coffee into the cups. "He will reach the airport in one piece."

"How can you be so sure?"

"I read this," Lilly replied and pointed at the dirty cup she had examined. "I took it from his room after his mother went downstairs. I don't see any danger in his path."

"Is it true? I mean, what you see? Or, are they-"

"Of course, it is!" Lilly said. "This is a gift I received from the Water. It's not only Storm what I am capable of doing. I also see accurate visions. Like the day when I first read your cup. You were chosen long before you met Jack."

"Then why does he feel so guilty about giving me the Water?"

"Think about it, Rose. When he gave you the Water, he made it official that you are in and bounded to the Blue Water. He regrets it and wishes that you followed Mark back."

"But, I will not," Rose said strongly. "I am not going to run away from who I am."

"I know you won't," Lilly said. "And, he does not expect you to either."

After she had drained her cup as well, Rose pushed it towards Lilly. "Read it, please."

Lilly did not move and stared at the empty cup for a moment. She looked anxious, however, she took it and rotated it between both hands. Rose studied her face, but Lilly was good at not revealing her feelings.

After a few minutes, Lilly put down the cup and looked at Rose. "It's you."

"Excuse me?"

"You are the one who will activate his symbol," Lilly explained, to Rose's confusion. "The Leader will sacrifice for the one who owns his heart, fully and completely."

Bill and Angelina entered the kitchen and stopped, looking at them. "Good morning, ladies," Bill said and looked at Lilly.

"Where is Anne?" Angelina looked at Lilly then at the used coffee pot.

"They left. Mark booked earlier tickets."

Bill frowned, but did not comment and picked up the newspaper.

"Stupid, Anne, she told me they booked for tomorrow." Angelina pointed at the cups before leaving the kitchen. "I'm not cleaning those. Luba is off today."

Lilly gave Angelina a warning look and put the cups in the sink before taking Rose by the arm and leading her upstairs to her balcony. "He is late."

But before Rose could reply, Jack soared right into the balcony. "Jack!" Rose threw herself into his arms. His embrace was strong, but he did not utter a word as they hugged. Rose released herself and looked up at him. The last time she had seen him was when he was attacked and there were two arrows sticking out of his chest, and when she thought she had lost him. Rose traced his bare chest with her eyes to where she believed the arrows might have been. No scars were left. She had performed it well.

Jack caught her eyes and covered the invisible scar with his hand. "You could have been-"

"It doesn't matter," Rose interrupted him and absentmindedly placed her palm over his hand on his chest. She was just thankful that she was once more able to look at his face and fall into his eyes.

"It did to me," he said in his deep voice and took her hands into his.

"Jack," Lilly said, cutting through their bond. "The doctor is a Protector."

"And Mark left," Rose added hastily.

He looked from Rose to Lilly with a confused frown. "What Protector?"

They told him everything that had happened with Dr. Liu and what he had informed them of.

"Was he saying the truth?" Jack looked at Lilly.

"He knew our grandparents' names," Lilly said, then jerked her head towards the forest.

"Let's continue inside."

"And, where is he now?" Jack asked as Lilly closed the balcony window behind her.

"He went back to London," Rose answered then something popped into her head. "Wait, the doctor knew that Mark would leave. Just before he left, he told me not to stop Mark tomorrow..."

But Jack's mind was on something else other than Mark. "Why did she not tell you, Lilly? She picked you to give the Water to..."

"Maybe we were not supposed to know then..."

"Wait," Rose interrupted. "The stories that people tell here in Nara, the myths and the legends, do they mention any Protectors? Maybe in some other form or wording... guardians maybe?"

"No, not that I know of," Jack said and frowned in concentration.

"We have to learn more about this," Lilly declared. "But, how?"

"I have an idea," Rose said, and Jack looked at her worriedly. "If this is history like you've said, Jack, then it is definitely written down, and that's also what Dr. Liu said... We need to go to the library. I am sure we'll find something there."

"Where is it?" Lilly asked.

"In the village."

"They can't go near the village," Lilly said and faced Jack.

"No," he said and leaned against the balcony door. "It's still dangerous."

"For how much longer are we going to wait?" Lilly glared at her brother. "I have had enough! We have to start doing something. We can't just sit here and wait for the rest, Jack. I know that's what you are thinking, but what if it's too late? We need more information, Jack, and we have to risk it. You just can't rely on the verbal tales... We have to go back to the original version."

Jack clenched his jaw, thinking. "We will have to be careful. Very careful." He made up his mind.

"What are the risks?" Rose asked, but realized the stupidity of her question a little late.

"What happened yesterday was the risk of stepping one foot out of protection!" Lilly replied, a little impatiently.

"What happened yesterday was nothing," Jack said and gave his sister a stern look. "This was the least of what they can actually do. It could have been worse... You know this better than us, Lilly. Those arrows were shot by only two Kalano..." He paused. "They are keeping a wide eye around the place, waiting."

"Hold on a second. What do you mean they are watching around the place?" Rose frowned. "Don't they see the house?"

"No. They don't see anything within the protection shield," Jack replied. "Just like the tree house... but, now we know where that shield extends to."

A faint creak of a floorboard outside the door caught her attention. There was a movement outside in the corridor, outside her door. Even Jack and Lilly noticed the moving shadow from the small gap between the floor and the door. *Angelina,* Rose thought as she made her way to open it and catch her red-handed. Spying!

"Luba!" Rose exclaimed when she found Luba crouched underneath a black cloak and her hands were shivering violently. "What are you doing here? Today is your day off."

"Rose! Stand back!" Lilly ordered and pulled her away from Luba. She seized Luba and pushed her to the ground, thrusting her right hand in front of her. "What do you want?"

"Lilly!" Rose hurried to help Luba off the ground, but Jack grabbed her before she was too close to her. "Lilly, she is just an old woman."

"Tell us why were you eavesdropping?" Lilly continued, "Speak!"

A deep moan came from under the hood and Luba started to shake violently. Lilly stepped closer and removed the hood from on top of Luba's head, and jerked backwards.

"Her eyes!" Rose shrieked and covered her face.

The old woman's eyes were two black spheres, like a crow, and her face was gnarled and squashed with pain. She looked at them one by one then smiled a smile that sent a chill down Rose's spine.

"Who sent you!" Lilly demanded.

The now strange woman started to slowly stand up on her feet, rising like a crouched bat with strained wings. She rose higher than her actual height, and Rose noticed that Luba was hovering above the ground with the terrifying smile still stapled on her crumbled face and her eyes fixed on Lilly.

"You will pay." A coarse voice came from Luba's slightly opened smile and shook the room walls. "Your master will be mercilesssssss."

"Finish it, Lilly!" Jack ordered. "Now!"

Obeying, Lilly held her hand in front of her and started to stir up a fierce wind against the now approaching body. But, Luba did not give in. She tried to go against the blowing wind and seize Lilly, but the wind was impenetrable. Suddenly she changed her target, seeing no way around, and jerked at Rose. Her black, skeleton hands were just inches away from Rose's neck when Jack leaped right in front of her. Luba smiled wider at Jack and sprang her hands eagerly to his neck instead. But, Jack was faster than those skeleton hands.

Lilly quickly stirred up a more powerful wind, causing Luba to glide away towards the corner. The wind had caused the windows to burst open, letting in more air to help Lilly, and the curtains danced helplessly against it. She managed to trap Luba inside a turning circle of angry wind that looked like a small version of a tornado. The smile was wiped off from Luba's face, and the skin crumbled more into a horrifying frown. Luba tried to penetrate the rotating trap, but what Lilly was doing was much stronger.

"I have no masters," Lilly bellowed.

Rose watched from behind Jack as Lilly drew circles in the air in which Luba gave a little jerk with every movement Lilly made. The speed of the roaring wind became fiercer that Rose suspected the shaking curtain rods would not hold on any longer. With a final draw from Lilly's rhythmic hand gestures, Luba opened her mouth in a silent scream, revealing black teeth, then her head dropped and wiggled down against her chest until it came to a halt. Slowly, Lilly lessened the intensity of the wind and died it completely away, causing Luba to smash into the ground with a loud crack of breaking bones.

"You choked her?" Rose emerged from behind Jack and looked over at the lifeless body. She could not believe what had just happened. How could Luba do this to her?

"Yes," Lilly said, panting a little. "It's hard to breath against air that forces itself up your nose. You can say I inflated her lungs." Lilly stepped over and knelt beside the corpse. With the tips of her fingers, she pulled the cloak off Luba's arms. There was something on the exposed skin. "Just like I guessed. An A-class spy for the Kalano. The Eagle Eye of the Spy mark justifies her high position."

"But, she had been working for us all year," Rose said in a low voice. "How could she betray us like that?"

"It was all planned and acted out perfectly," Lilly said, her tone was fierce. "But, not anymore."

Jack reached out for Rose's arm and pulled her away from the body, a frown traced his eyebrows. He looked at Lilly. "How did she get in?"

Lilly stood up and stepped out into the balcony, Jack and Rose followed her. "She was welcomed here. The owners of the house invited her in, discharging the protection against her. That is the only way a Kalano can penetrate a protection shield." She paused. "They know everything about us now."

The three of them fell silent, and stared at the night sky. Rose glanced at Jack and found his fist clenched into a hard ball. She reached over to him and looked at the emblem on his hand. The three parallel bars were clearer and sharper than the last time she had seen them. There was no doubt about it. It had been activated back there for the first time. And, it did so because Rose was in danger. Just like Lilly had said that it would be Rose who would activate Jack's symbol. But, at what price?

Jack met her eyes and managed half a smile. "I told you I would use it someday. And, I am glad at what it turned out to mean."

Downstairs the front door slammed shut, causing the three of them to jump. Lilly promptly soared to the roof to check who had come. "It's your father, Rose." She informed them as she made her way back to the balcony.

"What are we going to do with...?" Rose threw a glance at the dark figure lying in the middle of the room. "We need to hide it before anyone comes into my room."

"We'll have to burn it," Lilly said, making her way towards it. "But, it must be under the protection shield. They won't know if she is dead or alive as long as the body is inside it."

"The extension line stops at the edge of the pond," Jack said, recalling what he had seen on the day he was attacked. "We can burn it along that line. It's better to do it as far from here as possible."

"Rose!" Bill called from downstairs. "Are you alright? I think a storm is coming."

"I better go see him," Rose said and made her way to the door.

"We will go deal with the body then," Jack said.

"But, I want to come with you."

Jack shook his head. "You better stay here, Rose."

"Let her come, Jack," Lilly said, always impatiently. "We will be under the protection." He looked at Lilly for a couple of apprehensive seconds, then nodded to Rose.

"Rose!" Bill's voice came again.

"We will wait for you," Lilly said just as Rose was closing the door behind her.

Rose hurried down the stairs and found Bill sitting in the dimly lit living room. He was staring at a crumbled newspaper on the table in front of him. Rose gulped and sat next to him, trying to hid her anxiousness.

"Dad?" Rose said when she realized that he had not noticed her presence.

"Oh. There you are." He snapped out of his gaze. "Where have you been?"

"In my room, Dad." She tumbled over the words.

Angelina came out of the kitchen and crossed over to them. "What was that loud noise in your room?" she asked and sat down, putting one leg on top of the other.

"A strong breeze opened the windows," she said, curtly. "Dad, are you Ok?"

He took a deep breath and rubbed his face with both hands.

"What's the matter, dear?" Angelina asked.

"There is something going on in the country," he said. Rose stiffened. "The reports of missing girls have increased. Five young ladies were kidnapped last week."

"But, for sure the policemen-" Angelina said.

"The policemen can't find a single clue who kidnapped the girls or where to find them," Bill interrupted. "There are dangerous people in the country. So, from now on there will be no sidewalks in the forest and no visits to the Village except if I am with you. Are my words clear for both of you?"

"Yes, Bill," Angelina said. "Don't worry. We are safe here."

Rose nodded her head lightly. For the first time in her life she was right about something. *We are safe here.* She stood up and hugged her father. "Don't think about anything now, Dad. Just drink something warm and go to bed. I'm going to bed myself. Goodnight, Dad."

After giving him a goodnight kiss and faking a yawn, she climbed the stairs and headed to her room.

"You said they can't go anywhere near the village," Rose said once she locked the door behind her.

"They can't," Lilly said from where she was standing by the window and examining the night sky.

"What did your father want?" Jack asked, stepping over the unmoved body.

Maybe not that safe, she thought and tried not to look at it.

"He was warning me about the kidnappings that are happening in the village," she said. "Five girls have been kidnapped until now... without any evidence of who might be behind it."

Lilly turned away from the window and faced them. "No evidence?"

She shook her head.

"But, no one of them can enter the village," Lilly said.

"How do you know if that's true?" Rose queried.

"In the stories-" Jack started.

"There were no spies like Luba in the stories, Jack!" Lilly interrupted him. "In the stories there was a protection around the village that prevented anyone from the Dark Army to enter it. And, now we are hearing of people missing from the village. Doesn't that make you suspect the stories?"

He raised his eyebrows at her. "So, what...? Now you don't believe them?"

"They are not reliable anymore," Lilly said. "We have to go to the village and see for ourselves what's going on."

"Can we discuss this later?" he said with an edge in his voice, and stepped towards the body. "We have to get rid of this first before anyone enters and finds it."

"Step away, Jack," Lilly said and raised her hand in front of her. "I don't want anyone to touch it."

Under Lilly's command, the wind picked up its pace again and rushed in through the open balcony windows. The body started to shake a little as it was lifted off the ground by an invisible layer of air. Rose watched as Lilly twisted her hand elegantly and closed her fingers slowly one after the other. Obediently, the body glided towards Lilly and then out into the balcony. With another hand motion the body stopped, and the wind waited for its next order.

"Let's go." Lilly beckoned for both of them to join her out in the balcony. "Jack, you are the one who knows the limits of the protection. Tell us which course to take."

"It's about three-hundred meters high and extends until the pond," he informed them. "We will cross over as fast as we can until the trees become thicker. We'll land there then continue on foot."

Jack held Rose's hand and pulled her up into the air. "Rose and I will be ahead of you. Stay close, Lilly."

In a matter of seconds, they reached their landing spot and began walking in the pond's direction. Everything around them was quiet and dark as always, except for the soft cracking of twigs from beneath their feet. Jack led the way while Rose and Lilly followed close, keeping an alert ear for any peculiar noises. The-soon-to-be-burned body glided behind them.

When they reached the clearing of the pond, Jack stopped. "It ends just where the water hugs the shore, but it continues along that line and deeper into the trees on the right."

"Here would do," Lilly said, and started to slowly lower down the lifeless figure. "It's far enough from the house."

Jack looked at Rose, and she was sure he knew what was running through her mind. This place was very special to both of them and it could not be touched, should not be rubbed with such evil. No matter what happened and no matter what was yet to happen, this pond was theirs and should always remain pure.

"No, Lilly," Jack said, stopping her. He walked to the right, towards the path where he had disappeared once into, and stopped. "It's better to do it in a closed place. The clearing of the pond is too exposed, and we have to be careful no matter what." Rose met his eyes and saw the shimmer in them; she smiled.

Lilly nodded her head and let out an exasperated sigh, noticing their exchanged expressions, and guided the body towards where Jack was waiting. "Fine. As long as we get done with it quickly." With long, impatient strides, Lilly led the way this time and Jack slowed his pace to match Rose's. She did not go very far and stopped by a fallen tree overgrown with moss that blocked their path. Under her command, the body was lowered to the ground beside the tree.

"We need to find some dry wood," she said and cast her eyes around the dark forest. "That's if you see any in this darkness."

"Aren't we going to bury her?" Rose asked, looking from Jack to Lilly.

"Of course not," she replied. "We would be honoring her with a proper burial, and she does not deserve one. None of them do."

"You're going to burn her?" Rose said, watching her gather some dry twigs and any wooden block she was able to find. "But, she served me-"

"That's why I told you to stay back," Jack told her and held her hands. "I knew it wouldn't be easy for you, but we have to."

"Why? Can't we just leave her body in peace?" Rose heard her voice changing and felt the lump form in her throat.

"She was a Kalano, Rose," Lilly said, dropping wood around the dead body. "She was a helping hand in a plan that was designed to kill Jack. All of humankind, in fact."

"Lilly," Jack said with an edge to his voice and looked over at her. "Enough."

Rose was familiar with Lilly's boldness, but sometimes her words were sharp and harsh; however, she carried the bitter taste of the truth that Jack always tried to hide from her.

With two rocks, Lilly skillfully set the twigs on fire. They crackled slowly until the flames grew bigger and fiercer as they ate away at all the wood around the body, even under it, but it did not catch upon the flesh or the hair. The body was unharmed by any single flame.

"Why isn't it burning?" Rose asked and looked at Lilly through the smoke of the bonfire that by now had started to sting their eyes.

"It needs a Blue Water's power to do the job," Jack declared after contemplating the ground for a few moments. The fire refused to burn the body; whether it did not acknowledge its presence or simply sensed the cruelty of the creature that made it even more powerful than the fire's own flames. "This won't work, Lilly."

"I know," she said, sighing and throwing a twig into the last flames. "What are we going to do? Don't say we're burying her."

"No, Lilly, we are not going to bury her," Jack said with a voice filled with something familiar, something that Rose had heard before in his laughter. "We are going to hide her here until we know what other weapons are available among the army. As soon as we find the right one, we'll retrace our steps and finish the job. As for now, we are going to head back to the house and call it a night... End of discussion."

She opened her mouth to argue, but thought better of it when she saw the look on his face. After covering the body up with some leaves and dirt to hide it from any trespasser, which was unlikely to happen, they retraced their steps back to the house.

"Jack, what are we going to do?" Rose said, standing beside him in the balcony, where he was leaning against the railing.

"We'll make that visit to the library. Tomorrow morning." He sighed. "We better find something that'll explain all of this."

Ten: Answers in the Library

Time was running by faster than before, and there was nothing they could do to stop it. Nothing reassured them of their survival, not even hope or the dreams that used to sedate Rose. The young boy stopped visiting her, whether he felt the danger or sensed the change within the dreamer, she was not sure why. Rose woke up the next morning, unclear of what they would do or how would it be done. She joined Lilly in the balcony, who was contemplating their plan for the day.

"We need to go early," Lilly said, "and we must be quick."

"How are we going to get there?" Rose said, brushing the tiredness from her eyes.

"There is a way, but I am not sure your father will understand."

"Dad?"

"Yes, he could drive us there," Lilly replied. "Do you remember how I got here?"

"Yes, in the doctor's car."

"And, I was not caught. I acted normal and was patient, even though I could have just flown here."

"It's always better to stay low," Rose said, remembering Jack's words.

"Exactly."

"So, we should ask father to drop us to the village without giving anything away, right?"

"Yes, and I have found the best excuse to tell him," Lilly said just as a figure appeared in the sky. "But, first, we'll have to convince Jack."

Jack landed just beside Rose and took her hand into his. He brought it near to his mouth and kissed it. She was surprised at his action and her heart, as usual, made a soft skip. He smiled softly at her blushing cheeks and gazed deeply into her eyes, ignorant of his sister's impatience beside him.

There was something different in his eyes. Misery? Fear? Rose was not sure, but with another look she immediately knew the reason behind his abrupt conveyance of affection. It was guilt that swam in his eyes. Even though she had seen it before, this time it was evident, almost painful. She was not sure what to tell him, but she managed to pull a smile to comfort him.

"Jack," Lilly said, having lost her patience. "We must catch Bill before he goes to work."

Jack tore his gaze away from Rose and looked questioningly at his sister. "Why do you want to do that?"

"We need to go to the library in the village. The only way to do that is by driving there, so as not to draw any unwanted attention."

"And, how do you expect to explain yourself to Bill?" Jack's tone was unreadable.

"Rose will-"

"Rose?" Jack looked at Lilly with anxiety.

"Yes, Rose!" Lilly said curtly. "She'll tell her father that we want to shop for some women's things from the village. And, since he banned her from going there unless he's with her, it'll sound right to ask him to drop us there on his way."

Jack raised his eyebrows and pressed his lips. "I don't see myself in this plan."

Rose saw Lilly fidget a little before answering. "Jack, think about it. If you accompanied us, Bill might start asking questions. He'll wonder what are you doing with two girls going shopping for private stuff... or even worse, he might ask you to drop us yourself. I doubt you'll be capable of driving a car."

"Or, we could change the excuse, then I'll be able to come along," Jack said as he ushered the two girls to the roof. He immediately scanned the surroundings.

"Someone must stay here in case anything happens." Lilly said as she watched the driveway and made sure that Bill's car was still parked in front of the house.

Jack sighed. "I won't leave Rose behind and won't let her outside the protection shield unless I am with her."

"You won't," Rose shimmed in. "Didn't you say there is a protection on the village? They won't be able to enter it."

"I am not risking it." Jack looked at her with worry for a couple of tense seconds. "Don't forget the missing girls," he said, looking over his shoulder to Lilly.

"I did not forget about them," Lilly replied. "That's why we must go to the village and find out what's happening!"

Jack pocketed his hands and lowered his head, contemplating the roof's floor for a few seconds. Rose looked at him and instantly wanted to reach out and stroke all of his worries away. She didn't want to ever let go of him. "You go, Lilly. Rose and I will stay here." He raised his head back up.

"No, Jack," Rose said when she recalled her last visit to the library. "Akita, the librarian, will not respond to Lilly. According to her, Lilly is a total stranger who's coming to ask about an old legend in time when girls are missing. I don't think she'll take it cordially."

"Rose, please. Don't. I'll be less worried if you stayed here, safe inside the protection," he said.

"I have to go." She pushed herself to protest. "Akita has been my friend and confidant. She will be happy to help me. I'm sure the last thing she wants is a total stranger seeking for legendary information in her library," Rose added in hope of convincing him.

"She's right," Lilly said from behind him. He glared at her from over his shoulder. However, Lilly did not flinch and exchanged his glare. "You'll have to stay here." Lilly reached over and pulled Rose beside her. "Is it my ability or me that you don't trust?" Lilly snapped when she found a peculiar look on Jack's gloomy face. Rose had seen this expression before, on the day when he knew that the Kalano were after her.

"Take that back." Jack's voice was bleak.

"I see no problem now," Lilly said, looking fiercely at him. "Rose, catch your father before he leaves. You know what to say to him."

Jack grabbed Rose's arm and stopped her.

"Jack can't you see?" Lilly retorted. "You can't protect her! If something happens outside there, there is nothing that you can do to save both of our lives. And, I don't think sacrifice is the solution to keep her alive! At least I can protect her and not jump in front of an arrow."

"Will you watch what you are saying?" Jack said through gritted teeth. Rose sensed him throw a defensive look towards her, but she was incapable of lifting her eyes off the ground. Without another word from both of them, she reentered her room and went to find Bill. She knew Lilly's hurtful words were true. Her declaration had a meaning, a terrible meaning with harsh consequences. His affection was not enough to save or protect her life; towards her he was helpless and weak. And, just like his symbol had conveyed, the Leader can't save the Healer without paying his life as a price... and what a price it was. She felt a tear prickle down her cheek as she entered the bright kitchen, and she quickly brushed it away before Bill or Angelina could see it.

"Good morning, dear," Bill said as he flipped through the newspapers. "You're up early."

"Yes. I thought you could drop me and my friend to the village before you leave for work." Rose took the seat opposite him, trying very hard to conceal her current state of emotions. She caught a glimpse of the headlines: *Three More! Where Is The Police!* There was also minor article with a shocking headline: *The Government Acknowledges Various Kidnappings.* It was spreading rapidly.

"That friend, you say," he said and threw a glance at Angelina, "is not a serial killer on the run, right?"

"What?" Rose was disgusted. "No!"

"Oh, Bill!" Angelina snapped. "I was only wondering who this girl was and what she's doing in my house."

"Our house," Rose mused. She made a brief glance at Angelina and saw her puckered lips thin in repressed annoyance.

"Is it something urgent?" Bill asked, pretending that nothing had happened.

"Pretty urgent, yes." Rose nodded a little too enthusiastically than she had intended.

Bill raised his eyebrows. "Oh, that urgent...?"

"Girl stuff, Dad," she mumbled loud enough for him to hear.

Bill grabbed the papers again and pretended to read. "I'll be leaving in ten minutes. Make yourselves ready by then."

Throughout the bumpy journey, Rose kept recalling Jack's rigid expression he had when she entered the car. Even though he was crouching on the rooftop like an eagle, she had seen the worry on his sunlit face. Of course, he did not let them leave until he had surveyed the whole area and made sure nothing was lurking within the shadows of the forest.

You better help Akita, Rose thought just as the village started to appear at the bottom of the road ahead. It was unusually empty, Rose noticed. There were no children running around after each other, no shoppers bustling from one store to the other, and no girls sitting and gossiping. It was almost deserted except for a few traders scattered here and there with their products laid under the burning sun, hoping for any buyer to pass by. Bill drove into the second alley and parked right in front of the mini pharmacy store, just as he always did when he dropped Rose to purchase her personal needs. Lilly and Rose jumped out of the car and dashed into the store before Bill could even open his door. They quickly bought some stuff as proof and back up for their concocted story, and darted back out.

"All done?" Bill said when they came out hastily.

"Yes." Rose opened the door to the back seat and carelessly threw the shopping bags in. "Lilly and I just need to pay a little visit to the library."

"No problem," Bill said and locked his car. "Come on. I'll walk you, ladies, there. It's not safe to let two young and lovely ladies walk on their own, especially when the village is in this abnormal state."

Lilly and Rose looked at each other simultaneously, but Rose could not identify, as always, the expression on Lilly's face. They started walking alongside each other and Lilly unexpectedly took Rose's arm and tangled hers with it. "You must do the talking with this Akita," Lilly whispered, aware of Bill striding closely beside Rose. "She may recognize my Kalano accent and think otherwise..."

Rose nodded as they stopped in front of the library, hoping to find Akita in there. She let out a sigh of relief when she found Akita stooped over a pile of paper on her desk. Bill waited until both girls were safely inside the library before he went back to get the car.

Everything was the same since the last time she had been here; the same smell of paper and decaying book bindings, and the threatening stacks of high book piles that seemed to lean far too much out of balance. Mark was with her then, Rose recalled and gave a shudder; it seemed ages ago. However, she could perceive a new ambiance to the cramped place, but she did not know what it was. As they zigzagged their way to Akita, Rose made sure her necklace was hidden beneath her shirt and the emblem on her hand was concealed beneath the bandage and out of sight.

Akita was mumbling something underneath her breath and stopped when she realized there was company. She raised her head slowly and smiled when she saw her favorite customer. "Rose! I thought you forget me."

"I have been a little busy." Rose managed a smile.

"I hope you did not do danger to hurt your hand." Akita pointed at Rose's hand and threw a cynical glance at Lilly, who raised one eyebrow.

"I fell on it," Rose said and pocketed it. "We'll look around, OK?"

"Yes. Go," Akita said, waving them off, and went back to the paper on her desk. Lilly had already started rummaging through some piles when Rose turned to start her own hunt. A pile of thick and old books at the far end of the corner grabbed her attention, and she twisted her way towards it. She picked one up and was startled at its heaviness, its title read: *Nara, A History: The Old Age*. It was one of the translated Naryan books with no doubt. It was an interesting book with intriguing illustrations, but there was no mentioning of any 'Dark Army' in its contents. She put it aside and grabbed the next one, which was also completely useless. Rose looked over her shoulder and saw Lilly immersed in a book, but she quickly closed it with a puff of irritation. Lilly looked up at her and shook her head in dismay.

"Akita," Rose called as she retraced her steps to the old lady.

Akita looked up from an old paper she was examining, the dangling beads in her hair rattling. "I need your help to find what I am looking for..." Akita smiled at her and put the paper aside. "A book," Rose continued, "that has information about Nara's legends."

Akita's smile was now a little rigid and her eyes watched her cautiously. Rose felt as if those eyes could see right through her... just like Dr. Liu's used to. "Nara got many. Which one you want?"

"The Blue Water," Rose said and sensed Lilly come by her side.

Akita did not move at first and observed them with those eyes partly buried under wrinkled skin. She then swiftly turned away and went through a tiny door hidden behind an adorned blue canopy. Rose and Lilly heard some banging and crashing from inside and were about to go and check it out when Akita reappeared from behind the canopy with a book clutched tightly between her arms. She heaved it on the desk with a sigh and pushed it towards Rose. "All answers... here."

Rose picked it up and read its title: *Ako Nara*. It was in Naryan. "Do you have an English version?"

"Yo friend can read." Akita cringed her head towards Lilly.

Lilly took the book from her and flipped quickly through its old paper, sending a puff of dust in Rose's face. "It's the original version," Lilly whispered, her voice carried excitement.

"We'll take it," Rose said, eager to know what valuable information it bore.

"Yes. But," Akita said and pointed one finger at Rose, "yo must bring back. Three days. No more."

Rose and Lilly eagerly nodded and made their way out of the library where they found Bill waiting for them inside the car. Just as Rose was crossing over to the car, distant noises caught her ears. She jerked her head towards where the noises seemed to emanate from and saw a mob of police surrounding a man at the far end of the alley.

Lilly quickly seized Rose's arm and dragged her towards the car. As the car roared to life and the girls rushed inside, a policeman started to vigorously thrash the unarmed man with his booted feet and a thick stick. Rose watched in horror as the man whimpered and tried to defend himself against the ruthless blows until blood pooled around him.

"Goodness," Bill said, slowly driving out of his parking spot to get a good glimpse of what was happening.

"Sir," Lilly said impatiently, leaning forward in her seat. "I think we better move quickly. Now." Bill strongly agreed and stomped on the gas, causing the car to leap forward and bump its way out of the alley and onto the highway.

Rose looked perplexedly at Lilly, her eyes glimmering with fear against the afternoon sun. "Why did that policeman behave like that?" She asked in a whisper, the image of the bloodbath shining under the sunlight fresh in her mind. "The police here are civil and merciful towards the people."

"Must have been an outlaw," Billed answered instead, his face was crumbled in contemplation. Rose was sure that was not what he really thought and that he was just stating so to not frighten his daughter. Rose turned back to Lilly, waiting for an answer, but Lilly just looked at her gloomily and did not reply.

No one uttered a single word for the rest of the ride back home. Rose and Lilly were on edge all through the way and restless to get safely inside the protection again. They observed the road for anything strange, but everything looked normal. Once Bill drove the car into the drive way and into the invisible protection shield, Rose started to breathe again, just noticing that she had been holding it for a while. Upon parking, both girls jumped out of the car and into the house.

"What was that?" Rose asked Lilly while they hurried up the stairs.

"The police were not acting upon their own will. They are not aware," Lilly said with disgust in her tone, and stormed into Rose's room. "They are controlled, manipulated by the Kalano!" Rose's eyes widened with terror. "Now, I think I know who was kidnapping the girls..."

Both girls sat on the bed as Jack flew in through the open balcony door, and quickly took Rose in a hug. Just as quickly, he let go and started flipping through the book's pages, hoping it would have the answer to all of their questions. But, there was nothing in the book worth the journey they had made, except for authenticating the existence of the protection shield around the village. The book told the same story as the one Jack had once told her, nothing more or less. Its illustrations were pretty impressive as they jumped between the pages, foretelling the story without the need to read.

Rose, to her surprise, was able to understand the Naryan text. Jack had said that it was the Blue Water's effect, and she could consider it as another gift from it. Given her ability, Rose did not take her eyes off the book and read it from cover to cover in two days.

When the third and last day in borrowing the book came, nothing had been figured out. Their spirits had started to wear off as all three of them made their way down the stairs. There was no one in the house; Angelina and Bill went to the village, causing the house to have an eerie silence to it. They had the entire house to their disposal. Rose brought the book and sat in the living room beside the empty fireplace.

No one spoke much, especially after the realization they had about the policemen. It was the only acceptable explanation they had behind the mysterious disappearance of the girls. The Kalano forced the police to kidnap the girls, which they accomplished expertly, leaving no trace behind. Then they would sympathies with the heartbroken families. A perfect plan cooked by the Kalano, no doubt. Rose felt reassured when they found a hint in the book about mind controlling. It stated that the enemy had great and dark powers that could be used to enter one's mind through their dreams and gain control of the person. Rose had been frightened when she first read it, and a certain disturbing dream was fresh in her mind again, one she had thought she'd forgotten about.

Jack held her hand in his, which he did often since Rose had returned from the village. She couldn't forget how he had taken her in his arms and almost squeezed the breath out of her the moment he saw her, nor how he softly kissed her palm. Rose could still feel the warmth of his lips on her skin and blushed whenever she recalled it.

The book lay open on her lap as she flipped through it for the zillionth time now, in hope of deciphering any meaning or symbol. She was concentrating very hard on a few smudged words when the sound of the telephone ringing made her jump in her place, dropping the book and causing a couple of pages to rip out of the bindings.

All three of them froze in their places, irritated by the sudden break of silence. The landline rang for a few times until the answering machine beeped and someone spoke.

"Hey. This is Anthony Marcos." Anthony's deep voice filled the vast living room. Rose noticed the unusual uneasiness in his tone and rushed over to the telephone to pick it up.

"Hello," she answered, her breathing quickened.

"Oh. Hello, Rose," Anthony said. "How are you doing?"

"Great, Anthony." Rose was impatient.

"Good to hear that," he said, the uneasiness becoming more evident with every word.

Rose tightened her grip on the earpiece as Anthony continued, "I was wondering if Mark was still there? I've been trying to contact him for the past few days, but he either doesn't pick up or his phone is switched off..."

"Mark travelled a few days ago," Rose replied and dropped herself into a chair nearby. "He did not call you?"

"No. He did not return any of my calls," Anthony said and sighed, cursing underneath his breath. "There is something he has to know..."

"What happened, Anthony?" Rose felt her heart sink.

"Paul and Julio..." he paused and took in a deep breath. "They were found this morning... dead."

She gasped in disbelief. Jack and Lilly rushed to her side, and Jack managed to find and press the speaker button so they could all hear what was going on.

"How?" Rose forced her voice out as a lump in her throat tried to stop it.

"I... I honestly don't know," Anthony replied, his words echoing throughout the house. "The policemen said they found both of them lifeless in their bedrooms this morning, no signs of a break in or any struggle... they say whoever did this had done it clean."

"No evidence left behind." Rose half said to Anthony and half to Jack.

"No. Not a single finger print was found..." He exhaled. "Hey, listen, Rose. I have to go now."

"Yes, of course." Rose said, still gobsmacked by the horrid news. "I am sorry for your loss, Anthony."

"I'm sorry too... It's going to be harsh on Mark." And, with that, he hung up.

Rose stared at Jack, his face unreadable, and waited for him to tell her that her thoughts were mistaken, that it could not be as it appeared to be. But, his stillness only proved otherwise. Instantly, the sinister silence prevailed over them, thickening the air with cold and heavy agitation. Rose rubbed her face, trying to sweep away her fears, but only ended up wiping at her tears. Jack came closer and knelt in front of her, leveling with her face. He brushed away her tears with his thumb and took her hands into his. "I am sorry for Mark's loss..."

Rose bit her lips, gulping back a sob, and nodded to him. All sorts of what-if questions crept into her head and brought dark images with them. She tried to push them aside, but they were persistent, especially when she recalled one of her dreams.

"They're closer than I thought." Jack looked up at Lilly. She exchanged a disturbed expression with her brother, communicating with her eyes, and unconsciously let out a powerful exhale of apprehension, causing the torn paper on the floor to fly in the air as if made of feathers. Rose stared at the papers as they swayed down in front of her and noticed a single sheet laid heavily on the floor, unaffected by Lilly's exhale.

Without letting go of her hands, Jack stood up and gently pulled Rose out of her seat. He ushered her away from the telephone and out the terrace doors. A refreshing breeze blew at her face, blowing through her hair, and she breathed in the damp smell of the trees and blossoming flowers. But, even outside, the air transported the unfavorable feelings.

"Don't worry. Mark is chosen. He's protected by the Water."

Rose turned and faced him, always surprised at how he could fish out her thoughts. "I am so scared, Jack," she whispered.

He squeezed his eyes shut and clenched his jaws at her words, pulling her gently into his body and wrapping his arms around her. Rose's heart skipped at his action and felt his heart beat against hers. It was almost like magic how this simple act of affection drew out her fears. But, Rose knew it was only momentarily. The second she was out of his arms, her miserable thoughts would plunge into her mind again. And, for that, she did not want him to let go of her. She wanted to stay like that for the rest of her life, enveloped in him and protected from what was out there.

"Never be afraid as long as I am alive," he breathed in her ears, his warm breath tingling her skin. Goosebumps ran through her body. Whether it was from the chilly air or from the heat of his skin, she did not know. She closed her eyes and nuzzled against the hollow of his collarbone, breathing in his smell. She felt Jack's heart beat faster against his chest and he ran his fingers through her hair; her mouth twitched into a smile. They stood like that for what seemed to be a lifetime until Rose started drifting off, her head getting heavier against him.

"Rose," whispered Jack. But she only twitched a little and cuddled deeper into him, the drowsiness completely conquering her. He swiftly picked her legs up without awakening her, soared through the air, and landed in her balcony. With his legs, he pushed the glass doors aside and entered the room, where he gently put Rose on the bed and covered her with the bedcovers. He allowed himself to sit beside her and watch the innocence that dominated her face, her soft hair laying on it in wavy strands. Lilly entered the room, carrying the book in one hand and the unorganized stack of torn paper in the other, and walked to set them in the armchair near the balcony.

Minutes or maybe hours later, someone was gently shaking her out of her slumber and was whispering her name. That voice. That deep, sweet voice that had breathed her name into her ears was trying to wake her up, and she could not help but to oblige.

"How long have I been asleep?" Rose asked once she opened her eyes, and saw Jack's face emerging out of the blurriness. She tried to remember how did she fall asleep in the first place and blushed, recalling the sweet smell of Jack.

"For a couple of hours," Jack said, sitting in the armchair beside her, a plate full of bread and fruits was on the bedside table. He offered her a red apple. "Rose, did I not tell you to not forget to eat?"

It was more of a statement than a question, Rose realized. She pushed herself up and jumped out of bed, energy felt fresh in her blood. Accepting the apple from Jack, she munched on it, still recalling the unexplainable safeness she had felt between those arms...

Rose tried to put those feelings aside for now and looked around the room, noticing Lilly's absence. "Where is Lilly?"

"She went for a walk. Within the protection, of course," he replied. "She wants to clear her mind a little."

Rose took another bite and looked through the glass doors at the dark sky, where the moon shone like a silver gemstone amid the cloudless night. Her eyes hovered over the forest. "Jack, let's have a walk in the forest." She turned to look at him and was startled when she found him standing close by her side. He locked his warm brown eyes with her and smiled that irresistible dazzling smile of his. Rose couldn't help but melt underneath its radiance and exchanged his smile.

Without tearing his eyes away from her, Jack slid open the glass-doors and ushered her out. "I know where we could go," he said through his smile. Rose saw a twinkle of mischief in his moonlit eyes and raised her eyebrows in wonder.

"You've been trapped inside here for too long. And, I was afraid what might happen to you if you stepped out. But, I see no point in keeping you in anymore. Thank you for keeping your promise."

They pushed themselves up into the air and soared through the night sky and towards the dark forest. The mist was thick and heavy, and the silver moonlight penetrated the small gaps between the cramped trees, hitting the mist and creating an enthralling ambiance around them as they walked into it, the damp floor muting their pathless footsteps. She walked close to Jack, his hands not letting go of hers, and noticed his silence. Even though she always associated silence and deep thought with him, this time his silence had a calm feeling to it.

"Tell me your thoughts," Rose whispered.

A smile broke across his face and he chuckled his melodic chuckle. Rose was startled, she had not heard it for a long time and was stunned at the increased dominance it bore. "I remembered a special dream."

"Why is it special?" she asked.

He cringed his head and looked at her through gleaming eyes, a few strands of hair slid on his forehead and he brushed them back absentmindedly. "Always curious." He teased her.

She had used the curious tone again, Rose guessed. "I'm not curious..." She tried to stifle a smile. "Who said I am?"

He chuckled again. "Your face tells me everything."

Rose could not help but to giggle as well, discharging the worries into the air to be swept away by the breeze. She looked at Jack and found him staring at her, that breathtaking smile illuminating his face.

"I've missed hearing you laugh," he whispered. She smiled and felt her cheeks get warmer against the cold air.

They stopped when they found themselves in front of the pond, the mist crawling over its mirror surface. Rose was about to go to her favorite spot on top of the rock like she used to when Jack grasped her hand before she could take a step forward.

"The protection shield ends here," he told her. He picked up a long twig and kneeled down, and he started drawing an imaginary line in the pebbly ground just where the pond hugged the shore. "What lies beyond here is no longer safe to pass... at least for now."

Rose stood quietly for a few minutes and stared at the pond and the rock a few meters ahead of her. This used to be her refuge and where...

"I know what you're thinking..." he said and straightened himself back up. "I am sorry."

"This is where I first met you," she said, her eyes lost in thought, "and where I escaped from my bitter memories. How can it not be safe anymore?"

"Rose. Please... don't make this harder on me." He sounded as if he was in pain. "Don't make me feel more guilty-"

"Guilty?" Rose jerked her head and locked her eyes with his. "I am not blaming you, I would never blame you, Jack. And, I am not blaming anyone for the course my life had taken... On the contrary, I am grateful." Her mouth twitched into a smile, and she reached over to touch Jack's face to reassure him.

Jack gently held her hand against his cheek and brought her nearer to him. He stood so close to her that Rose could feel his breath on her face and his sweet smell filled her lungs. He softly kissed her hand, sending a shiver up her arm, and looked up into her eyes. Her heart hammered against her chest and she tried to elude his gaze. But, she couldn't resist the unfamiliar emotion arising within her and looked back into those fired up eyes. The shadow of his long eyelashes casted on his high cheekbones and his soft hair curled against his jawbones, she wanted to reach up and stroke it. She allowed him to pull her even closer, the heat of his body warm against her, and she was suddenly aware of his masculine arms and broad firm chest against the length of her body. Her breathing fastened and she felt lightheaded, uncertain of what might happen next.

He slowly leaned in when she did not show any signs of resistance, closing any space between them, and covered her lips with his in a soft kiss. His lips were soft and warm against hers, just like she thought they would be. She responded to him and kissed him back, surprising herself. Her breathing was short and quick, and her heart pounded in her ears as Jack continued to kiss her. She felt his hand cup her face and he kissed her harder, more hungrily. And, she responded, pushing herself more against his body, and reached to his soft hair she so desired to twist between her fingers.

A crack in the trees behind them made them jump, breaking their lips apart. Jack scanned the area with his eyes, not letting go of Rose. They stood in silence, clamped to each other, and listened. But, there was nothing audible except for the sound of their heavy breathing in their ears. Jack looked back at her and a smile drew on his face. He touched her forehead with his and brushed his nose against hers lightly. "You don't know how much I wanted to do this."

Rose giggled, her head was still spinning and she was shaking all over. "I love you, Jack Casper."

Jack closed his eyes and sighed with relief. "Finally you said it." He planted another kiss on her lips and smiled. "*Nakupenda*...more than anything."

She smiled against his lips. "*Nakupenda* ... I love how it sounds in Naryan."

"I feel it more in my mother tongue," he whispered. "But, I feel it more when I see you, Rose."

Her chest expanded with a deep breath, wishing that moment would never end.

Lilly had already arrived when they entered the room through the balcony. She looked at them with scrutinizing eyes, wondering what was the reason behind their happy faces in harsh times like these. Her brother eluded her gaze when she raised one eyebrow at him. Rose did not dare to make eye contact with Lilly lest she blush even more. Rose twirled around and started organizing the torn papers, trying to find their previous locations inside the book.

"We need to give the book back tonight," Rose said. "We need to find-" She stopped and frowned at one of the papers in her hand. A bend at its corner caught her attention.

"Rose?" Jack came close to her and looked over her shoulder at the piece of paper. "What is it?"

Her heart raced as she felt the thickness of the paper in her hand and realized how it was heavier than the others. "It's a double paper."

"What?" Jack reached over and felt the paper between his thumb and forefinger. Frowning, he took the paper and held it against the lit night lamp beside the bed, turning it between his hands and scrutinizing it. He looked at both of them with excitement in his eyes and said, "I need a pair of scissors and a wet cloth."

Rose quickly dampened a small towel in the bathroom and grabbed a pair of thin scissors. Jack took them to where he had set the paper on the dressing table and started to carefully separate the two papers from each other.

Fortunately, the papers split apart easily, without damaging the writing. When Jack set the two papers beside each other, they found the extra one to look different from the rest of the book's pages; it had an elegant, dark blue cursive and the paper itself had an unusual odor of... salt?

Jack moved the paper closer to the light and read out loud:

"The Founder is meant to be
For they will find me
Under the same as their color
Of power and given other.
Not East, not South, you march Until the ground below is damp.
A rock and a sister of the such will help with the forsaken hunt.
When the moon is in full camp Amidst the sinful night, guidance will appear to where the sister is near.
Bounded and out of sight, waiting for the moment to be held...
Beware of the Envious Eye
For it seeks whoever am I
That wakes from the seventh grave
When those words are grandly saved."

"What the...?" Lilly said and snatched the paper from her brother to read it for herself.

"Is this what I think it is?" Rose asked and looked at Jack, who was stirring what he had just read in his mind.

"It's a riddle," Lilly said. "But, why was-"

"Akita put it there." Rose blurted out of nowhere and gasped at what might be true. "We need to go to Akita. Now." She jumped up and hurried to grab her jacket.

"Rose, what are you doing?" Jack asked, following her around the room as she looked for a bag and stuffed the book and the paper in it.

"We need to go, Jack. I need to go and see Akita right now." She stopped running around and looked at him. "I think she is trying to tell us something."

"The librarian?" Jack frowned. "I am not-"

"No, she's right," Lilly said and hurried over to Rose. "Akita got us the book from a storage room. The book was hidden and so was this mysterious paper. There is definitely something special about it."

"Tomorrow in daylight will be safer for us to go." Jack reasoned. "We'll have to wait-"

"No, Jack," Rose protested. "I don't think we have enough time to wait." With the bag clutched tightly in her hand, she hurried to the door and out into the corridor.

"Rose!" Jack ran after her and grabbed her before she could descend the stairs.

"Jack, trust me. I need to go to her. I need to talk to her."

"Rose, you know it's dangerous out there. And, I have let you out of my sight once and I am not doing it again."

"Come with me, then."

"Of course I'm coming with you. But, what could be so important that you can't wait for tomorrow?"

"I... I think Akita is my Protector," Rose said. She did not know if her assumptions were correct or not, but she was following her instincts. She had to go and find out for herself. "Please, Jack."

Jack closed his eyes and contemplated for a moment, then he reopened them and faced his sister. "Lilly, go out to the back of the house and preform a strong wind through the forest. Make it look like you're checking the safety of the path for us. Keep at it for a couple of minutes, then go back inside until we come back."

"You want me to distract anyone watching the area?" Lilly asked, squinting her eyes in concentration.

"Yes. If anyone is near, they'll think we are heading that way and you are making sure it's safe for us. No one will suspect we are going the opposite direction," Jack replied.

"Jack, no-" Lilly started.

"Lilly," Jack said between gritted teeth. "Do as I say... Don't forget who I am." Lilly opened her mouth to argue, but thought better of it and went to do as the Leader ordered her. Jack held Rose's hand and headed towards her room. "We'll go through the window and land between the trees alongside the driveway."

"We are not going by car?" Rose asked as they stood in her balcony. Lilly looked up from where she was standing in front of the path and signaled to them that she was ready.

"No. We'll run to the village," Jack replied and pushed himself up into the air, pulling Rose up with him. "It's better not to draw any attention to us, especially if it's at night."

"But, the village is a half hour walk. It'll take us time." Rose stood on the roof and surveyed the trees immersed in inky darkness. She was sure they wouldn't even be able to see where they were going.

"It won't take time when you know how to fly. All you have to do is run very fast. Our bodies are light, and so is our step. We'll be able to make it in five minutes... Just stay close to me."

Rose took a deep breath and nodded. "Let's go."

It did not take her any effort to figure out how was she supposed to run and lift her body at the same time, keeping a low profile. They ran through the trees with unexpected speed without hitting or tripping into any of them, and the cold air bit their heated faces as they ran. Rose was surprised at how bright her surroundings appeared, even when they were running through darkness. She could not help but also notice the silence of their footsteps; they were so light that she was sure no one could ever hear them running. Suddenly she was aware of how strong she was and felt that there was still more power buried within her. They were much more powerful than this.

As Jack had said, they reached the deserted village quickly. Rose was about to run to the library when Jack grabbed her and pulled her beside him. He put his finger on her mouth to hush her before she could utter a word and pointed at the armed policemen standing at the end of the dark alley ahead of them.

"We must not be spotted," he whispered. They quietly moved to stand behind a shop where they could hide out of sight. Jack grabbed a nearby rock and threw it far away from them with so much strength that the wall the rock hit crumbled down. Jack stared with wide eyes at what he had just done. They watched as the patrolling policemen ran towards the racket, leaving the third alley clear for Jack and Rose to enter safely.

Rose sped to the library and was about to enter it when she heard the crunch of glass from underneath her feet. Confused, Rose looked up and gasped at the shattered windows of the library. She looked inside and was shocked at the mayhem: books were scattered everywhere, shelves brought down and cupboards broken. It looked like it was pillaged. Hurriedly, Rose ran in, finding her way to Akita's desk in the back.

Jack followed her. "Rose, I feel evil spirits in this place..."

The desk was thrown over in a corner where a huge bookshelf lay on top of it; the books scattered around like dead and opened bodies. Rose kept searching around the wrecked place, until something caught her eyes.

"Akita!" Rose hurried over to the broken desk where an old hand was visible between the stacks of books. "Jack, help me get her out!"

Jack quickly removed the books from on top of Akita, and Rose tried to get her out, but Akita's legs were stuck underneath the desk.

"Akita, do you hear me? Wake up!" Rose said and shook her shoulders, but Akita did not respond. "Akita! Please wake up!" Rose felt a lump forming in her throat and raised her hand to her mouth, sobbing quietly.

"Rose." Jack frowned at her. "Your hand..."

Her eyes widen with horror when she found blood covering her hand and staining the clothe around her emblem. But, she felt no pain. Jack bent over to Akita and reached her neck. He pulled out a small wooden dart with silver feathers and held it in front of him. Rose noticed the familiar silver feathers from the first time they were attacked in the forest.

With a loud gasp, Akita's old hands suddenly snatched Rose. She shrieked and tried to crawl away from those hands, but Akita kept a firm grip and brought Rose close to her face. "Solve it!" Akita said from between her unmoving lips, her eyes still closed. Jack jumped beside Rose and pulled her away from Akita. "Solve it!" Akita's hoarse voice said again, and with another gasp Akita's hands dropped to their death.

Her breathing was loud in her ears, and Jack's hand wrapped her tightly and prevented her from stepping close to the now lifeless body.

"She was my Protector, Jack." Her voice shook slightly. "She could have helped us. But, now she is dead. She had information, Jack. They killed her! Wait." Rose tried to unwrap his arms from around her. "I can heal her. Yes, I'll heal her!"

"Rose. Rose." Jack kept his grip firm around her as she fought to free herself. "You can't, Rose. It doesn't work that way. Only on the living."

She stopped fighting and allowed the tears to roll down her cheeks. "She was my protector. She could have helped us, Jack..."

"I know, I know," he said in a cracked voice, and held Rose tightly between his arms as she sobbed. "We must leave. Before they come back."

Eleven: The Riddle

Neither Jack nor Rose slowed their pace as they sped back into the protection shield of the house. A movement caught Rose's attention from between the trees as she ran. It seemed Jack also noticed it for he grabbed her hand and pulled her close to him.

"What did you find out?" Lilly said, suddenly appearing from between the trees. She gracefully ran towards them, catching up in a matter of seconds, and continued running until they all reached the clearing in front of the house. Rose stood and took a deep breath, feeling her head spin a little. She quickly composed herself before Jack could realize. *Akita,* Rose thought and winced at the last memory of her.

"Lilly, what were you doing in there?" Jack asked, his chest raising and falling as he caught his breath.

"I was too worried to wait for you in the house," Lilly said. "So I ran along the protection hoping you would show up any time soon."

Jack nodded and briefly scanned his surroundings. "Let's go inside first, before any-"

"Rose!" An angry voice came from inside the house and the front door flew open. "Where were you?" Bill stomped towards them like a raging bull, and Angelina followed him closely, scurrying on her tiptoes.

Rose darted a look at Jack, unsure of what she was going to say to her father. The truth? No. Bill was the last person to believe in such stories. But, she had to come up with something rational to explain her unplanned visit to the village.

"I made myself very clear when I ordered you not to step one foot, *one foot,* out of the house without my knowledge!" Bill stopped in front of his daughter and frowned down at her.

"Sir, it's my fault," Jack said and stood between him and Rose.

Bill jerked his head towards Jack and barked, "Shut your mouth, young man. I trusted you with my daughter... and this is how you repay me! Taking her into the forest when girls are being kidnapped. No, Rose! I don't want to hear you defend him."

"Mr. Peterson." Lilly took a confident step closer to Bill. "You need to calm down, sir."

"Calm down?" He stared at her, unbelieving their ignorance towards the matter. "No! I will not calm down until you, Rose, tell me what were you doing out here in the middle of the night."

"Sir," Jack said again.

"I said not a word from you." Bill cut him off and refaced Rose. "Get inside the house."

"Dad, I... I can explain." Rose looked at him and tried to figure out a way to approach the rather delicate subject she was about to surface to her father.

"No, Rose," he said, calmly this time. "I will not wait for your explanation. All I want now is for you to get inside the house... and pack up. We're leaving next week."

"What?" Rose scowled in confusion. "What do you mean by we are leaving?"

"I wanted to tell you under better circumstances, but you have left me no choice." Bill's voice went back to its fatherly tone. "Nara is not safe at the moment. With the several disappearances in the village, I can't stop worrying about you and can't imagine what I'd do if you were next. Even if we lived here for years, we will always be strangers here... It's time to go back home, Rose. I believe you are ready to go back home."

Rose slowly shook her head in disbelief, but also in defiance. "I'm not leaving, Dad."

"Rose, dear. We are not going to argue about this."

"I am afraid we have to, Dad." Rose felt Jack's eyes on her, but she did not meet them.

She was not going to allow him to influence her. This was her choice, and her choice alone. Bill sighed and looked at Jack and Lilly. "Excuse us, if you don't mind. I need a moment with my daughter alone."

"No. Stay." Rose reached out and caught Jack's hand. "Jack, I'm going to tell him." Jack looked into her eyes and nodded, giving her hand a light squeeze.

"Rose? What's going on?" Bill looked from Rose to Jack, and back again.

"I'll explain everything once she's out of earshot." Rose looked at Angelina, who had been watching with amusement.

"Excuse me, young lady?" Angelina started, but reluctantly stopped when Bill threw her a sharp look.

"Get back inside the house," Bill told her from over his shoulder. With a despicable glance at her stepdaughter, Angelina twirled around and paced slowly to the house in hope she would catch anything from the mysterious chat.

After taking a deep breath and exchanging a comforting glance with Jack, Rose started to explain that sort of thing that her father never believed.

"Dad, I need you to listen carefully to me. Please, without interrupting or getting angry. Just hear me out. Alright?"

Bill frowned in confusion and nodded. "Alright."

"You once told me how the people of Nara always blame the people on the other side of the mountains when anything bad happens, like the disappearance of the girls. And, that they speak of legends and myths...stories of great warriors in possession of great powers..."

"Oh, Rose," Bill said. "Now, don't tell me you believe in such nonsense?"

"It's true, Dad," Rose said, ignoring Bill's last words. "These legends and myths are true."

"Did he fill your head with this nonsense?" Bill pointed at Jack. "Has he been playing around with your head?"

"Dad. Please, you promised not to interrupt."

"What can I do, Rose. I was expecting something rational. Not some bedtime stories. I don't believe in them."

"Then you don't believe in me, Dad... Nor in my existence." Her voice did not shake, but her heart was jumping frantically inside her chest.

Bill stared at her, his mouth opened in perplexity. Rose seized his silence and continued her tale. After all her calculations and plans, she sought no other way than to bombard him with what he must know for his and her sake. She explained everything that had been going on for the last three months: what she had discovered the day after their summer gathering, her ability to ride the wind, the attack, Mark's illness and recovery, her healing powers, the incomplete army, Dr. Liu and Akita's hidden identities.

Upon hearing it all, Bill said, "I need to sit down." Jack and Rose helped Bill walk back into the house, and they seated him in the nearest chair by the fireplace. "How can this be true?"

Before Rose could answer him, Jack winked at her and quietly left her with her overwhelmed father. She was grateful that Jack had been there while she explained all of this to Bill. She did not know what she could have done without him. Even though Jack did not utter a single word on the matter, letting her handle it all by herself, his presence was enough to keep her going.

"I am not forcing you to believe, Dad." Rose crouched down in front of Bill and took his rough hands into hers. "All I am asking is for you to trust me."

"No, no." Bill vehemently shook his head. "I cannot let you do this. No, Rose. I can't..."

"Dad," she said. "This is who I am. It's my destiny. It's not a coincidence when you chose to bring me to Nara."

"Rose..." He looked deeply into her eyes and tightened his grip on her soft hands. "You are the only one I have left. I cannot lose you, too."

She pulled him into her arms and held him firmly. "You will not lose me, Dad. I'm not going to leave you." A tear rolled down her cheeks. "But, I must ask you to leave Nara."

He released himself from her embrace and looked at her, his eyes were bloodshot red. "I am not leaving you, Rose."

"Dad, please. Don't do this to me." She brushed her tear away. "You must take Angelina and go."

"No, I can-"

"She is right, Bill," Angelina said, coming out of the kitchen. She stood in front of them with a face that bore something new; fear, Rose realized. "I heard everything."

"I am not leaving my daughter behind." Bill looked at his wife, his expression weak.

"I can't leave, Dad. Even if I wanted to. Please, Dad. It's better if you leave."

"Bill, I am not staying here any longer." Angelina started to pace the room with exasperation. "No, I will not!"

"Dad, please. You must trust me on this one," Rose said and straightened herself up.

"Bill, I am calling the travel agency and will ask them to book two seats on the first plane tomorrow," Angelina said and scurried to the telephone.

"One seat," Bill said, looking over at Angelina as she dialed the number with shaking hands. She looked at him perplexedly. "I am not going to abandon my daughter."

"Bill, you may not see me again," Angelina said and slammed the phone down. "You might die if you stay here!"

"Then at least my daughter will be the last person I see..." Bill stared at Angelina, his face filled with defiance.

"So, you are choosing her over me?" Angelina said. Her voice shook, but she tried to compose herself.

"Of course, I will!" Bill roared back at her. "What did you even think? I was so God damn blind when it came to you, Angelina, but no more! Out! Out of my house!"

"So be it!" Angelina trembled under his gaze. "I don't want to die, I'm still young for such a fate. I'll travel first thing in the morning, and I will not wait for you if you change your mind! Why do I even care, Bill? I am your second choice, so go to hell, Bill! Go to hell!"

A ringing slap landed on Angelina's cheek, shaking her whole body. She looked up at Bill, her eyes wide. "That is for what you did to Rose," Bill said. "Now, out of my house."

With utter disbelief, she stomped up the stairs to her room where she slammed the door shut. After a few minutes, she came back down with a suitcase and marched out the door and into a waiting taxi.

Bill sat back down heavily, understandingly overwhelmed by all that had been occurring.

Rose ran to her father and hugged him tightly, her heart racing. "Thank you... Dad," she said, feeling as though she finally had her old dad back, and that the darkness of Angelina was finally gone.

She embraced him one last time and then walked up the stairs to her room. It was relieving to explain to her father all that was happening around him, lifting the load off her shoulders, but she was still worried about his safety.

Jack and Lilly were in the balcony when Rose entered her room. "He chose not to leave," she said.

Jack turned around and faced her. "I can't tell you not to worry about him, but I assure you he is perfectly safe."

She shook her head, staring at the black trees in front of her. "How can you say that?"

"He is," Jack said and mustered half a smile. "He's your father, Rose. The father of a main power. He's protected."

"He's protected?"

"The parents and siblings of a main power are protected from any danger," Lilly said as she stared at the almost full moon. "That way they could not be a leverage to the Kalano, or more of an obstacle."

"As long as Bill stays inside the house, nothing harmful will touch him. It's safer here, and I am sure that will cause you to worry less," Jack said and tried to give an encouraging smile, but he failed to convince Rose.

"He was not supposed to know." Lilly said, still staring at the moon, which by then was obscured by grey clouds.

"He had to," Rose said and stepped closer to where Jack was standing and leaning against the rails. "My father is a realistic person. Without any proof or explanation presented to him, he wouldn't have believed... and it's his right to know the truth about his only daughter."

Rose saw Jack clench his jaw as he ran a hand through his hair, sighing deeply into the chilly air of the night. She knew exactly what was worrying him, that topic which never evaded his mind. It hurt her to see him suffer like that, suffer over something he would never be able to change no matter how hard he tried.

Finding a way to dissolve the tension, she unzipped her bag and withdrew the old book and the mysterious riddle, drawing Jack and Lilly's attention. She reread the riddle to herself and tried to figure out what Akita was trying to tell her. Akita had saved her last breath to tell her solve it, and after what had happened to her that night it seemed that it was a very important piece of paper to possess. They were after it with no doubt. But, why?

The three of them studied those puzzling words silently, each hoping that the other would come up with something to start with. But, Rose felt as if they were looking for a needle in haystack. However, Rose started to decipher the riddle more as she read it over and over again, trying to trace the meaning behind the words.

"They will find me," Rose read out loud and frowned. "Find me as in finding this piece of paper or something else?"

"It's definitely something else," Jack said from over her shoulder. "'Under'. 'East'. 'South'. These are all words describing a location..."

"Under the same as their color'," Rose continued.

"Under the sea," Lilly said. They both looked at her questioningly. "Blue. We are the Blue Water Army. Blue is our color. And, the sea is blue."

Rose brought the paper up to her nose and sniffed it. "The paper itself smells of salty water... Like the spray of the sea."

With what his sister had just said in mind, Jack contemplated the riddle for a few moments. "It's leading to the sea coast," he said.

"North-west of the sea coast," Rose said, realizing the missing directions in the riddle. "And, the place is supposed to be marked with two identical rocks that 'will help with the forsaken hunt'."

They all looked at each other with excitement and fear in their eyes. This was all beyond the protection shield.

"We need to get there and find out what is waiting for us," Jack said and looked at Rose. "You are staying behind this time."

"What?" Rose was not surprised. "I won't leave you-"

"No one is going tonight," Lilly barged in. "It must be a full-moon night. 'When the moon is in full camp... amidst the sinful night'." Lilly read those couple of lines from the riddle in Rose's hand and looked up at the sky. "It's not a full moon yet. We must wait until tomorrow."

Rose took advantage of Lilly's interruption and focused on the piece of paper in her hand. "Whatever we are to find is going to be near the second rock... buried, I guess."

"Of course buried," Lilly said, taking the riddle from Rose.

"Seven holes must be dug," Jack said, pointing at the last couple of lines. "And in the seventh one is where it's going to be."

Rose frowned at the number. Why seven holes? It could be just a number to fulfill the necessities of the legend. She noted to bring it up to Jack later. However, the two lines before the last couple disturbed her. The riddle strongly warned about those who were also looking for the hidden object. And, it was clearly the Kalano who were 'The Envious Eye'...

'Whoever am I' made her heart make a few skips, and she wondered what might possibly be waiting for them beneath the sands of the shore.

"Prepare yourself for tomorrow, Lilly," Jack said and took the paper from her. "Like the riddle says, they'll be waiting for the right moment to attack."

Rose placed a hand on his arm and looked at his stern face. "I'm coming with you, Jack."

"That won't happen." He shook his head, folding the paper and pocketing it in the back of his shorts.

"Jack," Rose sighed. "Akita gave me this riddle and made sure that we solve it... It's just that I have a feeling that I should be there tomorrow with you." She was too wearied to try to convince him with a more reasonable answer. She eyed him as he clenched his jaws and contemplated their situation; he seemed to have second thoughts.

"I'll be fine, Jack," Rose said, even though she was perfectly sure that she might not make it back tomorrow. But, it did not matter. If Jack was not able to protect her with his body, she would protect him with her soul... Just like she had done before.

"Trust me," she whispered.

He looked into her eyes with a torn expression. He tried to conceal it from her with a frown, but to no avail. "If anything happened to you, I-"

She quickly pressed a finger against his lips, stopping him from continuing a sentence that might have caused both their dismay. "Nothing will happen," she reassured him.

"So," Lilly said, cutting their momentary bond as usual, "if both of you are going, that means I will be watching over the house until you two come back."

"Yes, Lilly," Jack replied and exchanged an understandable look with his sister. He knew his sister very well; she never liked to do the unadventurous jobs.

Lilly folded her arms and straightened her back, preserving her calmness. But, Rose saw something different in her eyes, there was a flare that gave away Lilly's capability to mask her emotions. When Lilly had noticed the wonder in Rose's eyes, without saying much of a word, she soared to the forest where she disappeared within the trees.

Rose and Jack stared at where she had disappeared, but neither of them said anything. She heard him sigh, but decided to keep her thoughts for herself at the moment. She was now certain there was a secret behind Lilly's rigid persona. Without further ado, Jack urged Rose to sleep early that night, but not before she had made sure that Bill was safe.

That night Rose had a fitful sleep filled with incoherent dreams. It was a puzzling night. Rose found herself once again stapled to the ground and watched the young boy running in front of her, and he came closer to her this time. She stretched her hands and was about to reach the little boy, but the image blurred and the boy disappeared in an instant. Her vision refocused again, and that time she found herself back in the devastated place where the women's scream pierced her ears. And just like she had seen before, Jack was in chains and kneeling on the ground. Rose was not able to handle such a scene, and she tried to close her eyes and block that image. But who had control over what they could dream?

At dawn, Rose woke up with a startle and tears ran down the corner of her eyes. She laid immobile for a couple of minutes until her breathing slowed down and the throbbing in her head ceased away. A cool breeze brushed her flushed cheeks, and Rose looked over at the glass door and found it open. She could see a tall and graceful figure standing in the balcony. Lilly held her head low and Rose thought she heard the sound of the faintest sob. She wanted to go over to her and comfort her, but Lilly might not be grateful to be caught in such a weak moment. So, Rose stayed in bed, feigning sleep, until the sun was out.

It was impossible to calm her thoughts that day. Ever since Mark had left, she tried not to think or worry about him anymore. But, he somehow found his way into her head. And after the last dream, she got more worried if anything bad had happened to him... Like what had become of Jade and Paul.

But, the distress was evident in her face, and Jack noticed it even after her efforts to mask them. However, she was grateful he did not inquire about their cause. He just gave her a smile and an embrace that lifted her spirits, but only for moments.

The night came tediously as the full moon conquered the sky with its silver light. It was time for Jack and Rose to go and fulfill the riddle's quest. Bill did not try to prevent her when Rose had informed him of her plan for the night. However, she had kept the details from her father. After grabbing a compass from her drawer, the riddle, and a flashlight and stuffing them into her leather bag, Rose went out the front door and met Jack right at the driveway. He wore a black shirt over a pair of black shorts just like they had planned; even Rose wore a plain black shirt on her dyed linen pants. It was Jack's idea; he said that it would prevent them from being noticed amidst the dark night in comparison to any other color.

Rose stopped and stared at Jack. The sword she once had seen hanging in his tree house was strapped to his waist and hung at his side. She was suddenly terrified. What if that was the last time she would see him? What if her dreams were not just her conscious playing around with her worries? It all seemed too... real? Not the fact she was living a legend, but that she might lose the light of her life at any moment. He could be gone in an instant just like he had entered her life unexpectedly.

When Jack saw the look on her face, he ran to her and kissed her lips softly without any introductions. And, that made all her worries more agonizing.

"Everything is going to be alright," he whispered into her lips. "I'll protect you." She used all her strength to restrain her tears and to show that she was strong. She had to be strong for him.

With the use of the compass to find northwest, Jack and Rose sped through the forest until they reached its edge where the trees mingled with the white sands of Nara's Atlantic coast. That part of the coast was almost deserted of people and fishermen alike. It was dark and very quiet except for the sound of the waves as they broke upon the sand. The full moon casted its light upon the dark water and helped Rose and Jack identify their surroundings.

Rose opened her eyes wide and observed the shore. There were stones scattered everywhere along the shore, and it seemed impossible to locate the two designated rocks of the riddle. She walked alongside Jack as they examined every two rocks alike, hoping to stumble over the right ones. But, it was hard to concentrate on finding some rocks in the darkness and at the same time look out for any ambushers that might appear at any moment.

"What if we're mistaken?" Jack asked in a whisper. He looked around and surveyed the threshold of the forest, gripping the handle of his sword. "What if they were not two identical rocks?"

"No, we are not mistaken," Rose said and stopped in her tracks. "There they are." She pointed at two identical rocks illuminated by the moonlight and half immersed in the water when the waves broke upon them, spraying salty water in their wake. The twin rocks were exactly the same in shape and size, and perfectly lined beside each other.

Jack hurried towards to them and started examining the ground around. There were holes dug all around the rocks, five holes exactly. But, they were all empty. That was definitely the right place. "They were here," Jack said as he looked into the hollowed sand. "They tried to find it, but they couldn't."

Rose looked around and frowned. There were seven holes in the riddle, not five. The Kalano had got the wrong number. She realized that they still needed to dig two more. With the help of a nearby wooden plank, Jack started hollowing out two holes close to the other five until they had seven holes in total.

A crack in the trees made Rose hold her breath and Jack quickly placed a hand on his sword and surveyed the dark forest.

"We need to be quick," he whispered.

Instantly, Rose fished out the riddle from her bag and held it out in front of her. The writings glistened against the moonlight that she did not need the flashlight to see. Was there anything to say after they dig the holes? Rose looked over the riddle, but nothing of such was mentioned.

"It doesn't say what to do next," Rose whispered. "It just says where the other rock is-"

Rose jerked her head towards the two rocks and sped over to them. A small space between the two rocks had created a kind of a pothole that preserved some of the water when the waves splashed on top of it. She leaned over one of the rocks and observed the flooded pothole. Something inside gleamed against the full moonlight.

"Jack, I think this is it," she said and looked up at him.

He nodded and quickly sunk his hand into the pothole. With a startle, Jack pulled his hand out of the water and frowned with puzzlement.

"The water is boiling hot," he said.

Rose grabbed his hand and eased away his pain. "Maybe I am supposed to do it."

"Rose, no. You'll-"

She held her breath and plunged her hand inside the pothole. She frowned; the water was cool against her skin. Her fingers touched the hardness of the immersed object and, firmly gripping it, she drew out an old book with frayed leather bindings. Rose and Jack exchanged a concerned look; they did not expect another book. She settled it on top of the rocks and examined the cover. And, just like the riddle, the writings on the cover glistened against the moonlight and read:

"I conjure thee, I conjure thee

For every Evil Spirit and every Insane

I shall be touched not.

Only the Seven Blue for they are Blessed."

Rose reread the title and frowned. The number seven kept popping up. Could it be-

"Hand us the book." A hissing voice came from behind them.

Rose felt the hairs on the back of her neck stand up and held her breath. She could feel Jack slip his hand into hers and hold it tightly. They had to turn around, but she did not want to lest what she might see. But, there was no choice.

Two cloaked figures stood meters away, their heads hidden by black hoods. Their black cloaks were long and the hems swayed against the breeze, making them appear as if they were bodiless with hallow faces underneath the hoods. They reminded her of Luba and she guessed that they were also Spies.

"Hand usssss the book," one of them said again.

Jack had a hand on the hilt of his sword, but did not unsheathe it. He knew that even with the sword he was completely powerless. What was he expected to do? What could he do? They would not make it if they flew; the figures were too close. They would be an easy catch.

With a disgusted look at those figures which had been haunting him for almost a decade now, Jack unsheathed his sword and took a step forward, making sure that he was blocking Rose and the Book out of their sight. "Go back to your master," Jack said in his powerful voice, "You will take no book tonight."

Upon hearing the voice of the Leader, the figures glided a little closer to Jack and Rose. One of them stretched out its bony hand, like a snake coming out of its dark hole, and pointed sharp fingers at Jack.

Rose suddenly felt Jack grip her hand tighter and saw his chest rise up and down. He clenched his jaws and shut his eyes in anguish.

"Rose, run," Jack said from under his breath. "Take the wind and fly back home."

"What are they doing to you?" Rose said, trying not to panic. "Jack. Jack, answer me."

"Run," he said again and opened his eyes, they were bloodshot red. "Run, Rose."

She shook her head. "No. No, I won't."

Figuring out what to do to save Jack from his anguish, she held his hand with both of hers and aroused the Healer within. Her aura infiltrated Jack through his hand and dominated his body. Within seconds, his breathing slowed and he released his grip on Rose's hands a little. Whatever dark power the figure was practicing on Jack had completely been defeated and ceased away.

The two Spies sensed the Healer's power, and they both turned their hoods towards Rose. And, in a swift move, the other figure raised its arm in the air and had a silver arrow in its hand. It aimed at Rose and threw.

Rose's eyes widened in horror as she saw the arrow speed towards her like a silver bullet. There was no time to run, and the shock caused her to freeze in her spot. But, suddenly her vision was obscured and she found Jack standing right in front of her, between her and the shooting arrow.

His eyes shut in pain as the arrow pierced his back. He reopened them and looked into her shocked eyes. "Fly back home," he said heavily.

Pulling herself out of her shock, Rose quickly reached over, pulled the arrow out from his bloodied back, and cured him with the softest touch of her hand.

"Ssssso you are the one," both figures said in union, and they raised their arms with more silver arrows to shoot.

"Jack, no!" Rose cried.

Jack seized the book from her hand and threw it far away from them, distracting the Spies. Once Jack found them looking away, he grabbed Rose and soared up into the air, towards the thick clouds. But, Jack stopped abruptly and looked down at the black figures. Rose also noticed the oddity of the scene. The figures had not leaped and seized the book.

Instead, they were standing right where Jack and Rose had left them, except they were shuddering and throwing the silver arrows at the trees behind them.

"Someone is fighting them," Jack said and looked around him at the clouds. "There is no wind, then it's not Lilly who's fighting them."

"Jack, look!" Rose pointed at the two figures.

One of the figures had collapsed to the ground and the sand beneath it was soaked, even though it was far off from the damp sand of the seashore. They lowered themselves closer to the scene just in time to see the other figure give a jolt and fall next to its friend, smoke coming from the depth of its hood. They casted their eyes for anybody, but the forest was inky black.

"Stay close," Jack said and led the way back to the ground, where Rose quickly grabbed the untouched book and packed it in her bag.

With his sword in his hand again, Jack stood and listened for any movement in the trees. Whoever had done this was certainly not the enemy. But, he still had to be prepared. A loud crack echoed through the trees and several hurried footsteps were heard. Rose stood close to Jack and held her breath as the footsteps came closer, followed by a voice.

Rose knew that voice very well. She froze in her spot. "No way."

Twelve: White Paper

"Look who we have here."

Mark appeared at the threshold of the dark forest and looked at Rose and Jack, his stare dark. Rose's mouth dropped open in disbelief at the sight of Mark. He turned around and signaled behind him. She jerked her head at Jack and found him frowning in utter puzzlement. However, a thin thread of comprehension could be traced in his frown, and that was enough to answer her unspoken question regarding the collapse of the Spies and Mark's unexpected show up.

The sound of more steps caught her ears and she widened her eyes in bewilderment as three more people came into view beside Mark.

"Bloody hell," Anthony said and walked towards the black cloaks lying in the sand. "What exactly are those?"

"Shit," Zane said, following Anthony. "You and Mark kicked their asses."

"Very appropriate, Zane." A high-pitched voice reached Rose's ears. Her eyes widened with horror this time as she caught a glimpse of Heidi standing beside Mark.

Jack glanced at her, his frown still conquering his face. It was all clear to him now, but he was still surprised. The four of them, Mark, Anthony, Zane, and Heidi completed his Blue Water Army. Finally, they were seven.

"Mark?" Rose asked, "How did you-"

"How did we know that you were here?" Mark finished her sentence. "Or how did we save you from a terrible fate?"

"Not here," Jack said, taking Rose by the hand and walking hastily towards Mark and the others who had by then rejoined their friend again. Jack casted his eyes at them all and said, "We must go back before they discover the failure of the ambush. I believe you have some explanation to do." He addressed Mark.

Mark gave a snort, but he remained quiet and stared at Jack with a sharp look. Jack clenched his jaws and nodded, most probably foretelling the problems he would have.

"Stay close everyone," Jack said and crossed over into the forest.

Rose met Mark's eyes, unsure to smile or not, but he had saved her the worry for he rapidly looked away. Confused, she turned around and took Jack's waiting hand.

Without looking back, Jack and Rose broke into a run and sped through the trees. Confirming Jack's expectations, the rest of them followed up with the same speed. She caught sight of Mark running, his steps as light as feathers, close to her. Even though a lot of unfavorable things had happened between them, she could not deny the relief and happiness she had felt upon seeing him. They did not stop running until they were under the protection and had reached the house. To their surprise, Bill and Lilly were not the only ones who were waiting for their return.

"Did you get the book?" Dr. Liu rushed over to Rose once they entered the living room. His eyes had dark circles around them and his clothes were haggard.

Jack eyed him a little, suspicious, nonetheless, he nodded for Rose to take it out of her bag.

"Keep it safe," the doctor said. "I am not one of the Blue members, therefore, I cannot touch it." He looked around at them and addressed Mark. "I have done all that I could do to help you. It's time to take care of yourselves now. And, I am sorry for your loss, gentlemen."

"What happened, doctor?" Jack asked.

"I believe it's best if your members explained to you themselves." The doctor put a hand on his chest and lowered his head in a bow. "You are the Leader, Jack Casper. And, I believe you will lead the Blue Water Army, your army, to glory. You have all my respect and service as long as I live."

Rose examined Jack as he stared at the Protector for a few moments and then turned around to face his main powers. She, too, observed them and noticed their drawn and red eyes; they looked as if they had not slept for days. However, there was something different about them, especially Mark. She was not sure what was it, but they seemed to be standing taller and looking much more stronger than they had... Even Heidi. Rose was not sure how she would tolerate her presence.

"Before anything else, I want to know what you did to defeat the spies," Jack asked.

"Well," Mark started, but was interrupted.

"One was drowned in its own body water," Anthony explained, his face completely expressionless, "and the other was burned from inside out."

"Water." Jack pointed at Anthony who gave him a nod. "Fire." He looked over at Mark.

"Yeah," Mark responded, with a smirk.

Jack said. "I need to know what happened."

Anthony nodded with a sigh. "Right after we left Nara, strange things started to happen. Frequent nightmares and strange voices at night. None of us slept properly."

"We were all going through the same thing," Zane added, "But, no one had the guts to tell each other. I thought I was losing my mind."

"I sometimes woke up and found the bed soaked with water and the bathroom flooded," Anthony said.

Jack frowned and folded his arms. "What about your Protectors?"

"Dead," Anthony replied in a croaked voice.

"All of them," Zane said and glanced sideways at Heidi, who was suddenly tearful. Her shoulders started to shake and she burst into tears. Zane held her between his arms and tried to calm her. "It's going to be OK. Crying will not bring Robin back."

Robin was Heidi's nanny, Rose remembered. She was everything to Heidi as her parents were extremely busy people; they had no time for their only child.

"I am sorry for your loss," Jack said to them.

Anthony half smiled, almost sarcastic, "Right."

"You don't have to be here if you don't want to," Lilly said from where she was standing by the empty fireplace. She looked at Anthony with her sharp eyes, and he looked back curiously. Rose noticed his eyes had become bluer.

"As if we had a choice," Anthony replied. "You gave us the Water yourself."

"You chose to drink it!"

"Lilly," Jack said and threw her a sharp look. "You really don't have a choice. Take it from me." He paused. "Dr. Liu told you to give them the water?"

Lilly nodded in reply.

"You tried running before?" Zane asked.

Jack nodded and exchanged a glance with Rose. "Several times, but in despair. You can't run away from who you are."

At those words, Mark slowly walked out the balcony doors to sit on the terrace. Rose followed him out as the rest talked. She wanted to know his side of the story and what had happened to him to change his mind and come back. And, she owed him a thank you for what he had done that night. She sat beside Mark and found him examining the emblem on his hand. The mark of the Fire was a complex mark, just like its owner.

"Thank you," she said softly. "You saved our lives."

He smirked, trying to be his sarcastic self, but there was hurt evident in his eyes. "You're welcome."

She hated his tone. "And thank you for coming back."

He tilted his head and looked at her, a faint frown tracing his forehead. "I didn't come back for you." Rose stayed motionless, trying not to show her surprise. "I came back to avenge my friends," he said and looked away. "I came back to make sure my mother wakes up from her sleep every morning. You heard what happened to them, they did not wake from their sleep."

The loss in his eyes was heartbreaking, and Rose was not able to restrain a tear. She raised a hand and touched Mark's arm, and he did not coil away from her. "I am sorry," she whispered. He lightly nodded, staring aimlessly at the ground beneath his feat.

Just as Rose was straightening herself up, Anthony, Zane, and Heidi stepped out into the terrace. Anthony glanced at Mark and then at Rose, giving her a nod. She gave him one back and re-entered the house, brushing away one tear. She found Jack talking to Bill.

"I hope we are not bothering you, sir," Jack was saying when Rose reached them. "I didn't know they were part of this. And here is our only place of protection. I apologize for the intrusion."

Bill pulled Rose into his arms and kissed her forehead. "The guest room is empty," he said. "Is there anything I can do to help?"

"Thank you." Jack nodded. "The most important thing is to stay inside the house."

"I hope this will be over soon," Bill said. "After that I will take my daughter and go back home."

When Bill retired to his room, Rose turned her head back to Jack and found his eyes buried under a frown which traced his face in agony. It was hard to see his beautiful face contracted into such an expression. Holding his head with both hands, Rose straightened his eyebrows with her thumbs until she completely erased the scowl away. "I am not going anywhere," she said softly.

"Don't foretell events," Lilly said coldly, interrupting their moment as usual. "We never know what might happen tomorrow." She walked to the front door and turned around. "You better check the book now."

"Come on," Jack said and pulled her hand. "Let's see what we can learn from the book." Leaving the others, Jack and Rose went upstairs to her room and sat on the edge of the bed. She retrieved the big book from her bag and laid it on her lap; it was relatively heavy. Careful, she opened the first page and found it filled with script:

I am revealed
When Seven is One,
For I hold their Destiny and how it will become.
Their great powers were once a myth
But history will repeat this.
Every age the faces change,
The Power remains the same.
The End is open between two Conclusions, the Healer will choose.
The Results will be recorded
For the very last page is still unfolded.

They looked at each other, the same question evident in their eyes. Rose flipped to the second page, but it was completely empty. Shaking her head with irritation, she flipped through the whole book. There was nothing in it except for white paper.

"What are we going to do?" Rose asked, exhaling her vexation.

"As the book says," Jack replied, standing up and walking to the glass doors. "We have to unite in order for the book to reveal itself."

"Why is it testing us?"

He took a deep breath. "It's testing us as much as it's guaranteeing our victory. We won't be able to succeed if the army itself is broken apart."

Rose watched him as he stared into the night sky, his eyes faraway. It was not difficult for her to guess what was worrying him other than the white pages of the book which they thought was going to answer all their questions. She peeked at his back and found the spot where the arrow had pierced; dried blood stained the fabric around it. Catching her eyes, Jack pulled off the shirt, baring unharmed skin right where the arrow had been, and threw it in the nearby bin.

Rose could not help but to break him a smile. "You saved my life."

He closed his eyes and took a deep breath. "I did nothing."

Before Rose could open her mouth, Jack slid open the glass-doors and soared up to the roof. She jumped off the bed and hurried after him. She found him standing at the edge of the rooftop with his arms crossed over his chest, a painful look on his face. He looked away when she stood in front of him and tried to catch his eyes. With her hand, she held his chin and pulled his face back to her.

"Let's take a walk," she softly said and held his hand. She was grateful he did not show any sign of resistance, and they flew to the forest, not noticing the four pairs of eyes following them from below. She ushered him down the path until they reached the clearing of the pond, and she waited for him to speak his mind.

He stood idle for a few minutes, doing nothing except for staring into her soft and curious eyes. "I could've lost you tonight," he said in a croaked voice. "And, I was not able to do anything."

Rose shook her head. "You saved me, Jack." Slowly, she stood on her tiptoes and brushed her lips against his. "That's what you did. You saved my life. I'm alive because of you."

"No, Rose," he whispered into her lips. "You'll die because of me."

"Don't say that-"

"Can't you see, Rose?" He frowned. "I am the Leader of the Blue Water Army, and I can't even stop two, powerless spies from harming you... I thought I would know how to protect you. But, all I did was plead you to run, to fly away."

"Jack-"

"You will not take part of this anymore," he interrupted her.

"What?" Rose knew that this was coming, but she was still appalled upon hearing it.

"I won't be able to live if anything happened to you."

"Jack, you cannot do this to me!" She took a step away.

He inhaled and brushed a hand through his hair. "Do you know what those Spies did today?"

"They were hurting you," Rose said, noticing his now bloodshot eyes.

"They tortured me with my fears. All my fears came visible in front of my eyes as if they were really there." He rubbed his eyes; pushing away the images he had seen and feared since the moment he had met Rose.

She was shocked, and did not know what to say to him. Her dream of Jack plunged into her head, and her heart sped. She grabbed his hands and pressed them tightly. "I will not leave you to do this alone! Even if you've already found your main powers, I will not turn away from what we have started," she said, looking deeply into his eyes.

"What if I don't make it, Rose?" His tone was strong, but only to try to convince her. "What if I die at the end? You know it doesn't work on the dead."

"You will not die!"

"There is no guarantee!" He let go of her hands. "What if our story has no happy ending, Rose? What if everything we have built falls apart? Maybe this time the good won't vanquish the evil."

"Jack, stop it!" She took in a deep inhale, trying to gulp back a lump in her throat.

"Even if I do survive," he continued. "Your father will take you back home. And, he has every right to do so. What will happen to us then?"

"Here is my home," Rose said, "I belong here with you."

"I may not be around anymore, Rose," he breathed heatedly.

"Stop saying that!"

"I won't!" he said. "You need to know that this is not a fairytale! I am not a superhero..."

Rose stared at him. "You are Jack Casper, the leader of the Blue Water Army... *My* hero."

At her words, the lonely tear trickled down Jack's cheek. This was a moment she thought she would never witness. A single tear of the Leader was enough to tell of the pain and suffering within him.

Incapable of seeing his tormented face, she tenderly brushed away his tear and pulled him into a tight embrace. She felt his heart pounding against his chest from the intensity of their conversation.

"Jack-"

"Will you marry me, Rose Peterson?" He whispered in her ear.

She ceased to breathe.

Uncertain that she had heard right, Rose stood still in Jack's embrace, her heart skipping inside her chest. Her mind was spinning, and her heart was soaring.

Gently letting go, Jack regarded her with a small smile that shined out of his face. He took hold of her right hand and kissed the inside of her palm, his glinting eyes never dropping from hers.

"Rose Peterson, will-"

"Yes," she said, the word leaping from her lips. She wanted to say it before he asked again, but still couldn't believe this was really happening.

With eyes glistening with ecstasy, Jack covered her mouth with a soft kiss, entangling his lifetime promise with her lips. His arm wrapped around her small waist and pulled her more into the length of his body as they both sank into the kiss.

***

The house was completely silent when Rose awoke just before dawn crept into the sky. With the events of the night before, everyone had collapsed straight into their beds. Crawling out of her bed and tiptoeing, Rose stepped out into the balcony and leaned against the rails. Her mind was very occupied that she gave up trying to sleep and allowed her thoughts to take control. She was still light with happiness. Rose shook her head and smiled; she could not believe what Jack had asked her a couple of hours ago. It was a completely different feeling than the first time he had confessed his love. He fully wanted her to be his for the rest of his life, and she could not possibly want him any less than he wanted her.

Everything was already planned in her head. She could picture herself in a white dress and a tiara on her loose hair while Jack would be all dressed up in a crisp, black tux, them arm in arm. They would have the most adorable house with a perfect garden where their kids would play while she and Jack watched over them. And at night, they would hold each other until they drifted off to sleep, without fearing the shadows ever again. Everything would be perfect.

But, at the same time, Rose knew that not every story had a happy ending. What guaranteed theirs? A soft sound of footsteps coming from behind her cut through her thoughts. Lilly appeared from the darkness of the room and joined Rose, her eyes heavy with pain.

"You must have a Plan B," Lilly said as if she knew what Rose was thinking of. "You never know what might happen to Jack."

"Lilly, please. Not you too," she whispered.

"Stop denying it, Rose." Lilly's tone was different. "Don't turn away from what is true. Don't take all that is good and disregard their consequences. I was in your place once."

Rose was surprised at this other side of Lilly. She regarded her as Lilly's eyes became slightly tearful.

"What happened?"

"I fell in love with someone. I loved him with all my heart, and that rarely happens with me. I was always strong, looking after my brother and mother when father was gone. I was in total control of my life and accepted it even after I found out about who I really am." Lilly paused. "Then Baas came into my life, even though he had been around since I was a little girl. He was Jack's childhood friend as well. I tried to put out my feelings for him, but he got the best of me."

"Did something happen to him?" Rose could not believe she was hearing those words come from Lilly.

Lilly pressed her lips hard. "He is the Leader of the Dark Army."

Rose covered her mouth in shock.

"That was my reaction when I first heard the news," Lilly said. "I couldn't believe it at first. But, then I realized that I had been blind. It was all there in front of me from the first time we met. I believed he would change to the better, at least for me." She paused to take a deep breath. "But, I was completely wrong. When the Dark Army legacy triggered in his blood, he was completely lost," Lilly continued and wiped her tears with her slender hand. "What I am trying to say here is that never disregard the truth. Expect the worst and you'll live better. Love is blind, Rose, and a double-edged sword. Either you control them or set them free. Love can be freedom."

Lilly did not wait for Rose to gather herself and speak. Instead, she turned around and went back to bed. Her story had left Rose standing in total bewilderment. What happened to her was unfair and unbearable. It was already harsh to live knowing that one's love might die someday before your own eyes, let alone fight in a war where they would kill them with their own hands. Love was blind, but was it that blind?

Pulling her clothes closer to her body, she leaned again on the rails and caught a glimpse of someone standing in the adjacent terrace. She leaned a little and caught glimpse of Mark and Anthony and instantly hoped they did not overhear their conversation, or else Lilly would be very displeased. Before Rose could make herself unnoticeable, Mark met her eyes for a moment before he looked away.

When the first rays of sunrise had washed over Rose's face, she went to get some sleep before Jack would arrive to gather all the members.

Thirteen: Past Pardons

The smell of Lilly's coffee filled Rose's lungs as she made her way down the stairs.

Everyone had woken up early and sat in the living room, their eyes sparkled with questions. Their expressions reminded Rose of herself when she first knew of her destiny, so she could not blame them for their worries.

She spotted Jack resting against the wooden rails of the fireplace and smiled. He smiled back at her and winked. Rose had found a red rose lying beside her on the pillow when she had awoke that morning, and she had not been able to stop smiling since then. But, she had to compose herself for her smiles were not appropriate in their grave situation.

Jack pushed himself out of his relaxed position and stood before the six members, crossing his arms firmly against his chest.

"Now that we are complete," he addressed them. "It's best if you all understood why we are here. There is a war-"

"We already know why we are bloody here," Mark said from where he was sitting beside Anthony. "The question is why us?"

"I don't know," Jack replied, looking at Mark. "Believe me I am surprised at this turn of events as much as you are."

Mark pursed his lips in an amused smirk. "And do you know what are we supposed to do, Jack, the Leader?"

"The book which we found yesterday," Jack said, turning away from Mark, "holds the answers to many questions, at least I hope it will."

"You hope?" Mark raised one eyebrow at him. "What do you mean you hope? Don't you have it already? What? You can't read?"

Rose was about to open her mouth and reply back at Mark's imprudence, but thought it better to let Jack deal with him. It was his army after all, and Mark was a member of it.

"No, Mark," Jack said, maintaining his composure. "I can't read it because the book is empty."

"Empty?" Anthony inquired. "After all that happened yesterday."

"Unfortunately. But, we can fix that," Jack said. "The book will reveal its contents the moment we are all united."

"Do you mean there are more members?" Zane said. He was standing by one of the windows and had been examining the surroundings outside.

"No. We are seven and complete."

Finally, Rose thought.

"So?" Mark said. "We are united, then. We can't possibly unite more than that."

"Our powers, Mark," Anthony said and looked up at Jack. "We need to unite our powers."

Jack nodded.

"And how are we going to do that?" Heidi said. Rose pretended to be interested in the cup of coffee in her hands. "I still don't know what my power is."

"Neither do I," Zane added.

Jack contemplated the ground for a few moments then said, "Very well, then. We'll sort that out. Let's go outside and see what we can do."

Rose walked over to Jack, and they all stepped out into the clearing in front of the terrace. "Where is Dr. Liu?" she asked when she noticed he had not been around since Jack and her had came back from their walk yesterday.

"He left very early this morning," Jack answered. "He said he had important business to do. I think it's Protector kind of business."

Rose glanced at Lilly as she made her way over to them. Her face was still sunken. She gave her half a smile, but Lilly only returned it with a light nod.

"And by the way," Jack said before he turned to his members. "Before you start, you must get inside and have some breakfast." He glanced over at Mark then turned back to Rose. "I think you'll be practicing your power a lot today. And you're going to need some energy for that."

"Jack, are you planning for a practice class?" Rose whispered back.

He nodded.

"Good luck with that," Lilly muttered as she regarded the four members in front of her, and Rose saw her throw a skeptic look at Heidi who played with a lock of her blonde hair and examined her nails. Moments later, Rose emerged from inside the house with a fruit basket, knowing they would all need to refuel their energy.

"First thing," Jack said once Rose had rejoined them in the clearing. "Did all of you use the one common power that we all share?"

Mark suddenly looked amused. "We can do that?"

"Yes," Jack replied.

"And, what is that?" Anthony asked, looking to Mark and Jack. "The fast running?"

Without bothering to explain, Jack decided to show them and flew up to the roof.

Anthony, Zane, and Heidi dropped their mouths in wonder as they looked up at him.

"I love the Blue Water," Zane said, eager to try it for himself.

"You must concentrate on the wind around you and forget your fears," Jack instructed from where he was crouching at the edge of the roof. "You are the one in control of your body, not the wind."

Rose watched them as they concentrated. Mark was the first one to get it as he had made it clear he was up for the challenge. Zane reached the rooftop next, with some kicking in the air, but he made it. And, then Heidi, who was, to Rose's surprise, graceful at it. It was Anthony who had some trouble; he stopped when he had made it halfway. His face turned pale and he looked very anxious.

"Anthony," Zane called. "You can do it, man."

"Come on, now. It's not that high, Anthony," Mark said. "You'll get your adrenalin daily dose. It's a rush."

"I prefer my bike for that," Anthony said, still in midair.

"What a soft boy," Lilly muttered, her face clearly finding him pathetic.

He tried to slowly lower himself down, very careful not to lose his balance, but, he stumbled to the ground and landed on his knees instead of his feet with a thud. Before anyone could realize the seriousness of the fall, Zane was at Anthony's side, and already helping him up.

"That was fast," Anthony said as he leaned on Zane's shoulder and limped to the nearest chair in the terrace, cursing under his breath.

Rose hurried over to him as the rest descended from the roof. "Here," she said and crouched beside his injured leg. His black jeans were torn where she could see a bloodied scratch below his kneecap. "Let me help you."

"No, I am fine," Anthony said and reclined back in the bamboo chair.

Ignoring his refusal, Rose covered his wound with her hand and left his knee unscratched. Anthony looked at her in amazement.

"I couldn't help it," she replied to his gaze.

"Woah," Zane said. "That was fantastic, Rose."

"Gentlemen," Jack said. "Grab-"

"Ladies here." Heidi looked at him with a hand on her hips.

"Ladies," Jack slowly said and gave a little nod. "You might need to eat as much of that as possible." He pointed at the basket full of food on the table. "Always keep yourselves energized."

At the mention of food, the boys jumped up and attacked the basket. They relaxed for a while, entertaining themselves by provoking Anthony's fear of heights who gave them one of his dark gazes.

They kept practicing throughout the day. But, Jack was still determined to understand their powers and what they were capable of. He summoned them again into the clearing, where the sun was starting to set.

"Zane," Jack said, holding a fist-sized rock in his hand. "I am going to throw this towards those trees. And, I want you to gather all your strength and catch it before it hits the tree."

Zane looked at him and scratched his head. "I'll try."

With his strong arms, Jack pitched the rock so hard that Rose heard it whizz through the air. Suddenly, Zane flew and caught it in his palm. Upon landing, he seemed confused at what he had just done.

"Wow," Mark cried. "That was bloody amazing!"

Anthony looked at Jack and said, "Speed?"

Jack nodded at him, and a smile drew the corner of his lips. He glanced at Rose, where she and Lilly were sitting and examining the training session, and winked at her. She silently giggled, but stopped when she saw Mark's eyes on her. Rose tried to give him a soft smile, but he only nodded and turned his back.

"Watch out," Lilly said, keeping her voice low. "That Heidi gave you a fierce look. I think she's in love with Mark."

Rose did not say anything on that topic. It was outraging for her, and she could not ever imagine Mark and Heidi as a couple. She did not deserve such a loyal and loveable man like Mark.

"Ms. Butterfield," Jack said, cutting through Rose's thoughts. "Let's-"

"It's Heidi," she said.

"You always hated that name." Mark laughed. "Remember, Anthony, how she used to – Ouch!" Mark clasped his forehead where a rock had smacked his temple. "You mental!"

Heidi appeared to be shocked from what she had done. "I-I'm so sorry, Mark. I didn't mean to hurt you."

"What were you thinking, Heidi?" Anthony frowned at her.

Upon seeing this, Rose leapt from her chair and sped over to them. Jack signaled at Mark's temple, which by then had blood trickling down the side of his face. Rose looked sharply at Heidi as she stepped in front of Mark. He eluded her eyes as she softly touched his forehead, and she could not help but remember the last time she had healed him and when she had almost thought he was gone.

"Alright," Jack said once Rose had gone back to join Lilly in the terrace. "Everyone needs to stay calm. We still do not know what our limits are. The last thing we need is to hurt each other. Now, Heidi. Grab that rock and try to hit that branch on the third tree."

Heidi looked at where he was pointing and opened her mouth in uncertainty. "You want me to hit that with this?"

"I bet she won't even throw it anywhere near the first tree," Zane said to the other boys.

"Count me in," Anthony said.

Heidi raised her eyebrows at them and pressed her lips in determination. Squinting her eyes in concentration, she tossed the rock in her hand before she threw it with all the strength her lean arms could muster. All seven members followed the rock as it broke off the branch with a loud crack.

"Woah," Zane said. "Now that's one good throw." He turned to Mark and Anthony. "See? I told you she would hit it."

"The Shooter," Jack answered Heidi's amused look.

Testing her abilities, Jack made Heidi shoot at some bizarre targets that were nearly impossible to hit. But, she did not miss one of them. Her power was vital for the war, and her accuracy was lethal.

After numerous trials with the Shooter, Jack turned his attention towards Anthony. "Do you understand your power?" Jack asked.

"Pretty much," Anthony replied. "I had to deal with my flooded flat."

Jack signaled for him to demonstrate, and Anthony obeyed. With his hands at his sides Anthony started to make circular motions in the air, as if he was skimming his fingers in invisible water, which he only could see. Very slowly, tiny and twinkling water drops arose from the ground beneath Anthony as he continued swirling his hands. A million water drops froze in the air at their master's command, like hovering diamonds in the last rays of the ceasing sun. With another swift motion the droplets fell to the ground with an audible splash like that of the last drops of rain.

"That's it?" Lilly said loud enough to reach Anthony.

He broke her half a smile and raised a finger in front of him, drawing the same circles in the air. For a second nothing appeared to be happening, but all of their attention was suddenly grabbed by the sound of gushing water coming from the depth of the forest. A huge wave of water burst from between the trees, drowning the trees and bushes in its way. The wave reached the Blue Water members in the clearing and halted a few paces in front of them, looking like an enormous monster, which was about to devour anything in front of it.

Rose gasped at the water as it twirled and swirled within itself, and Lilly rushed over to it and examined it up close with impressed eyes.

"Don't get too close," Anthony said, restraining a smile.

Lilly didn't smile and walked away from the preternatural mass of water.

Having seen enough, Jack signaled him to stop and restore the water from wherever he had extracted it.

"Impressive," Jack said and nodded at him.

"I can tell," Anthony said, darting a look over his shoulder at Lilly.

"Why don't you, Jack, show us your mighty powers," Mark said. "You are the Leader, aren't you?"

Leaping out of her chair, Rose hurried over to them and stood beside Jack. "I think you all had enough for today. Why don't we continue training tomorrow?"

Mark and Jack stared at each other, electrical vibes seemed to jump around them.

"Not before he shows us his leadership powers," Mark said, a smirk forming on his lips.

No matter how hard she tried to catch his attention, Mark did not look at her and continued glaring at Jack. Whether he did not notice her pleading eyes or he was simply ignoring her, she realized that he was not going to make this easy on Jack.

"Come on, Mark," Anthony said and pulled his arm. "Let's grab a drink."

Once they were back inside, Rose stepped in front of Jack, who had been quiet, and regarded his gloomy eyes.

"Don't mind him," she said. "He'll come around."

He sighed. "This is not going to be easy."

"I know. But, you did a great job today."

"They did." He corrected her. "I can't deny; they are fast learners. But, Anthony has to overcome his fear."

Rose smiled in a way that Jack knew held something behind it. He raised his eyebrows in query.

"Leave that for Lilly," Rose said in a low voice lest Lilly might catch a word. "You'll find him soaring around very soon."

He frowned and glanced at Lilly as she sat staring into space with a blank expression on her face. He did not say anything, but his eyes betrayed him and exposed his worries. Since the time Lilly had confined her with Baas's story, she wondered why Jack had never mentioned him before. He could have just told her that he was his childhood friend and kept his sister's love life out of the picture. But, he did not, even when she had told him about Heidi. There was no reason to blame him; she knew how he was feeling about it.

The night had fallen upon the house, immersing it in total darkness as the Seven Blue lingered in and out of it, each one of them deciphering their sudden change of identity. Rose entered the kitchen to prepare a decent dinner to fill the stomachs of the members. Zane volunteered to help and cook some of his favorite Naryan recipes. Even Heidi gave a hand in distributing the plates around. They scattered themselves in the living room, some on the floor and others on the couches. The seasons seemed strange this year; it felt like the summer had ended early and winter was beginning. A chilly breeze rushed through the open windows and bit the cheeks of the Seven Blue as they devoured what was on their plates.

Rose shuddered and felt goosebumps all over her arms, she regretted her choice of the light cardigan for warmth. Looking to the side, she saw the empty fireplace just beside her. The old wood was in no shape to produce a sufficient fire, and she was too tired to go and fetch some new ones. Before she could look away, smoke started to ascend from between the cracks of the firewood. They started to crackle until a single, red flame arose, igniting the whole fireplace. She darted her head towards Mark, who was sitting far away from her and the fireplace, and met his eyes. He threw her half a smile that briefly lingered on his mouth and turned his head back to Anthony.

When Rose looked back at the fireplace, she found it containing a warm fire that casted its heat upon them and threw a red hue across the room. Her mind drifted off to her father, who was in the kitchen eating away his worries.

"When are we going to tell him?" Rose whispered to Jack beside her.

"When the time is right," he said.

She bit her lips and nodded. Even though she yearned to tell her father about Jack's proposal, she knew the time was not appropriate. After the war would be better, at least she would be assured that Jack would be alive to marry her in the first place. But, it was not her father's response that she feared. She was more concerned about Mark's reaction when she would eventually expose to him her plan for the uncertain future. No, it would be a harsh act if she told him anytime soon. He was already going through so much, and she did not want to deepen the wound in his heart more than it already was.

One by one, they retreated to their rooms after Jack told them there would be another training session in the morning. Rose and Jack stayed back to clean up after, and then Jack sat and contemplated his emblem on his hand for a while. As she placed the last plate in the kitchen cupboard, Rose glanced at a pair of black boots descending the staircase.

Anthony stepped into the kitchen, still in his black pants and navy-blue shirt, and briefly glanced at Jack before he turned and spoke to Rose.

"Could I have a minute," he said and exited the kitchen.

Rose looked at Jack and went after him, wondering what he could possibly want from her. Maybe he wanted to tell her something about Mark. If that was the case, then Mark was being unreasonable not to come and talk to her personally. When she reached where Anthony was waiting, she stopped with a startle. Heidi was standing right beside him.

"Rose," Anthony said. "Heidi feels uncomfortable sleeping in the same room as three guys. And, she wants to sleep in your room with you and Lilly."

Not expecting Anthony to put her in that situation, he was the one who knew how deep the wounds between her and Heidi. She looked at him with irritation and folded her arms.

"I told you I'll sleep down here on one of the couches," Heidi said. "They've got quite a lot to choose from."

"You won't sleep down here," Anthony said and threw her his sharp eyes to shut her up. She rolled her eyes and he turned back to Rose. "Look, I know that you two don't get along well. And, I know that you are mad at me."

"I'm glad you know that, Anthony," Rose said, nodding her head.

"Yes, I know," Anthony said, keeping his strong voice low.

"But, you need to know that you were not the only one going through a hard time."

Rose frowned at him, and for the first time noticed a scar across the left side of his neck, barely visible underneath his long hair. She pulled her eyes away quickly when she realized that he had noticed what she was staring at.

"You've been distant for a long time," Anthony said, containing his impassive face. "And you have no idea how hard Heidi's life has been."

She bit her lips and nodded. "Yes, Anthony. Maybe I don't really know, but I do know the meaning of friendship."

"Oh, my goodness!" Heidi said. "Can't you let it go already? We were children, for crying out loud!"

"Say that to yourself," Rose said, trying very hard to compose the pain arousing from the old memories. "You were the one who betrayed me after my mother died!"

Upon hearing Rose's voice, Jack appeared from the kitchen and beckoned for Anthony to come and leave the girls to settle their old disputes by themselves. But, Anthony refused to leave them and made sure to stay until they got through.

"I was a jealous, little girl, alright!" Heidi said. "I confess it, but stop judging me on my past."

"You weren't there when I most needed you, Heidi," Rose said and heard her voice change. She gulped back the lump in her throat; she was not going to let herself cry in front of Heidi.

"I know I wasn't, and I am sorry!" Heidi gasped; she appeared to be surprised at her apologetic words just as Rose was.

"I'm sorry too," Rose said and shook her head. "But, you are too late. You lost my trust years ago. And I don't know how I'm going to trust you now. But, I've learned to heal..." Rose pulled her eyes away from Heidi's tearful ones and looked at Anthony. "She can sleep in my room, but that does not mean anything."

Before Anthony could open his mouth, Rose turned away and reentered the kitchen where she fell into Jack's arms. Jack held her as long as she needed and then walked her up the stairs to her room without saying anything to her. In front of the door, he kissed her forehead and told her to sleep well and told her tomorrow was going to be an interesting day. Just as he was about to leave, the guest-room door opened and Mark stepped out into the corridor, wearing a black jacket on top of his white shirt from the morning. He looked like he was going outside.

"What?" Mark asked when he saw them both looking at him.

"Where are you going?" Rose said.

"I need fresh air," he curtly said and headed towards the staircase.

"Mark," Jack said, stopping him in his tracks. "Do you mind if I join you?"

Mark smirked. "Yeah, I do," he said and descended the stairs.

"I'll see you tomorrow," Jack said and quickly followed Mark, leaving Rose puzzled in his wake.

Wondering what Jack wanted to talk to Mark about, Rose entered her room and found Heidi had already set up a bed on the floor in front of the balcony and in her pajamas. She was on the phone and did not notice Rose's entrance.

"This is Heidi," she said in a weak voice. Rose guessed she had been crying. "If you are ever wondering where I am, that's if you even noticed my absence, just know that I'm ok. And, if you are worrying, don't worry. I'll be back soon. Yeah." Heidi paused and breathed in a sob. "Love you." She slammed the phone shut and sobbed quietly as she hugged her legs to her chest, rocking herself slowly back and forth.

Taken back at what she had just heard, Rose shut the door to announce her presence. She regarded Heidi who quickly dried her tears and turned her head towards the door.

"How long have you been standing there?" Heidi said, regaining her provoking tone. Nevertheless, Rose could not miss the pain in her eyes, and immediately suspected that Heidi had spoken to none other than her parent's answering machine.

"I just came in," Rose said and climbed onto bed. "Are... Are you alright?"

Heidi glanced at her and sniffed. "I will be. I always am."

Rose was not sure what drove her to ask, but she could not help how pitiful she felt.

"I'm sorry for your loss. I know what she meant to you..." She paused for a moment thinking about Heidi's nanny, before continuing. "A broken heart is never an easy thing to deal with, especially when they're so close... yet so far."

To her surprise, Heidi was quiet.

"Don't hold onto something that brings you pain, Heidi. Forgiving and letting go is the only way to go. But, believe me, your destiny will guide you." Rose frowned, noticing how her words were not only meant for Heidi, but for herself as well. It was time to let go of her anger towards Heidi, and maybe the rest of the pain that she carried with her since her mother's passing.

"Mark loves you," Heidi whispered. "He always did."

Rose was quiet for a minute, knowing how painful it must be for Heidi to be the second choice. "I know, but Mark's love is a little bit misguided. Love is freedom, and he only tried to force me into his cage." Both girls met each other's eyes, and a silenced understanding was instantly shared. "Get some rest, Heidi. You need it."

They both got into bed, and then Rose noticed that Lilly was missing. Once the room was quiet and Heidi had fallen asleep, Rose entered the balcony and looked at the trees, wondering what Jack and Mark might have been up to. But, before her worries could paint situations, a shadow caught her eyes. She leaned over the rails and cranked her head, but the shadow had quickly disappeared. She had thought it was Lilly's, but the shadow was too broad to be hers. Leaning more against the rails, her eyes caught two figures clasped onto each other in passionate heat, almost devouring each other with their kisses.

She recoiled back for a moment to comprehend what she had just seen and looked down again. As she had guessed. Anthony had Lilly between his arms until she pushed him away and slapped his smirk off his lips. But, before Anthony could react, Lilly grasped him by his shirt and caught his mouth in another kiss right before running off into the darkness of the forest. With a hand on her blushed cheeks, Rose stared after them for a moment until she made her way back to bed.

***

In the morning, the splash of cold water swept away the fogginess from her head and helped Rose shake the memories of last night's dream. That incomprehensible dream had returned, just like she had feared it would. She glanced at her reflection in the mirror and wiped her face with a towel. What was going to happen to them? Jack had indeed found the Blue Water Army, but were they ready to crush the Kalano? Rose buried her head in the towel, trying to escape from her thoughts. But, she could not help thinking about the book lying inside her wardrobe. What could it possibly hold that was so important it refused to reveal it to them until they united? And what choice was she, the Healer, going to make? She buried her face deeper in the towel as her thoughts whirled inside her throbbing head.

A knock on the bathroom door made her look up. "Are you going to stay in there all day?" Heidi said.

With a last glance at her reflection, Rose replaced the towel and opened the bathroom door. Heidi was waiting in her pajamas and rubbing her puffy eyes when Rose passed her and entered her room.

"Rose?" A warm voice reigned in her wondering mind. She darted her head and found Jack standing at the doorway, his eyes fixed on her. "Are you alright?"

She nodded lightly and went into his arms. He took in a deep breath, Rose realized, and tightened his hold around her. "Don't squish me." She mumbled softly.

Jack met her eyes with a smile. "I want to hide you and keep you safe, but I know I can't do both."

Her smile lingered more on her lips, and she tiptoed to reach his mouth. "My heart and soul are safe with you." Noises downstairs brought them back to reality. "Where did you take Mark yesterday?"

"To where the Spy's body lay," Jack said as they made their way down the stairs.

Rose stopped in her tracks. "Luba?"

Jack nodded slowly and sighed. "It had to be done, Rose. Mark is the Fire, and his fire is the only one that could burn them."

"I should have gone with you."

"No." He pulled her hand and walked towards the kitchen. "I have to make him trust me and know me as his leader, not his competitor."

"Oh," she said. "And did you achieve that?"

"No." He broke a light smile full of doubt. "I don't think he'll ever forget."

She looked down at the floor and gave a sigh just as they entered the kitchen. The few sun-rays penetrated the small window on top of the sink, casting a yellow shade on the oak table scattered with empty mugs and crumbles of bread and fruits. Mark was sitting and staring into space while Zane beside him tossed fruit pulps into the empty cup in front of him. Opposite them, Anthony stood leaning against the counter, his blank expression contrasting her last image of him. Rose hid her blushing face with her hair.

"Sawubona, Rose," Zane said. He looked behind her at the stairway. "Is Heidi still asleep?"

"No," Rose said. "She's just freshening up."

"Mark," Jack said. Mark did not look up from where he sat. "Do you have any news from Dr. Liu?"

"He's on his way," Mark mumbled and stood up. He threw Rose a glance and walked out of the kitchen, making it a point to walk between her and Jack. She instantly understood the request in his eyes. She looked at Jack and raised her eyebrows questioningly.

He eluded her eyes and folded his arms. "Tell him we'll start training in half an hour," he said.

His tone was not blunt, and that relieved Rose. She went out of the double-glass doors and reached where Mark was standing in front of the forest path, his hands buried in the pockets of his grey jacket.

"So, he let you come out after all," Mark said.

Rose dropped her shoulders. "What is it, Mark?"

"Nothing is wrong," he said. "In fact, I'm having the best time of my life."

"Mark, please." Rose shook her head. "Give me a break."

"I am giving you a break, Rose."

"In what way exactly?"

Mark sighed and looked over at the house. "Come," Mark said and stepped onto the path. "Let's have a walk. The last thing I want him to have is incredible hearing abilities."

She peeked at the house before following him and bit her lips.

"What?" Mark said, frowning at her hesitation. "You don't trust me now?"

"Don't be like that," she said and walked on the path.

They walked silently as they wandered deeper into the forest within the protection. Rose stared at her shoes as they sank into the ground, cracking tree twigs and crushing dried leaves, and waited for Mark to speak. When he did not utter a word, she raised her head and looked at him to find a faint frown on his face. He seemed to be choosing his words carefully, to her surprise.

"Mark?" she said and stopped before they could reach the clearing of the pond. She was definitely not going there. "What is it?"

He straightened his head and locked his rusty eyes with hers. She tried to escape them, but failed to. "I can't do this anymore," he said with a deep sigh. "I tried to 'give you a break', but I just can't."

She frowned. "What do you mean?"

"I tried not to love you anymore, Rose. For your sake and mine. So, I won't get in the way of you and your love-chump."

Rose sighed softly. "What stopped you?"

He broke a soft smile. "I realized that if I killed my feelings for you, I'll be killing everything that had to do with you and my childhood. I'd end up hating you. And, I don't want that to happen."

She opened her mouth, but no words came out. There were no words to say to such a broken, young heart. She had thought he was stronger, but he only came back crawling on his knees for survival.

"Don't look at me that way," he said. "I'm not asking for your help. I'm just making things clear for once in my life." He buried his hands deeper in his jacket as a strong wind whistled passed them, blowing leaves and dust across the ground.

Rose shuddered and hugged her bare arms. She watched as Mark took off his jacket and held it out to her. She looked at him for a moment and took the jacket, grateful for its warm texture against her skin.

"Forgive me, Rose," he said, his voice shaking a little.

"For what?" She said. "For loving me? I can't blame you for that..."

"I was selfish." His gaze was fixed on her. "I never really thought what might become of you if you had accepted me. How would you have lived after my death?"

"Mark, stop-"

"Let me finish what I've got to say," he said a little strongly. "Trust me it's not easy to say this. But, I see a different person in front of me other than the weak girl I'd known. Yes! I'll give him credit for that. Jack made you stronger. Something I had been trying to do for a long time now." He paused and ran a hand through his soft hair, breathing in. "I just – I just," he said, looking for the right words. "I just want to say that I will not stop loving you, Rose Peterson. But... I will not try and destroy what you already have. I learned that love is freedom."

Rose took a deep breath, realizing that he and Anthony had indeed overheard her conversation with Lilly the other day on the balcony.

A small smile appeared on her lips. "I'm so sorry, Mark," she said softly. He turned his head away from her and broke a weak smile. "You know that I always cared about you, and always will."

"Good to hear that," he said and turned his eyes back to her. "But, of course. I am just your brother. Naturally, you'll have to care."

Upon hearing his hurt tone, Rose slowly approached him closer and rested her arms on his shoulders. She saw his eyes sparkle with surprise, but he did not pull back from her. "Forgive me, Mark." She stood on her tiptoes and hugged him tightly, locking him inside her arms. But, she did not feel Mark's arms wrap her back. He was stiff like a cold statue embraced by the bitter warmth of remorse.

Sensing his rigidness, Rose could not stop the sudden flow of tears that brought with it a reality that she had been trying to crush with her hopes. She gasped and started to sob, but Mark remained stiff.

"Promise me," she said between gasps. "Promise that you'll never leave me."

He stayed silent.

"Please, Mark."

"I can't promise you that," he said. "But, I bet Jack can. He's the Leader. I'm only a member."

She gulped back a sob and dropped her hands from around his shoulders, taking a few steps away from him. "You want to know Jack's 'mighty' power is?" she said, her face full of pain.

Mark eye's softened a little when he saw her face, but he kept his mouth lined firmly.

"He will sacrifice his life to save me. I will be the cause of his death, and I won't be able to use my power to save him," she paused for breath, "It doesn't work on the dead. I'm not ready to lose anyone, Mark."

Breaking out of his stiff stance, Mark covered the space between them in a wide stride and pulled her hard into his arms this time. She allowed herself to lose control again and let out every tear she had been trying to hide for the past few weeks. All her worries and doubt involving Jack and the future came pouring into her tears, dripping into Mark's chest and soaking his shirt. Her body shook as she buried her face inside his embrace, clenching onto his shirt like she had used to when she was a lost, little girl.

"I promise you," he said, his tone solemn. "And... I promise you that I will make sure he lives... for you."

The wind gushed against them once more and infiltrated the trees, sending a piercing whistle throughout the forest. It sent a chill down her spine, and she felt the hair on the back of her neck stand up. She instantly released Mark and looked around her. The blow of the wind was so strong that it swept away the dried leaves and shook the tree branches, threatening to break them at any moment. Mark covered his eyes behind his arms as dust blew into their faces, stinging their eyes and sticking to their lips. She squinted against the brown screen of dusty wind and scanned the vacancy, but the leaves obscured her vision. Quickly, Mark grabbed her hand and retraced their steps back to the where the path was. They ran as fast as their light feet could while the tree branches slapped at them, the wind pursuing them like an angry spirit.

It suddenly ceased away once they reached the end of the path. Rose hurried out from between the trees and almost bumped into Jack. She felt his strong arms support her and let out a breath of relief.

"What the hell was that?" Mark said, looking behind him at the trees as they once more stood tall.

When her heartbeat returned to normal, Rose looked around at the rest and saw Lilly standing in the terrace with a frown on her face. *It was definitely not Lilly's wind,* Rose thought.

"Zane," Jack said in his powerful voice that always evoked a sparkle of admiration in their eyes. "Run along the protection shield and make sure no one has penetrated it. Be quick. If you did not come back after thirty seconds, I'll assume something has happened."

Zane gave him a nod and disappeared into the forest before Rose could even blink. She glanced at Jack and locked with his stern eyes. But, before she could question him with hers, Zane reappeared.

"All clear," Zane said, his breathing was remarkably stable even after running around a huge area in less than half a minute.

Jack nodded, his face solemn.

"They are getting ready," Lilly said, approaching them with an urgent spring in her stride. "Jack, they are practicing their own powers. You and I know very well who is the Storm."

"Who?" Anthony said, his eyes fixed on her.

Lilly eluded his sharp gaze and looked at Jack. "The Leader of the Dark Army."

Rose's heart made a jolt inside her chest. She saw Jack clench his fist, a vein in his inner arm popped out, but he succeeded in restraining his temper within himself.

"Only storm?" Zane said as his eyebrows rose in skepticism. They all turned their heads and looked at him. "Um, I just think that the Leader of the Dark Army should be much more powerful than Storm."

"Don't underestimate him," Lilly said, her tone blunt. "It's enough his wind had penetrated the protection. He's much more powerful than you think."

"You sound like you know him," Mark said.

Lilly gave him a piercing glance and kept her mouth shut.

"Training will begin in five minutes," Jack said, his face so solemn that it was almost impassive. He tore away from them and strode to the terrace where Dr. Liu had just arrived.

"Zeyum," Dr. Liu said and put a hand across his chest when he saw Jack. "The Wise, as the Naryans call the Leader."

"Are you alright, doctor?" Rose said, looking at him closely. His once plump face was sucked in and haggard just as was his muddied clothes and stained shoes. He had a huge fabric sack at his feet and a single sheet from the local newspaper clutched in his hand.

"Better than expected, Rose," he said and pulled her a smile. "The hunting years have passed now that the Kalano are determined to capture the Leader for the Blue Army. Fortunately, the streets now are much safer for the Protectors to roam than it had been for the past ten years. Niago Siathe is preparing itself."

"Yes, we figured that out," Jack said. "And we are preparing as well."

"That is why I brought these." The Doctor heaved the sack up and put it on the nearby mahogany table, where it made a sound of clashing metal. He reached in and pulled out a silver Longsword with a leather grip that could fit both hands. Its silver blade glistened in the few rays of sunlight and its point shone threateningly. Rose saw that there were more of them in the sack. "Akita had kept them for the right time, but, as I had expected, she had no time to witness the union of the Blue Water."

"Why do we need swords?" Mark said, approaching them.

"It's a crucial weapon, Mark," the Doctor said, handing the one in his hand over to him. "Niago Siathe," the doctor said, "does not only fight with their powers. They have a certain number of main powers, just like the Blue Water Army. However, they do have a well-trained army that is made up of thousands of Kalano warriors, all equipped with the traditional weapons of Nara. Fighting with these will become handy, the Longsword is a foreign weapon to them and they are not familiar with its nature. I believe that you are familiar with the basics of it, Jack. You have one yourself."

"Yes," Jack said and a gloomy cloud covered his face, but he quickly shook it away. "I made it with my father. We used the very same metal they used for their spears and arrows."

"Ah, the crossroads of the world. It only happened once when the Wise Man was one of them, and he was the only weapon that could destroy them."

"What do you mean, doctor?" Rose said once she saw Jack's face still upset.

Dr. Liu looked at her and opened his mouth in hesitation. "You don't know about the crossroad that happened that time? I see the book has not yet revealed its pages to you."

"The crossing of the roles," Jack said. "The union of a Power and a Protector in marriage."

Rose looked at him in confusion, but his eyes were lost in his thoughts. She waited for the doctor to continue, but he only nodded and said that the book will explain everything to them. Dr. Liu spread the crumbled newspaper on the table and pointed at some photos of young and beautiful girls. They all gathered around it. A couple of them were familiar to Rose; she had seen them once or twice in the Village. "Thirteen girls were kidnapped during the last couple of weeks, with no evidence left behind."

"Are we going to look for them and save them?" Zane said, cringing his head from over Anthony's shoulder.

"You won't need to search for them, Zane," Dr. Liu said. "They will come to you. How or when? I cannot answer that. The book carries all the information you need."

"And how can we make this book reveal itself?" Mark snorted.

"By practicing," Jack said, his tone bleak. He grabbed the rest of the swords and hurried over to the clearing.

She felt Mark's eyes on her, but she decided to ignore the questions that he would surely ask. Instead, she followed Lilly to where Jack was waiting for them.

"Does anyone know how to handle a sword?" Jack said once all six of them stood in front of him.

"A fencing sword," Anthony replied, grabbing one with a single hand. He plunged its point into the ground and leaned on it.

"Very well. Anyone else?" Jack looked at the rest of them.

"Well," Mark said and plunged the one in his hand into the earth as well. "I don't see the importance of using a sword."

"Like Dr. Liu explained," Jack said, distributing the swords among the others, "it's important to know how to fight in close combat." However, Jack did not hand Rose one and kept the last sword on the ground.

She tried to catch his eyes, but he was deeply explaining the nature of the sword and how to wield it. He couldn't do this to her, Rose thought; she had to learn how to defend herself as well. Grabbing a chair in the terrace, Rose sat and watched as Jack demonstrated the right position of the legs in relation with the grip of the sword. But, she was not satisfied by just watching them train, so she noted the basics of Jack's moves and positions.

Jack had appointed Lilly, who turned out to be a graceful sword-fighter, and Anthony to help him with Mark and Heidi. With the obvious coldness between him and Mark, he had left Lilly for Mark and Anthony for Heidi. Jack observed them and corrected any wrong moves, and sometimes demonstrated a brief combat between him and Lilly, the sound of clashing metal made her heart give a jolt every time it echoed in the clearing.

Fourteen: The Seven Blue

The night slowly crept over them, and the stray clouds hovered above like white ghosts. They had been practicing for over four hours by then, and fatigue had started to tire their muscles and squeeze out their energy.

She had watched every minute of it, until her own back ached from the bamboo chair she was sitting in. Her eyes had lingered over Mark and Lilly from time to time, and she was grateful that he worked with her smoothly and without any provocation, so as not to provoke Lilly and her aggressive side.

With red faces and clothes soaked in sweat, they all entered the house and devoured what Dr. Liu had prepared for dinner, dashing off to the bathrooms afterwards. Rose was busy cleaning after dinner when Jack gently touched her arm and stopped her. She looked up at him and stared into his eyes, a gloomy expression casting a shadow on the vitality in his flushed cheeks.

"Come," he said.

There was nothing she could possibly do other than to leave what was in her hands and follow him out to the terrace, where the sword she was supposed to practice with lay on the table. He took it and handed it to her. Surprisingly, the sword was light in her hand. "I was saving you for a private session."

Before she was able to open her mouth, he entwined her hand and ushered her deep into the forest path. She tried to ask him where were they going, but he only smiled at her from beneath the gloominess in his face. However, she could guess where they were heading.

The pond was silent, its surface grey with the reflection of the clouds in the sky, allowing only some few gaps for the moonlight to bless the darkness below. Jack and Rose reached the clearing and stopped before the barrier that protected them from harm. She stared at the pond for a while, breathing in the air that had used to calm her and blow away her worries. Sensing Jack's eyes on her, she regained her wandering thoughts and turned away from the compelling pond.

He sighed. "First thing," he said and repositioned her hand on the sword grip, "you should know about a sword is how to hold it properly."

She did as he instructed all the way to how to deflect a thrust and was thankful for paying attention to the basics. Even with the sound of clashing metal, she could not stop wondering about the cause of his worries.

"I can't believe I'm doing this," he said as both swords met, the moonlight reflecting in the silver blades and illuminating his eyes. He made her preform a thrust towards him and he deflected it with a swift move of his wrist.

She lowered down the sword and looked at him, her muscles screaming with every move. "We will get through this. And after that, we will get married, have a wedding, and live happily ever after."

"It sounds easy when you say it." He thrust the sword into the muddied ground. "Rose, I need you to promise me one thing."

Her heart skipped; she feared his promises.

"If this doesn't end the way you are expecting it to, I want you to promise me that you won't live in mourning. Don't ever go back into the dark room again. I need you to live happy and loved."

"Please." She shook her head, trying to shake his words out of her head. "Stop talking!"

He opened his mouth to continue, but closed it when he saw the look on her face.

"We will get through this, Jack Casper! And, we will live happy and in good health. Together."

"Rose." He gently pulled her into his arms and enveloped her shaking body, his lips kissing the top of her head.

"You are the one," she said, "who must promise to stay alive for me."

He brushed his fingers through her hair, soothing her. "I will do everything in my strength to stay beside you."

His tone did not quaver, and that made her fears rest a little. With reluctant hands, she pushed herself out of his embrace and picked up her sword again. "You need to prepare me in every way for whatever is out there."

"In every way?"

"Yes."

He took a few steps away from her and picked up his sword as well. In a swift move, Jack grasped the edged blade in his palm and sliced it against his skin. Her eyes widened at the blood slipping from between his balled fingers. She hurried over to him, but Jack soared backwards and was far away from her in seconds.

"Jack!"

"Don't come closer," he said loud enough for her to hear. "Use your power from where you are."

Her breathing got faster as the image of his bloodied hands quickened her heartbeat. She closed her eyes and concentrated on that feeling of helpless love, the strong affection that bound their souls, and was surprised at how the Healer within her responded to the sudden emotions. She watched him as he came back to her, a faint trace of a smile on his lips.

"I may not be around you all the time, neither Mark nor any of us. That's why you have to practice healing from a distance."

Before she could reply, she glanced at his hand and found it unwounded. "I need to learn how to defend you and myself from any harm."

"That's my job," he said, his voice torn.

She reached her hands up to his face, straightening his frowning eyebrows.

"I know," she said. "But, that doesn't mean you leave me completely defenseless. I need to stay alive for you."

Jack closed his eyes at her touch and took a profound breath. Without saying anything more, he reopened his eyes and clanged his sword with hers. They did not reopen the subject again during the couple of hours of Rose's training, and she succeeded in focusing all her attention on how Jack was telling her to move and switch her legs.

She kept practicing until her muscles could not take it anymore, and her arms became completely numb from wielding the Longsword. She knew she would have to do this every day until she could master it, only if time allowed her to. She just hoped that her body would accommodate quickly and the fire in her muscles would lessen.

***

Day after day passed, the weather changing in an unnatural way such that Rose did not believe it was only the beginning of July. The sky poured rain during the day as they trained their sword fighting and blew horrible wind at night, where most of their power training took place. She could not deny that they were all getting stronger and better by the day, even Heidi mastered her shooting power with closed eyes. And, just as Rose had predicted, Anthony overcame his fear of heights with Lilly's midnight help. Rose had seen them train all alone a couple of times.

Her special training sessions with Jack took place every night. The Longsword became an easy tool in her hands, almost like a paintbrush where she stroked it in the air rather than on a canvas. Her healing power became stronger as well, and she was capable of arousing the Healer within much faster than she used to. Even Jack noticed her growing strength and complemented her with a soft smile. And, sometimes, he let her join the others during the combat fighting they performed when the moon was at its highest.

However, this miraculous progress only provoked their patience. The pages of the book were still bare of any words, and they yearned for the information it carried. After flipping the empty pages one last time, Rose returned it safely into her wardrobe and went out of the room. Though she was meant to take part in the sword-fight session that day, her muscles ached from all the training so she decided to rest for the day. She was amazed at the muscles forming in her arms when she surveyed herself in the mirror. They gave her a different shape that she almost thought those arms belonged to someone else.

Lilly and Heidi were sitting on the terrace when Rose joined them. The ladies were watching Mark, Anthony, and Zane in combat against Jack. They were trying to beat him, but Rose knew his fighting skills were well nourished with years of experience.

"Look at them," Lilly said. "They took off their shirts to try to impress us."

Rose indeed noticed the change of the scene. Even though she liked the sight of Jack's bare skin, she felt slightly uncomfortable when she found the young men lacking shirts as well, their skin glistening with the rain droplets.

"It's working," Heidi said, her eyes following Mark.

Rose looked over at them and spotted Mark, still the skinniest among them. However, she could not deny that his arms had taken a nice shape and his stomach became firmer. But, the shadow of his ribs and backbone could still be seen even after the noticeable changes of his broadened shoulders and chest.

"I can't take it anymore," Lilly said and picked up her sword from beside her. "I won't sit here and watch them have all the fun any longer." With long strides, Lilly walked over to them, the rain soaking her once she had stepped from underneath the terrace's roof, and clashed swords with Anthony without any introductions.

From the corner of her eyes, Rose watched Heidi as she fixed her eyes on Mark, who seemed totally ignorant of the longing evoking from them. Heidi played with a strand of her blond hair, and Rose saw a cloth wrapped around her wrist. She cringed her head to get a better look, but Heidi noticed and folded her hands to her chest.

"What happened?" Rose heard herself say.

"Sword cut," Heidi said. "I was practicing with Mark yesterday."

Somehow those words worried her.

"It was an accident." Heidi blurted out when she saw the look on her face.

Rose eyed her as Heidi's blue eyes tried to evade hers, and she started to twist a strand around her finger again. With a sigh, Rose looked over at Mark. He couldn't do this, she thought. Heidi shouldn't be harmed due to his misplaced anger. She turned her head back to Heidi and reached over to her wounded hand.

Heidi frowned at her, but did not draw away from Rose's touch. When Rose released her hand, Heidi unwrapped her wrist and stared at the healed skin. Rose saw the faintest smile on her lips and gave her a nod in return.

A strong clang of metal echoed above the sound of gushing rain, causing Rose to jerk her head at the others. Her heart made a faint skip when she found Mark in one-on-one combat with Jack.

Rose stood up and moved towards them. Rushing under the rain, her hair and shirt instantly getting plastered to her face and body, Rose went over to them just as Mark made a thrust at Jack who deflected it without any imposed effort.

"You think you're strong, Jack," Mark said, performing another failed blow.

"Mark-" Rose was about to go over to him, but Anthony blocked her way.

He looked at her and shook his head. "Stay out of this for once."

Jack remained calm, only deflecting Mark's blows.

"You say you're the Leader." Mark's sword met Jack's in another loud clang, red flames sparkling off of the one in Mark's hands. "Why don't you share with all of us your power? Who says you can save her, Jack!"

With a swift move of his sword, Jack sent a blow towards Mark, causing him to stagger a few paces backwards. When he had regained his balance, Mark looked at him and breathed out a heated breath, letting smoke out of his mouth. Rose sensed the Fire within him rise like a raging monster.

"Have you thought about how she'll live when you're gone?" Mark stomped towards Jack again and raised his sword high, aiming for his chest this time.

Jack deflected it again, and inflicted another blow, causing his raged opponent to stumble again.

"Or are you using her just as a weapon for all of this!"

"Mark!" Rose said, and tried to reach him, but Anthony kept her a hostage behind him. "Anthony, do something!"

With a stern gaze, Jack took a step towards Mark this time and slammed his sword against his. The force of the blow caused Mark to slip on the muddied ground and fall on his back. The rain poured restlessly on them, and the wind rushed by, howling in their ears. Mark got up with a lurch and rubbed his eyes from the obscuring rain. He squinted his eyes at Jack and held the sword with both hands, raising it above his head again.

"You have no idea what you're talking about," Jack said through gritted teeth.

Mark attempted wide blows at Jack, one after the other with nothing but rage and fury. Seeing there was no way to defeat his stronger opponent, Mark levitated up and aimed a thrust down at him. This time the sword point was so close to Jack's face that it slit the skin beside his right eye, blood poured out and mixed with the rain crawling down the side of his face.

"Mark!" Anthony finally intervened, but his friend gave him no attention and focused on Jack.

He watched as the wound in Jack's face disappeared. "Of course! She will always save you from any harm. You'll keep her close by so she can heal you."

"Why can't you forgive, Mark?" Jack said, his powerful tone echoed over the wind. "Can't you see she's not meant for you?"

"Oh, I forgave her. But, really, tell me." Mark soared over him, trying to get another successful blow from above. But, Jack prepared himself this time. "Is she really meant for you, then? After you realized she was part of your army or before that!"

"She chose her own path!"

Mark dropped back to the ground, pushing his wet hair away from his eyes. "Just like I chose mine." He breathed.

Jack lowered his sword when he found Mark's at his side. "You know what I mean."

She knew Mark needed this fight. It was his way of getting rid of the last emotions he held towards Jack. But, before his irrationality could take him far, Anthony and Zane intervened and seized their friend.

"Mark, you've made your point," Anthony said and tore the sword from Mark's firm grasp. But, Mark was not yet done. They tried to keep hold of him when suddenly they lurched away from him, clutching their hands and cursing.

"Don't forget that I burn," Mark said, looking at his friends.

"Mark, no!" Anthony plunged to catch Mark, but he had already sped from his reach and aimed at Jack, leaving smoke in his wake.

Before he could reach Jack, a sudden blow of wind pushed him out of balance. Lilly stood with her hands extended in front of her and a scowl on her face. She kept Mark prisoned within her wind and watched him as he tried to fight his way out. But, his Fire extinguished every time he tried to gather it in his hands.

Rose rushed over to Lilly to prevent her from harming him, but the sound of a huge splash of water stopped her in her tracks. Helped by the rain, Anthony used his power on Lilly, causing her to lose her focus and soaking her more than she already was. Standing there for a second, her mouth opened in surprise, Lilly regained herself and sent a wave of wind towards Anthony. Fortunately, Zane was fast enough to push his friend out of her line.

With her heart beating in her ears, Rose darted her head towards Mark and found him straightening himself up and stomping over to Jack. "Mark!" Rose raced and stood in front of him, preventing Mark from stepping any closer to Jack. She looked up at him in anger.

"Get out of my way," he said through gritted teeth. He placed a hand on her shoulder and was about to push her aside when a hand suddenly seized his in a bone-cracking grasp.

"Don't you ever touch her again." Jack's voice hissed through his clenched teeth. He gazed at him for a couple of cold moments.

Mark sneered and looked at Jack's hand. "I told you to be careful, Jack. Don't ever play with fire, you might just get burned."

"That's the privilege of being the Leader, you don't get burned or harmed by any of the members."

Rose found herself breathing again, and watched Mark try to smolder the hand clutching him to no avail.

Jack released Mark's wrist, but did not pull away the gaze. "Can't you see? You'll have to hurt her first to get to me. You can never kill me unless-"

"Oh, I don't want to kill you. Just hurt you little." He paused and met Rose's eyes for a brief moment. "I love her, so I won't do anything to harm her."

The three of them stood in the rain, their breathing heavy as they looked at each other. Breaking the icy silence, Anthony pulled Mark away from Jack and forced him inside the house, cursing at him. Rose went to her room as well. It took her some time to regain control of her feelings. She needed to avoid everyone for the time being. Her fears were gradually choking her and her brain would not rest.

All of them were still disturbed with what had happened earlier in the day, so Jack did not carry out their power training at night. Rose let out a deep breath. *Why, Mark?* Rose thought, staring aimlessly at the floor and listening to the howling of the wind outside. At least the rain had stopped. With another sigh, she got up and opened the cupboard where she had kept the Blue Book safe.

She gasped.

The cupboard was empty.

She rummaged through the pile of clothes and behind some boxes, but it was not there.

Without losing another minute, Rose dashed out of the balcony and soared to the roof.

"Jack!" She knew he was up there. "I can't find the-"

Upon her arrival, Jack bolted up on his feet and faced her, the book clutched between his hands.

She sighed. "I thought someone took it." Jack frowned and looked at the book.

"Jack?"

He looked up at her again and drew up half a smile. "The book is complete. Everything has been revealed."

Her mouth dropped open. "Finally!"

She rushed over to him and reached for it.

But, before she could touch it, Jack held it away from her. She frowned, confused, and regarded his eyes. There was something horribly different about them. "Jack, what does the book say?"

He tried to evade her worried eyes. "Some information about the Niego Siethe, their powers, and tactics. It's very helpful for our strategy outline."

Rose saw him pocket his free hand deep into his shorts. She sighed. "Please, don't try to convince me there is nothing awful in this book."

He did not reply.

"Jack, if something bad is going to happen, I need to know." Silence. "Don't do this to me." She shook her head. "Don't do like what they've done to me ten years ago. If something is going to happen, I need to know."

He closed his eyes and sighed.

"Let me prepare myself this time, Jack. I don't want any more surprises, I won't be able to handle them."

Jack nodded slowly and placed the book in her waiting hands. "Before you choose," he said, preventing her from opening it, "promise me that you'll choose wisely. Consult your brain this time, Rose. Not your heart."

He pulled her closer to him and planted a gentle kiss on her forehead. "Whatever your choice will be, I'll respect it."

Rose watched him as he flew into the night and disappeared within the dark forest, leaving her shaken with fear in his wake.

***

Her face was pale as a withering rose when she regarded herself in the mirror the following morning, and her eyes were bloodshot red with dark circles around them. She had been unable to steal a few hours of sleep the night before. What she had figured out was unbearable, and could prevent any soul from rest. Her head throbbed. No, she was not able to recollect the words that had butchered her upon reading them.

"Rose?" Lilly appeared in the doorway.

"Y-yes." Rose pulled a smile.

Lilly scrutinized her for a moment. "Jack is waiting for you downstairs. He has something important to say to the members." Her heart lurched inside her chest. "Hurry up."

Rose gulped and followed her downstairs where she found them gathered in the terrace. Her legs shook a little as she joined them, making sure to hide her face behind a few strands of her hair. She felt Jack's eyes on her, but she was not able to meet them lest her tears exposed her.

"Now that we're all here." Mark spoke. Rose felt her heart squeeze with pain. "Why don't you save us the suspense and tell us what's in the Blue Book."

Rose heard Jack take a deep breath.

"The book," Jack said, "has some valuable information about the Dark Army. Things that we need to look out for in the war."

"Do you even know when that is?" Mark said.

"Very soon, Mark," Lilly said.

"Now," Jack continued. "Dr. Liu has mentioned before the crossroads of the World, something which only happens once every thousand years. Once a member of the Blue Water marries a Protector, the roles shift; the Warrior becomes the Protector while the Protector becomes the Warrior. And, that's how the bloodlines change."

"Do you know who?" Zane said.

"No, the Book did not mention any names. No one knows about their bloodline unless the Niago Siathe rises back. Other than that, they're just normal people."

"You mean," Anthony said, "they could be any two normal people ignorant of the truth of their bloodlines?"

Jack contemplated the ground before answering. "Yes, they could."

Rose stole a glance at Jack from beneath her hair. Could it possibly be what she was thinking of? She had read it last night, but what she had reluctantly found out stopped her from looking further in the book.

"There is also," Jack said, and Rose felt him approach her, "a necklace that serves as a weapon for the Protectors. This red necklace was once in possession of a Protector. The book says that it has the ability to take back our powers, just like how the Water gave it."

Rose touched the necklace with her fingers and observed it. Could it take her healing powers in any minute?

"Wait," Mark said and pointed at the necklace on Rose's chest. "This could take back our powers just like that? We won't have them after the war?"

"It will take back our powers only if we win the war." Jack said. "We only must fulfill a purpose."

Rose took in a deep breath, suddenly feeling the heaviness of the necklace around her neck. It was the core of their powers, the source of it all. The Water only activated what the necklace already designated for them.

He paused before continuing, "There is something we have to take care of besides the necklace. The Dancers. One of the Dark Army's traditions is to perform a spiritual dance before the beginning of the war, and these may be one of the most dangerous obstacles we'll deal with."

"The Dancers?" Zane said.

"Yes, Zane, the Dancers. They are a group of young women with a lead dancer. Don't enjoy yourselves, gentlemen. These Dancers can mesmerize you, making you unable to move or even think. They'll try to lure you to them with their grace, but you must not let their charm control you. If you do, then you won't see the sunlight ever again. Fortunately, that doesn't apply to the ladies. Rose, Lilly, and Heidi, your job will be to prevent us from laying an eye on them."

"We'll have to kill them," Lilly said.

"Yes, you do. But, you can save your energy and bring down the lead dancer, she's the one controlling them."

"How will we know which one is her?" Heidi said.

"She won't be hard to point out," Jack said. "She'll probably be the most beautiful of them."

Rose looked at Jack and caught his eyes, but she quickly tore them away from him. She held her throbbing head, the image of her horrible dreams jumped into it again.

"Talk about fatal beauty," Zane said, and Anthony smacked him on the head.

"The other thing we all need to watch out for is the Execution Sword, or commonly known as the Ngulu."

"The what?" Anthony and Mark said in union.

"It's the weapon of the Dark Leader."

"Baas?" Anthony said.

Rose glimpsed Lilly beside her take a deep breath and fold her arms.

Jack frowned.

"Exactly. The Ngulu is a symbol of power and leadership, so the Dark Leader uses it only to kill his equal."

"You?" Mark said.

Rose tried to throw him a sharp look, but she could not bear to look at him like that, it hurt her heart. She glimpsed Anthony nudging him to hold his tongue.

"Yes, me, Mark."

Her breathing was loud in her ears, and the tears gathered in her eyes, but she contained them as best as she could, fighting the provoking images of her nightmares. She stared aimlessly at the ground, unable to look at the face that had been her guardian and savior for the last couple of months. The idea of his probable death being argued was too much for her to listen to.

"We won't," Lilly said, breaking the sudden silence, "allow him to touch you, Jack."

"You can't do anything, Lilly, none of you can. The Leaders fight each other until one is dead, that's how the winning side is known."

"So," Anthony said, straightening himself, "you have to kill the Dark Leader in order for the Blue Water to defeat the Dark Army."

"But," Lilly said, "it won't be that easy."

"I didn't say it bloody will, Lilly."

"I am just saying he is very powerful and manipulative."

"Don't worry." Anthony eyed her. "We'll kick Baas's arse."

"I guess we'll need a plan for that," Zane said.

"And, I have one," Jack said.

"Hold it right there," Mark said and stood up from his seat, running a hand through his hair in confusion. "Aren't we forgetting something here?"

Rose frowned just like the others.

"That we are only seven people fighting?" Zane blurted out.

"Exactly!"

They all exchanged glances, and Rose found Jack contemplating the ground with his hands in his pockets.

Mark approached Jack. "Do you think we can fight a whole army, Jack? Seven members-wait, make that almost six, regarding the lack of powers in one."

Before Lilly could unfold her arms, Rose grabbed them and gave her a pleading look not to do anything irrational. She was surprised that Lilly did as she wished.

Forcing himself not to lose his calm, which seemed to be on the verge these days, Jack said, "No, Mark. I don't. But, if you have any solutions, why don't you tell us."

Mark smirked and went back to his seat without another word.

"Well," Zane hesitated. "Mark has a point. We can't possibly fight them all by ourselves."

"Don't tell me you're doubting your own strength!" Lilly said. "We are the Seven Blue!"

"Yes, we are," Anthony said, "but, who the hell said we're the Blue Water Army?"

"So, what?" Mark straightened. "We're only a part of the Blue Water Army?"

Jack frowned; he seemed to be thinking carefully.

"So, does that make us incomplete?" Heidi said.

"Yes, it does." Dr. Liu entered the terrace, his clothes muddied and his glasses askew. But, there was a sparkle in his eyes that made Rose sense there was something coming.

"Doctor?" Mark said, regarding him. "Blimey. You look like you haven't slept in days."

"That's because I haven't, Mark." He faced Jack and smiled. "I've been awake for the past days talking to the chieftains of every village in Nara. Don't worry, Zeyum, you're army is now complete."

Jack looked around at them. "Doctor, we are only seven."

"As you should be. You are the Seven Blue of the Blue Water Army, the main half."

"And, the other half?" Mark said.

Dr. Liu smiled and walked to the clearing where they held their training sessions.

He beckoned Jack to join him and pointed at the forest. "Meet the rest of your army," he said.

Rose hurried over and stood beside Jack. She looked at where the doctor was pointing, but she did not understand what they were supposed to find until six figures approached them from between the trees. When they came closer, she noticed that they were three old men and three old women. Their elaborated outfits and wooden canes designated their high status. Once they were right in front of Jack they bowed their heads in courtesy.

"Zeyum," said the oldest man. "I am the Great Chieftain of Nara, and I have the honor to meet the Wise One."

Jack looked at him and back at the doctor in confusion.

"Bringing," the doctor said, "the other half of the Blue Water Army is the Protectors Job as well, Jack. We've been meeting in secret for the past ten years, seeking out contacts and checking old scripts to prepare for this day."

Jack came closer to the doctor. "Thank you, doctor. But they are only six. We are still incomplete."

"They were supposed to be seven chieftains, but the seventh is regrettably the enemy."

"Oh, now it makes much more sense," Mark said, appearing beside the doctor. "Let's see, that makes us thirteen now. What a lucky number!"

"Mr. Parker, would you be more sensible."

"Then show me the rest of the bloody army!"

The Great Chieftain observed Mark. "You possess the spirit of the Fire, I believe. Remarkable how the spirit of the human reflects their power, impatient and fierce. You can burn without flames. I come from a village which once gave birth to the Fire some hundred years ago."

Mark raised his eyebrows, trying to hide his amusement.

"You may calm your soul. We are here to help when The Day is decided, but, for now, we must go." He bowed to Jack again. "Zeyum, we will meet again." The six chieftains turned around and disappeared within the trees again, leaving Jack, Rose and Mark staring in their wake.

"The Great Chieftain," the doctor said, "is also the Keeper of the Legend. I record the events and the Seven Blue progress to power and give him the documents. He will be a great help to the army, but all in good time."

"When that time comes," Mark said, throwing Jack a glance. "Is there anything else in the book?"

Rose jerked her head towards them and gulped.

Jack remained expressionless, and looked Mark right in the eyes. "No, there isn't."

"Good," Mark said and turned away from them, heading back to the terrace, "because I'm starving."

Jack locked his eyes with hers, and she hated the dullness she found in them. She was sure they were an exact reflection of hers.

"You should eat something," he said, his voice full of repressed pain.

She replied flatly, "Yes, I should."

A strong thunderbolt echoed in the cloudy sky, illuminating a flash of silver light just as they went back into the house and joined the rest. It was going to be a wet night for their power-training session.

Fifteen: Last Words

There was this unexplainable sensation that told Rose the time was sooner than they were expecting, that Day was about to arrive. It could have been from the endless nightmares that choked her in her sleeps, or the faint screams she heard when the wind rushed through her hair. Either way, it was about to happen. That was for sure.

Since the time when the Chieftains came, the Seven Blue trained like never before. They were fiercer, faster, and much stronger than they had ever imagined. It became a simple task to guess each other's next move, as if mind reading was another gift from the Blue Water.

Rose made sure not to miss a single training session. Whether the Power or sword training, she found it easier to shut down her thoughts during these intense hours. Once again, she had fallen into the silent days where she rarely opened her mouth. She kept all the words in her brain, thinking about them day and night. It was much easier to contain her ever-growing worries when Jack was some distance away. He was always capable of fishing out her thoughts, and that was the last thing she wanted him to do. She had made her choice, and hoped she was not mistaken. But, it did not matter. The Healer had made her choice, and there was no turning back now.

Rose stood in her usual place in the balcony, the faint screams noticeable in the cool wind. The hairs on her arm stood up. Jack was on the roof, torturing himself with the thoughts that never left his mind, and she was thankful he felt her need to be alone. She heard the soft sound of a sliding door and saw somebody enter the guest room balcony.

"You're still awake," Mark said, leaning with his elbows on the rails. She straightened herself and faced ahead.

He snorted. "Of course, I'm the bad guy in this place."

She replied quietly, "No, you're not."

He came closer to her and stopped when the rails prevented him from going any farther. "Does that mean you've changed your mind about us?"

She sighed. "Mark, please don't start again."

"I was just asking, there is no harm in hoping a little. Just like you used to hope that Neverland existed."

Her lips were on the verge of a smile.

Mark dropped his head and giggled. "Come on, Rose. Show me that smile. Don't hold it back. Come on, now."

She turned her head the other side to hide the smile on her face.

"Very discreet." Mark smirked.

Her shoulders shook a little, and a few chuckles escaped her, ringing in the air like bells.

"That's better!"

Her laughter increased until she was unable to stop herself. She laughed until her stomach hurt and her eyes teared up.

"Blimey, I haven't heard you laugh that hard in such a long time."

She wiped her eyes, and stood silent for a moment, sensing the sudden tremble all over her body. The tears came rushing down again, but this time they were not from laughter.

"Rose?" Mark hovered in the air.

She held her hand out. "No! Stay where you are. I'm fine." He hesitated, but touched back down.

"Rose?" Came a deep voice from above her.

"I'm ok, Jack," she said and brushed away the tears, stifling the sobs. "I'm going to bed."

Once she entered the room, she buried her face in the pillow and gulped back the few sobs that tried to escape her. She tried keeping quiet to avoid waking Lilly and Heidi up, and lay motionless in bed, wrapping herself in the pleasant silence of the dark. A soft ringtone disturbed it.

"Yeah." Rose heard Heidi's sleepy voice whisper in the darkness. "Zane, it's three in the morning... You woke me up just to ask me that? Well, right now I'm not OK because I want to sleep... Oh, you will be sorry in the morning... Zane, go to sleep." The sound of the phone shutting echoed in the room, and Rose heard Heidi groan. She could not help but let one corner of her lips draw up into a smile.

The next morning, Rose went to check on her father who had been very supportive throughout these past few weeks.

"Dad?" Rose knocked on Bill's door. "Dad, are you in there?"

She found the door unlocked and entered the room. The curtains were closed and the bed was unmade. A few empty glasses laid on the table and some on the floor. She called him again and checked the bathroom, but there was no sign of him. Her eyes wide with shock, she raced down stairs and bumped into Dr. Liu.

"Where is Dad?"

"Mr. Peterson is somewhere safe."

"He's outside the protection!"

"There is no need to worry, Ms. Peterson. Your father is perfectly safe, even safer than here."

"But, he must be under the protection."

"The protection won't last for much longer. Once the Day arrives, it will lift from this house. Anyone could come and cause harm. I am a Protector, Rose. Your father is safe."

"I-I did not get to tell him goodbye."

"You will have all the time after the war, there is no need of farewells, Rose."

She looked the other way and gulped. "When did you take him?"

"This morning. He refused to come at first, but I did what was necessary to get him out of the house."

"You should've told me first, doctor."

"I'm sorry, Rose. I wanted things to go quietly, drawing the least amount of attention for his safety."

"Is everything all right?" Jack said, entering the house through the opened terrace doors and approaching them.

"No, it's not. Dr. Liu took my father away."

Jack nodded to him. "It's for his safety, Rose. He'll be fine."

"I wanted-" She broke off and looked at Jack's face. No, she could not give him the slightest hint of her choice. He had kept a lot of secrets from her before, and now she was keeping hers. "Very well. Come on, then, Jack."

"Rose?"

"I need to train. There are some weak moves I need to concentrate on-"

"Rose, you are pushing yourself too hard." It pained her to hear his concern, but she did not let it control her.

"I must be prepared to defend myself; that's the only way to keep you alive."

He opened his mouth, but quickly closed it. He nodded and ushered her out into the terrace where Lilly and Anthony were already partaking in a fierce combat composed of sword and power fighting. Heidi, Mark and Zane were training on some moves that required flight.

The rain had stopped for now. The grey clouds had very few gaps for the sun to prove its presence and shine its rays on the Seven Blue. Rose quickly grabbed her Longsword and walked into the clearing and beckoned for Jack to clash blades. But, before he could another blade met with hers.

"What's wrong with you?" Mark said, crossing his sword with hers. She was not gentle, and made a counterattack, causing him to defend his torso. "I can see that you're very calm."

"I don't want to talk, Mark." She deflected his thrust and attacked again.

A second blade clashed with hers, and she saw Mark take a few steps back, rolling his eyes, and rejoined Zane and Heidi.

"You still don't want to tell me what is your choice," Jack said, deflecting her blows.

"Yes," she said and evaded his deep eyes.

He remained silent for most of the training session.

But, Rose could tell that his mind was busy thinking about all the things he wished to ask her.

"Did you tell Mark?" He kept his voice low.

She suddenly stopped and looked at him. "No, I didn't. And, I'm not planning to. Jack, promise me you won't tell him."

He pressed his lips together and nodded. Their swords met again just as a loud thunderbolt echoed in the sky, startling them all.

"Here comes the rain again," Zane said.

"Lilly?" Rose heard the urgency in Jack's voice. She looked over and found Lilly scowling at the sky. Another thunderbolt struck. Suddenly horror conquered Lilly's face. Jack raced over to her as another thunderbolt cracked the sky open.

"They are ready," Lilly said. The wind picked up its pace and howled past their ears like a wild, raging wolf. Thunderbolts, one after the other struck in the sky, creating a constant web of them, almost like a pattern.

"Lilly." Anthony hurried over to her and held her.

"They have made their decision," she said, her wide eyes following the thunderbolts. "The Day is decided." She gasped.

"When, Lilly?" Jack cried over the deafening sound of thunder.

Her expression hardened and she turned slowly to Jack.

"Tonight."

Rose's heart dropped to her knees, and her breathing quickened. She stared at her mark.

This was it. The day she had been waiting for to complete her duty, and the one that Jack feared. It was all going to end, whether in tragedy or in happiness.

The wind stormed past the Seven Blue and sped up into the sky, pushing the grey clouds closer together and obscuring the setting sun. Everything fell into the twilight. They all stood looking at one another, as their minds digested their situation. But, there was no time left for them to waste.

"What-"

Mark was about to speak, but Jack held his hand out and ordered him to stop. Jack stood silent; he seemed to be alarmed.

Rose knew that look very well. It was the first expression she had seen on his face when he had first appeared mysteriously by the pond. He was listening to something. She held her breath and tried to listen over the howling of the wind. There were noises coming from within the trees, it sounded like the rattling of metal. Jack raised his sword up and the rest did the same. They clustered together, the sound getting closer.

From between the swaying trees, Rose saw a dozen of faces emerge. Their big, round eyes surveyed them like ghosts from the hallows of the trees. She casted her eyes around and saw that the rest had also noticed them. She found Jack's eyes locked with one of them and started to lower his sword.

"They are here," Jack announced.

One of the face owners stepped out from the shadows of the forest. He was an old man with an elaborated wooden cane. Rose recognized him at once.

"Zeyum," the Great Chieftain said. "The Day has been decided, and your army is ready. They are indeed normal sons of Nara, but do not forget we are people born with fighting skills the Spirit thrust upon us. Our great ancestors have served the Blue Water just the same, and we are ready to do it once more."

"Great Chieftain," Dr. Liu said, rushing over to them. "Is the Army ready?"

"Yes, Protector," the Great Chieftain said. He looked behind at the trees and raised his arm. "Zeyum, meet your warriors."

More faces popped out from between the trees and advanced towards them. Young and old men appeared in battle gear, local wooden shields in one hand and long, sharp spears in the other. They had war paint spread over their faces and bare chests. Traditional-leather war bracelets were strapped around their muscled arms and legs, giving them a certain look of belonging and strength. Their faces were strong and, now that they were closer, their eyes carried determination and courage. They stood tall against the restless wind, while the knives and weapons hanging from the belts around their waist rattled. When Rose casted with her eyes deeper into the forest, she found out that nearly every single tree sheltered a dozen brave warriors. They seemed to exceed a thousand.

Jack looked around at them, disbelief evident in his eyes. She only guessed how he must have been feeling. Finally, he was going to face the pursuers that had haunted him for most of his life. He nodded at his warriors and they all bowed their heads to him in return.

Tears gathered in Rose's eyes.

"Zeyum," Dr. Liu said, "may I have a word with you and the Great Chieftain in private."

Rose watched as he took Jack and the old man a couple of paces away.

"Not thirteen, Mark." Rose heard Zane say.

"Blimey," Mark said in awe.

"Lilly," Anthony said. Rose turned around and went over to her. She was still in shock from what had happened. "Was that Baas, Lilly?"

She nodded. "He drew out the patterns in the sky. He knew I would be able to read them."

Anthony cursed.

"Do you know where they are?" Mark asked.

"Down in the valley."

Rose frowned. Could it be the valley bellow Jack's tree house? But, the thought dwelled only briefly in her mind when she saw Jack approaching them, his face stern.

"Seven Blue, are you ready?" he said in his powerful voice as they all nodded.

"Good," Jack said, "because in a few hours we will put everything we learned to the final test. Those brave warriors will join us, and every one of us will be surrounded by an appointed team. That was their ancestor's duty, and today they will complete theirs, just like us. Seven Blue, get yourselves ready. We will meet the Niago Siathe in the valley at midnight."

Rose counted the hours and realized that they only had five hours left. There was still much she wanted to do before everything turned into darkness. The others went back to the terrace and started to prepare; the color had disappeared from their faces.

"Rose," Jack said, grabbing her attention. "Dr. Liu has especially handpicked a team of the finest warriors to protect – prevent any harm from touching you." He clenched his jaws.

She locked her eyes with his and allowed herself to sink into their amber color one more time, maybe the last time. She took in every detail of his face, engraving his image in her memory in case everything she feared happened this dreadful night. She felt his hands grab her waist and he pulled her against his body, their lips brushing against each other.

"I won't ever forgive myself if anything happened to you. Please tell me you've made the choice with your mind."

She pressed her lips to his and took a profound breath, filling her being with his smell. "I will always love you, Jack Casper."

He replied back with a firm kiss and looked at her, his eyebrows woven in agony. "You have no idea how much I love you."

She pulled her lips into a feeble smile.

"Zeyum," the Great Chieftain called Jack. There were more than a dozen of young ladies standing with baskets full of bright fabric. "These daughters of Nara will help the Seven Blue prepare for the Great War. They will dress you in the traditional war colors, they bring good luck and may the Spirits be by your side."

The girls also had the traditional clothes strapped around their ankles and wrists, and some had them embroiled with their braided, black hair. One very thin girl, but beautiful with catlike eyes, started wrapping Rose's right wrist with a wide threaded strap with the colors bright blue, red, and green. She also put a similar, but thinner, one around her ankles. Rose watched another girl do the same to Jack. When they had finished, the girls turned around to Jack and bowed.

"Zeyum," one of them said. "Please, bring us our sisters back. They were kidnapped."

Rose tried to hide her shock. These were the sisters of the compelled Dancers. She noticed the grave disturbance on Jack's face. He forced a smile and nodded.

Reassured with that, both girls joined the others who by then had reached the rest of the members in the terrace and started to bless them with the colors. Without exchanging another glance with Jack, Rose turned around and headed to her room, locking the door behind her. Opening her bedside-table drawer and pulling out a blank paper and pen, she sat down and started to write.

She wrote for half an hour until a knock on the door sounded. She hurriedly wrote down the last words, folded the paper, and pocketed it in her pocket. When she opened the door, she found Mark standing in front of her, all dressed and ready with his sword strapped around his waist with a leather belt. His face was familiarly pale.

"I just wanted to," he started, "say that I'm sorry... I know that it's kind of too late, but you know me."

She half smiled.

"What is it?" he said.

"I remembered the last time you knocked on my door just to apologize. I was so mad at you that I had to fight the urge to punch you right in the face."

He twitched. "You mean this resembles a bad memory?"

"In some way. You never meant it back then. You were never sorry."

He looked to the ground, unable to meet her eyes. "I'm really sorry, Rose."

"I know," she said. "I'm sorry, too. For all the pain I caused you. Forgive me, I never meant to hurt you."

"Rose-"

"Promise me, Mark. That you'll live happy."

"Let's not jump into the future. We don't know what will happen tonight."

"I know, but let's just say that – that you won't get harmed and made it out alive. I need you to promise me that you'll move on with your life."

"Not that same talk, Rose. Nothing is going to happen to you. And, stop make-believing. It won't work here."

She kept her mouth shut. Only if you knew, she thought, what was written in the last few pages of the book. Stepping closer to him, she wrapped her arms around his torso, and felt his arms lock her inside his hug.

"I called Anne," he said.

She released him and stared up at him.

"I had to listen to her voice, in case I don't." He gulped. "I don't think I ever will again."

"You will, Mark."

"No, I don't think so. Let's face it. I've used my second chance in this life. Of course, it's a kind of a blessing, a way out. But, second chances are usually shorter than the first."

"Don't say that," she said, a lump forming in her throat. "It doesn't have to be that way."

"Well, if it is that way, take care of Anne for me. Will you?"

She nodded, although she was sure she would not have to.

At the end of the corridor, Anthony popped his head out of the guest room and called Mark.

"Wait." Rose stopped him before he could turn away from her and kissed over his cheekbone lightly. He stood there for a minute, smiling, then left her doorway.

She went back into her room and crossed to the balcony. It was night by then, only three hours left until midnight. The wind had stilled slightly, but there was still a strong stream of biting cold air. The moon was barely visible amidst the thick clouds. Rose hoped it would not rain.

The warriors had started to spread around the house, and some stood guarding it. She spotted Jack immersed in deep conversation with the Great Chieftain; he was possibly informing him of the war plan.

There was one thing she wanted to do before the Protection fell, something she had always done when her head was filled with worries. A visit to her old friend, the pond. She soared in the air, making sure that no one spotted her, and landed somewhere in the middle of the path. But, the path was not empty, the rest of the warriors extended deeper into the forest. She just hoped that none of them had invaded the pond.

Fortunately for her, the pond and its clearing were empty. As if nothing had changed, the mist had risen and danced on top of the sweet water like white ghosts, radiating silver light against the gleam of the moon. She walked to the protection's border and knelt down, yearning for a last dip into the pond's clear water. Her tears could not resist, and fell down her cheeks. She was going to miss everything about this place, its people and the memories it held.

"Rose." She heard Jack's deep voice behind her. She quickly wiped her tears away and straightened up. He had a soft smile on his lips. "Here was our first meeting."

She achieved a smile and nodded. "I was uncertain if you were real or not."

He raised his eyebrows, and stepped closer. "I thought so, too. You talked quite freely to a total stranger."

"Well, you made me feel safe. You always do."

He lowered his head. "If only I could make you feel that way for the rest of your life, I'd be the happiest person."

Her heart skipped. "You do, Jack. You saved me from many things."

He entwined his hands with hers and touched their foreheads together. "Please, tell me that you made the choice with your mind. I will love you no matter what you choose."

She remained silent.

"Don't do something that you'll regret later."

"Don't worry about that," she said. "I won't."

He knelt down where she had been sitting and pulled her with him. They sat beside each other, sharing the silence before the storm, and allowed their thoughts to dwell on this moment. She knew it may very well be their last.

***

"Seven Blue," Jack said, standing in front of his army.

"The time has come to face what we have been destined for. In a few minutes the protection will lift. We will no more be protected, only our Power and swords will do so." He eyed every one of them. "We are powerful as one. We won't make it alive if trust is not our backbone. We need to trust not only in one another, but also in ourselves. Forget the past. Don't let it be your downfall. What was done is done, and all you can do is change the future. Not the present for all of us are stuck in this mission, and there is no way out except by fulfilling our destiny."

Rose listened to him like the rest; even the warriors had turned their ears to him. Closing her eyes, she tried to push away the images of her night dreams, the ones which she always saw Jack in — No. She was not going to give into her fears anymore. She had found a solution, and she would carry it out no matter what. Jack had a heavy price to pay for her protection, and she found a way to pay him back.

"We have trained day and night," Jack continued, "for this day. I know we are ready. We will fight tonight for avenging what was taken from us; our families and loved ones, our moments of joy, and our dreams for life." He paused. "Every drop of blood we'll spill tonight will be for what we have lost. After tonight, we will be free from the shadows that haunted us. Fight for your freedom!"

A loud roar echoed through the air. The warriors had raised their spears and shields, praising and crying with excitement.

"Blue Water Army!" Jack's voice dominated their ears. "To the valley!"

The thousand warriors turned towards the forest and marched, the sound of drums reverberating the war beats. Rose heard their song, their tones vibrating in the wind which had picked up its pace again. She spotted Dr. Liu and ran over to him before he could follow the warriors into the forest.

"Rose?" he said. He, too, was fully armored and dressed in the war colors.

"Doctor," she said and removed the paper she had written earlier from her pocket. She handed it to him. "Please, read this if things do not go as planned."

He frowned at the paper. "I don't understand."

"Just read it in the presence of Bill, and the Seven Blue when the time is right. Make sure that Jack and Mark know what's inside."

"Rose, is this your will?"

She ignored the statement. "Promise me you'll do that."

He sighed, understanding. "Very well. If that's your wish." He buried the paper deep into his pocket.

"Thank you very much," she said, "Dr. Liu, for everything you've done to help Mark and Jack."

He smiled. "That is my duty. I'll see you soon."

She watched as the forest swallowed him into its darkness. A loud rumble of thunder struck the sky, sending her heart lurching inside her chest. She turned and rejoined the Seven Blue. Jack stood in front of the path and faced the Seven Blue. Rose made a last survey of her friends. They were all wearing the same war colors and the leather belts that held their Longswords. The boys had war colors painted on their bare chests, indicating bravery and courage in front of death. And, the girls had war accessories in their hair and ankles.

"Are you ready?" the Leader said. They gave him a strong nod. "I hope to see you all again here."

Rose squeezed the hilt of her sword.

"Let's keep hoping," Mark said.

"No farewells," Lilly said. "They bring bad luck. Let's get this done with."

Another thunderbolt cracked the sky. "To your places, everyone," Jack said.

Simultaneously, Mark, Anthony, Lilly, Zane, and Heidi soared up into the sky and waited for Jack to lead. Her eyes followed Mark as he took off.

She looked back at Jack and found him rushing over to her. With a single move, he cupped her face and laid a kiss on her quivering lips. It was like no other kiss he had ever given her. There was something different about it, as if he knew it would be the last kiss they would ever share.

"Remember me, Rose," he whispered. "You'll find me in your dreams like you always do."

"I will." The words trembled out of her mouth. She did not want to let go of him, and was ready to give all that she had to freeze this moment in time.

He held her hand and pulled her up with him to where the others were waiting. They hovered in the air for a little, watching the process of the warriors as they curved their way through the blackness of the forest and towards the valley. At the far side of the valley, black smoke rose from the mountains ahead. There was motion visible among the trees descending from those mountains.

Jack let out a low whistle, heard over the cry of the wind, signaling their procession. As planned, Rose went over to Mark and flew beside him. That was the plan; she was under Mark's protection.

Sixteen: The Battle of the Valley

The valley stretched under the moonlight like a black carpet. The waterfall was clear from where they were hovering above the valley, its water snaking a river at the far side just where the thick trees marked the continuation of the forest. Beneath them, the warriors had halted at the bottom of the cliff and clustered together in neat formations. The Seven Blue landed in front of them.

Rose watched the clearing of the valley in front of her, the silver moonlight throwing its rays on it as though it understood the significance of this event. The clearing stretched out until it reached the mountains ahead. Squinting, she saw some movement from where the black smoke seemed to emanate. The sound of war drums echoed across the wide stretch of land so that she did not know which side was playing it.

"Places everyone," Jack said. "The Dancers are almost here. Men, remember don't look at them under any circumstances."

She raised her head and glimpsed a dozen or so figures making their way towards them, moving in soft steps. As they got closer, Rose saw the figures appear to be tall, young women in striking white dresses that seemed to glow their own light, contrasting with their ink-black hair that flowed behind them like a sheet of silk. Pulling her eyes away from them, she quickly turned to Jack and made sure he had his back to the seducing gestures of their hands. She saw Lilly guarding Anthony's eyes, and Heidi held Zane and Mark's arms, preventing them from turning their bodies around.

When the boys seemed stable, Lilly and Heidi came over. "Jack, I see the lead dancer. Heidi will strike her down with a spear."

Rose looked back at the Dancers and, sure enough, the lead dancer was the most elegant one of them. However, her hair distinguished her the most; the tips of her hair seemed to radiate a silver light. She moved in ways that were so graceful that Lilly's grace seemed meaningless beside it. Her legs and arms danced to the beats of the drums, the bracelets around her ankles chimed as she stomped the ground. The other dancers imitated her every move, as if their hands and feet were strapped with invisible wires, which only she could control.

Darting her eyes towards Jack, she saw the copper strands in his hair reflect the faintest silver light, almost like in the hair of the lead dancer. She moved closer to him and touched a single strand, realizing the irony behind it. He was one of them. Their blood ran in his veins, the same blood which nourished their destroyer's body. They had given birth to the very person whom they wished to kill. To him, the son of one of their members.

He certainly knew what was going in her mind for he feebly smiled and removed her hand. "I don't consider myself one of them. We are very different."

Suddenly a dreadful cry vibrated in their ears. A long spear had pierced the lead dancer right in the chest. She cried out, signaling the war cry, and dropped to the ground. Her dead body fell; the white dress stained with blood. The war had begun.

From behind Rose, the warriors banged their spears on the shields and let out an excited cry. However, the other side of the clearing remained silent. Nothing could be heard or seen other than the black smoke which seemed to act as a shield.

A silent minute had passed when suddenly a rain of ignited arrows soared in the air from amidst the black smoke and aimed at the Blue Water Army. With her sword clutched in her hands, Rose watched Lilly gather a fierce wind and shot it at the arrows, bombarding and sweeping them out of range. She then sent a blowing wind at the Dark Army and blew the smoke away, revealing what was beneath. Even though they were far enough that Rose could only see a cluster of figures mingled together, she saw how Lilly's eyes were fixed on a certain figure, a look of disgust on her face.

Steadily the figures glided forward like the black smoke, which had covered them. They came close until Rose could identify them. The Niago Siathe wore black hoods just like the ones she had seen before, except they held spears and large axes that winked at her under the moonlight. Behind them stood warriors with silver feathers wrapped around their arms and legs, Rose guessed these were Niago Siathe's war colors. The army continued until the mountains ahead. She hoped they did not extend beyond them. The Blue Water Army was barely half their size.

A tall man stood at the very front, dressed in a black cloak that swept the ground behind him as he alone marched a few steps to the front. His skin was dark, and his hair had the same lit tips as Jack. A great hooked blade dragged on the ground as he held it with one arm by his side. If Rose had thought Death could not be personified, she would have believed that Death itself was walking in front of her. She tried to pull her eyes away from the Execution sword that was especially designed to decapitate Jack.

"Jack Casssssper," the Dark Leader said, his guttural voice echoing throughout the valley. "It has been a long time, my friend."

Jack glared at him, his face dark even under the moonlight.

"Do not," the Dark Leader said, "tell me you have not enjoyed the last ten years. It was fascinating to watch you run like a puppy back to your filthy pit to hide. However, the best part was your sister. Of course, I knew she was the little bird that flew to you with the news. Yes, Jack. I made sure the fabricated news reached you."

"You will pay, Baas!" Jack bellowed.

Baas opened his mouth and shrilling laughter filled the air, accompanied by a crack of thunder. "I heard that you are the one who is ready to pay a heavy price for a sssspecial Rossssse. Well, good thing I brought the *Ngulu* on this glorioussss event."

Rose felt her hands grasp her sword tighter. Baas's white eyes lingered on her for a brief second, sending chills down her spine. Just then she remembered those pair of eyes. She had seen them once a long time ago from her window, watching her from the darkness of the forest. She turned her head to Jack and found it difficult to describe his face. He was glowering at him with unfathomed loathing.

A great stream of fierce wind roared at Baas, but he was not affected, his cloak merely swayed. "Always fierce," Baas said, facing Lilly. "Just how I like it. But, my fight is not with you. I am here to discard of your little brother. There is a world waiting for me to control, and I am very impatient."

"You bastard!" Lilly retorted.

Baas punched the ground with the *Ngulu* and the clouds rumbled, crying its first few drops of rain. They fell on Rose like sharp pieces of shattered glass, scratching the skin on her arms and shoulders. But, that was nothing compared to the pain they had trained to endure.

The wind rushed past them, reverberating the thunder of drums in their ears and the rumble of the clouds. Baas retraced his steps back to his army, allowing them to surround him. The hooded warriors raised their spears and swords and walked forward, lessening the distance between the two armies. The Blue Water warriors marched as well.

The sound of soaring arrows filled the air one more time, but this time from their sides. Mark lit them on fire as the arrows pierced the air and fell upon the Niago Siathe, the front line falling to the ground. But, there were more coming from behind the mountains. She looked at Jack just to see him race to the other side with his Longsword raised on top of his head. His fight was with the Leader, but first he had to find him.

The sound of clashing metal boomed in the valley as the warriors from both sides collided with fury together, the sky cracked with thunder. Rose held her sword firmly, ready for anything. She darted her eyes around, looking for any of the injured to heal. She glimpsed Anthony fighting a group of the feathered warriors. Rose paid attention to their moves and was shocked at how fast and light they were; she had to make sure to avoid clashing swords with them.

Nevertheless, Anthony's strength won over them and he soon swept them off their feet with a beating from a wave of water. Close by him, Rose noticed Heidi shooting down some warriors with throwing knives and fighting a couple of the feathered warriors at the same time. A spear came rushing past Rose's waist and sank into Heidi's thigh.

"Cover!" Rose yelled and sped to where Heidi had fallen, twisting in the muddy ground with pain. Anthony, as he was the nearest, conjured the rain within his control and blasted Heidi's opponents into a swirling wave that instantly prevented them from breathing.

"Hold on." Rose held the spear and tugged at it, her hands shaking as she tightened her muscles. She pulled it out, trying as best as she could to prevent it from tearing up any more flesh. Covering the deep, bloodied hole in Heidi's thigh, she took a deep breath and focused on the wound. Her head spun for a second as a chunk of energy left her body.

Quickly the girls stood up before any blade or spear could pierce their backs. But, before Rose could turn around, Heidi abruptly pulled her behind and thrust her Longsword forward. Rose heard the sound of metal penetrating flesh. When she looked at the ground, she found a dead warrior who was about to strike her down with a short knife.

"Thank you," Rose said to her over the roar of the war. "Watch out!" Heidi pointed at two hooded warriors approaching them, their bloodied swords clutched in their hands.

Her heart raced. She felt her muscles contract as Rose met their blades and deflected the blows. She tried to recall her training with Jack, but her fear chased the memories away. The first warrior tried to unarm her with a short knife, with force on the middle of the sword. He increased the weight on her blade, intending to tear it out of her grasp, but she propelled it upwards and sent the knife flying from his hand. Relieved that she had remembered her training during the fight, she used the flexibility of the Longsword to surprise him with a blow to the legs, injuring him, while the second warrior aimed at her throat with determination; but the blade miraculously missed her skin. The wet ground was not helping her keep her footing, but she successfully blocked his blow and shifted to the right, causing her opponent to scatter aimlessly forward. Taking advantage, she struck him in the back and instantly turned just in time to ward off the injured one's wide blow with a second knife that she had seen emerge from beneath the cloak.

But, before she could finish him off, the man shook inside his cloak and smoke rose from his mouth, ears, and even his unseeing eyes. She stared at him, letting her breathing catch up, and winced at her blood-stained sword. She could not believe she had killed a person with her own hands.

"Rose, are you hurt?" Mark jumped in front of her. There was a slash across his arm, and his is face was covered in dirt.

She hurriedly grabbed him and took care of the wound, sensing more of her energy dissolve. "No, I'm OK. Where is Jack?"

"He's alive, don't worry."

"Where is he, Mark?" Her voice was loud.

"Where he should be, fighting the Dark Leader. Jack was right, the Longsword is a great advantage to us. Until now, we are ahead."

Rose allowed herself to breathe again. A thunder rumbled far in the distance and the rain thickened. Mark grabbed her hand and hauled her across the wet ground and over some dead bodies; some were the Blue Water warriors. She tried not to look at the chopped off heads and pieces of limbs scattered all over. Mark shoved her to a group of about twenty strong and young warriors standing under the cliff and partially hidden behind the trees. They encircled her once they saw her, trapping her like a bird inside a human cage.

"What's this?" she said.

"They'll make sure no harm reaches you," Mark replied.

"How am I supposed to fight if I'm trapped like this?"

He pressed his lips.

"Mark?" She tried to look at him, but the warriors were taller than her that she could barely see Mark. "You better tell me what is happening right now."

"These are Jack's orders, Rose." She heard him say.

"Since when do you obey Jack's orders!"

But, he had already dashed off. She could not stay here, she must get out now before it was too late. Her eyes must be kept on Jack and Mark all the time to be prepared when the time arrives. She wouldn't be able to carry out her plan this way. Rose tried to push her way through the warriors, but they would not budge no matter how hard she tried. Finding there was no way out like that, Rose looked up and lifted herself off the ground. However, her escape plan did not work. Two warriors grabbed her feet and prevented her from flying up any farther. But, at least, she was able to see the battlefield from the top of their heads.

Every one of her friends had at least five swords battling them. Mark alone was surrounded by a dozen. His sword swung in the air, warding off blows, and his power burned them down like dominos. Once he had finished them off, more hooded and feathered warriors encompassed him.

A little more deep into the Niago Siathe side, Lilly stormed away her assaulters and choked them like Rose had seen her do before. In the middle of the valley, and where the hooded warriors condensed, Jack fought Baas in one-on-one combat, putting him off balance with the use of the Longsword. But, Baas was fast and a cunning fighter. He got up faster than he fell, and swung the Ngulu in the air. Jack lurched backwards and defended his neck with his sword, holding it with both hands on top of his head. With both swords coiled together, Jack sprang into the air and whirled above his surprised opponent, bringing Baas along with him. He tugged at the *Ngulu* and Baas fell under the implied weight.

However, his opponent possessed great rebound moves and twirled back up like a snake would from its hole to snare its prey. With his arm raised above him, Baas lashed Jack with a sharp stream of wind and sent him stumbling away and smacking his head on a rock.

Rose cupped her mouth and gasped. Instantly, she aroused the greater force of her healing abilities and discharged them to Jack. She swayed a little out of balance, and her eyes tried to see through the rain, but her image was a blur. She could only glimpse the shadow of Jack bolt up again.

An arrow whizzed by her head, narrowly missing her ear and deafening it for a few moments. One of the warriors holding her tugged her down and forced her feet to the ground. When she regained her balance, she tried to shake him off, but he was stronger than her and determined not to let go.

It was more horrifying to hear the sound of clashing swords and the cries of the warriors as they were struck down than to watch it as it happened. Rose had no idea who those screams belonged to, and who was dying. All that she could see were the backs of the warriors surrounding her in a very tight circle. Her unconscious mind filled with her fears and threatened her hopes with the images of her nightmares, flashing Jack's chained legs and arms in front of her. What if by then she won't have enough energy to save him from an impending doom? What if her powers disobeyed her desires? Adrenalin rushed through her blood, and her heart hammered in her ears. What if she drank from the Water a second time to double her strength? She had to break free of this prison. Now!

The sky above her roared, sending constant rain down upon them. Even though it collided with her skin like sharp razors, it washed down her sweating back and hair, helping her refocus. The wind sped by, and Rose raised her head, pleased to sniff fresh air only to find it carrying with it the scent of blood and water mingled with the wet odor of mud. Shielding her eyes, she glimpsed the tree house on the cliff above her. She stared at it, a plan forming in her head. She tried again to shove the warriors away, but it was hopeless.

A sudden booming sound vibrated from somewhere near her. Rose jerked her head around, but she could not see a thing. The warriors surrounding her started to shuffle, and Rose heard the clash of metal. They were being attacked.

The very front row tried to fight off the feathered warriors, but they came in with fury and determination and blasted off some the warrior's heads. The ones behind them quickly hurried to take their place and protect the Healer, but they too were massacred. She had no time to pull out her sword for a couple of the Blue Water warriors grabbed her and tried to hide her. A knife plunged into the back of the one holding her, and he dropped dead to the ground.

Finally free from their protection, however, terrified of the five warriors that were now chasing her, she ran with her sword drawn to the verdant side of the valley. She raced into the dark trees and flew over the river to its other bank. The feathered warriors in pursuit haltered and regarded the water with hesitation. For a second Rose thought they were afraid from the water, but they promptly leapt the river's width in one jump and landed in front of Rose's pale face.

She gave a shriek as her sword met theirs. They were five on one, there was no way she could defeat them all and still survive. For sure they had sensed her waver, the closest one to her thrusted a hand forward and scratched her arm with a short knife. She felt her energy draw, healing herself.

Her image blurred, almost unseeing the wide blow that was about to pierce her between the ribs. She concentrated on defending herself, until she could find a way out. She deflected them off until they reached the thicker trees. Rose plunged behind a tree, fleeing a wide blow by one of their spears. She took a deep breath and soared behind another tree, trying to distract them. She leaned against the wet moss crawling on the bark and listened as more steps approached her. Trying not to produce a single crack, she placed her hand on one of the massive tree roots and turned to look from the corner of her eyes. Three Blue Water warriors had followed her chase and come to save her.

The fight broke out again between them. Rose clutched her sword and hauled herself up, but stayed concealed behind the tree. She darted her eyes around and found her exit. Twirling away from the tree, Rose raced back to the river and jumped over it when suddenly an excruciating sensation burned her body, throwing her out of balance.

She fell head down on the other bank of the river; her lower body plunged into the freezing water. A cry escaped her. She clasped the wet ground, embedding her nails in it, and tried to take a deep breath. But, when she tried to move a severe pain hit her, sending electrical shocks through her body. Her eyes watered and felt her side was about to split open. Whenever she made an effort to move, her arms shook under her weight and her legs were already numb.

The water around her lower body had turned scarlet red. Looking down, she saw a short knife had stabbed her in the side, just below the ribs. It belonged to one of the warriors that pursued her. She forced in a deep breath, gulping the pain. She must not be heard in case the feathered warriors back there had defeated the Blue Water and came back to find her. Rose reached to her side and drew the knife out with shaking hands. She waited while the wound healed itself, the excruciating pain slowly leaving her body.

With what little energy left in her, Rose heaved herself up and leaned against a tree. The ground under her feet spun and her already blurred vision degraded further. She raised her head up and looked at the towering cliff, but she only saw its great shadow lurk above her. She had to get there, but she was not sure how she would with barely any energy left in her. But, she must. The energy she had won't be enough to carry out her plan. She must be prepared before it was too late.

One thing she was sure of was that it was nearly dawn. The dark sky of the night started to turn violet. However, the rain continued showering them, and the wind promised an ill-fated end. She stood leaning against the tree, staring at the battle scene and trying to identify the figures, but that was impossible for her now. What if she was too late? She thought, pushing herself off the tree and heading towards the cliff. What if they had already killed him? While she was staggering from one tree to the other, she heard a soft noise from behind her. Her heart quickened, and hurried her step.

"Zane!" Rose breathed out with relief. He had bloodstains all over his body and his black locks were grey from the faded black ashes it inhabited.

"Rose." He held her falling body. "What happened?"

She forced herself to stand straight, but her last healing process had depleted all her strength. "Take me to the tree house," she whispered.

He looked at her as if she had lost touch with the world. Before they could waste time, Rose told Zane of what was written in the book and of her plan, and asked him to help her. She pointed up at the tree house and allowed him to carry her, closing her eyes in case his abnormal speed further dizzied her.

And, it was a good thing she did. Rose felt her heart jolt as Zane took off. The rain smacked them harder as he sped against it, and the wind roared in their ears, freezing her face. Then almost instantly everything settled at once as Zane put her down on the wooden platform. She surveyed the tree house, but had no idea where to look. The small room was where she searched in first. She had to be quick for her strength could only make her move her arms, and she had to go back to the valley as soon as she could.

She started rummaging underneath the bed, but there was nothing. She surveyed the room for any hidden cabinets, but also, none were there. The wind outside howled louder, swaying the tree a little. It terrified her to know that Baas was behind the wind, and that Jack was fighting him all by himself.

Concluding that it was not in there, she exited the room and dug through both shelves with Zane's help. Their hunt was fruitless.

"Um," Zane said, holding something in his hand, "is this what you are looking for, Rose?"

"Yes!" She snatched the flask of Blue Water from him. "Where did you find it?"

"Surprisingly in my pocket."

She dropped her shoulders.

"You had it with you all this time!"

"No," he said, puzzled.

"Never mind," she said. "I need my energy back, doubled if I can. I hope this will work." She had a theory that like before, the Blue Water would give her renewed energy. Rose gulped down a mouthful and felt the bursting energy explode within her veins. Her image cleared out and sharpened, and the color returned to her face. It had worked!

"Rose." Zane's tone was urgent. "We have a tiny, little problem."

She held her breath and looked to where he was pointing at half a dozen floating hooded warriors, their huge axes swaying from their hands like a pendulum. Tik tok, tik tok. They had come to take her, to use her as a weapon against Jack. That was certain, but she must not allow them to take advantage of her.

"They can't see us," Rose said. "They know that we are inside, but they can't see through the protection shield. The Blue Water protects itself."

Zane paced the platform, noting every possible way to get through them as fast as he could without giving them a chance to catch up. Rose looked down at the valley bellow and saw that a cloud of fog had crept over the battlefield, preventing her from seeing whom was who. Where was Jack? And Mark? She looked up to the mountains ahead, and her heart dropped. There were more warriors approaching the valley from behind the mountains.

"Zane, I must get down there now!"

His eyes opened wide. "Got it!" he said and rushed to her. He carried her and flew vertically down the cliff, surprising their opponents. Rose felt her heart jump to her throat as they fell down with extraordinary speed. She hugged her sword, fearing it would suddenly fly out of her hands. They landed at the bottom of the cliff, amidst the shadows of the trees.

Seventeen: The Healer's Choice

Rose leaned against her sword, trying to catch her breath. She made a note that if she ever survived, she would never fly with Zane again.

"Rose, hurry!" Zane said, holding out his sword as he watched the hooded figures descend.

Her head jerked around the battlefield, but she found no sign of Jack or Mark. Terror stabbed her hammering heart. She helplessly squinted through the fog and glimpsed a familiar mass of blonde hair stained with blood and mud. Heidi stumbled across the valley, throwing arrows and spears as she went. At the side, near the forest, Rose saw Anthony use the river as a weapon, blasting the massive number of his attackers, and Lilly was close by him circling her hands in fierce strokes and sweeping her assaulters away. The Seven Blue were still fighting, but there was something different about them; the color in their faces started to fade and their muscles were for sure screaming under their skin.

"Zane!" She cried over the rumble of the thunder. "Go find Mark and stay with him." He nodded and promised her he will after he finished off their pursuers.

Nourished with fresh energy in her blood, Rose raced through the fog, jumping over heaps of dead bodies and abandoned weapons. The ground was more slippery than ever, muddy with wet dirt and blood. There were several trees on the other side of the valley on fire. Her heart gave a bolt, and she froze in her tracks. Black smoke mixed with the fog stung her eyes, and she felt the taste of ashes in her mouth. Even though the rain was vehemently pouring on them, it failed to wash away the fog and cease the fire. A terrible sensation filled her cells as she darted around for Mark, but he was nowhere to be seen.

"Rose!" Came a voice from behind her, and she heard the sound of blades.

Lurching around, she found Dr. Liu soaked in mud fighting off two feathered warriors that were coming at her. She quickly joined in and blocked a blow that aimed for the doctor's back. With a swift inflection from her sword, Rose caused her opponent to stumble to the ground. Making sure her feet were fixed to the ground, she raised her sword to strike, but the feathered warrior leapt back up with a spear in his hand. He thrust his weapon at her. Rose winced as she felt the cold metal slit her arm.

The feathered warrior took advantage of her surprise and crouched to the ground, spinning the spear in his hand and striking her knee. Rose felt her leg sway out of balance and she slipped on the wet ground, falling into a mud puddle. Her Longsword flew from her hand as she tried to break her fall with her arms, but the wet ground was not helping at all. With the rain slashing into her eyes, she barely could see above as she lay on her back. A great shadow lurked above her, and she saw the point of her opponent's spear flash against the thunder. He raised it above his head and lunged it at Rose.

The spear plunged into the ground, missing her by seconds. She had rolled away from the strike and plunged for her sword. The feathered warrior removed the spear and re-attacked before she could take a breath. Holding the sword above her head with both hands, she blocked the blow again. Her hands shook as her opponent pushed down at her with his spear, he had the advantage of his upper position.

She tried to stand up, pushing him away, but she was fighting from a weak angle. Her muscles screeched under the pressure she forced, and her arms started to lose their strength. The silver point of the spear came closer to her neck, ready to pierce her throat at any moment. She was upholding it with all her might that she barely could breathe. At any moment now her arms would give up on her.

A splatter of blood suddenly spurted on her face just as a sword protruded the feathered warrior's torso. Rose quickly rolled away before he could fall on her and leapt to her legs, catching her breath.

"Thank you, doctor," Rose shouted above the gushing rain.

He ran up to her, breathing heavily. "Did you make your choice?"

She frowned and looked around, making sure there were no assaulters hiding in the fog.

She nodded at him. "Yes, I did."

"Remember, you can choose only one, or you'll pay your life as a price!"

"I know," she said and escaped his eyes.

"I am aware that it is a hard choice, but you must make a sacrifice."

"I am making one!"

Four hooded warriors materialized from between the black fog and glided towards them. Dr. Liu grabbed her arm before she could raise her sword and told her to leave.

"I'll take care of them," he said. "You must go and keep an eye on your choice."

She stared at him, unable to leave him outnumbered.

However, she turned around and forced herself away. Before she could go any further, she heard the doctor yell, and found her legs taking her back to where she had left him.

Dr. Liu lay on the ground, his face up towards the sky and his hand free of any weapon. Her eyes widened as a pool of blood poured from behind his head. Rose knelt beside him and found his eyes opened in shock, reflecting the last images of horror he had seen.

"Doctor!" She shook him, but he was already gone. She could not help the dead. Two pair of cold hands grasped her arms and squeezed it. Her shock pushed her to flight, but the hands tightened their clench, the nails plunging into her flesh like the sharp claws of an eagle. She jerked her head and found the hands belonged to two hooded warriors.

Even though she knew there was absolutely no use to try and escape them, Rose tried to push them off with her arms and legs, kicking at them. One of them released a hand and put it against her throat. Rose froze when she felt a cold knife set on her throat, right above her main artery that throbbed with fright. That was it; they had caught her. She dreaded what was about to happen.

Anthony, Lilly and Heidi could not believe their eyes and rushed to fight them off, but the hooded warrior threatened to slice her throat on the spot. Her captors dragged her to the middle of the battlefield and forced her down on her knees, the knife still on her throat. Rose looked up from the ground and saw Jack and Baas a little further engaged in fierce combat. Her eyes widened with shock at Jack's appearance. Several cuts and slits covered his bare chest and back that dripped blood to the ground as he forced himself to continue fighting Baas. She dropped her head down, feeling her heart in her mouth.

One of the captors grabbed her hair and tugged her head up. She gave out a shriek of pain thinking her scalp was about to leave her head. The wind carried her scream and roared passed Jack. He instantly froze in his place and stared at her, unseeing Baas aim a blow with the *Ngulu* to his head that sent him flat to the ground.

She opened her mouth to call his name, but her voice had abandoned her.

Jack! Get up! She yelled in her mind.

Two hooded warriors hustled to him before he could force himself up, and pinned him to the ground. A third warrior approached him, trailing long, black chains behind him. Rose gasped, and the captor pressed the knife deeper on her skin. Baas stood over Jack and placed his foot on the side of his face, pressing his head in the mud. He looked at Rose and drew his mouth into what Rose believed to be a shadow of a smile. His free hand appeared from beneath his cloak and signaled them to bring her closer. They did not bother to straighten her up, instead, they dragged her to where Jack was, the skin on her knees peeled off as it scraped the sharp remnants of broken blades scattered in the mud. She winced and resisted screaming for Jack's sake.

The sound of rattling chains echoed in the sudden silence of the vacancy, both armies surrounded the scene to witness the significant moment of the legend. The hooded warrior tugged Jack's arms to his back and shackled them and did the same with his legs. When the chains were fastened, Baas forced him on his knees and pulled his hair back, bringing his head upwards.

It was like suddenly being pushed back into her nightmares. She had seen this scene many times that for a second she thought she was about to wake up and find him by her side. But, the pages of the book had proven the harsh facts. She locked with his tired eyes and his exhausted face pained her heart. Her tears mingled with the pouring rain down her face, almost blinding her.

"What kind of leader are you," Baas said and let go of his hair, looking down at him, "so weak and fragile in front of some pathetic feelings."

Jack's chest heaved up and down with helpless anger, and looked at his enemy a long and disgusted look that was evident under the mud and blood staining his face. He tried to resist the restraining chains.

"There is no way out," Baas said, placing a spear point vertically against his throat. "The game is over."

"This was just a game to you?" Jack said from behind gritted teeth.

"Something like that." He brought the point closer to his skin. "You have no idea how glad I am to finally destroy you."

Jack closed his eyes, expecting the spear to pierce his throat at any moment. Rose wanted to call him, to tell him not to worry and that everything would be just fine. But, even after all that time revising the plan in her head, she was not sure how things would eventually turn out. No matter how her fears pulled her down, she wouldn't turn away from her decision.

"There will be more time for you to close your eyes," Baas said. "Yes, I will not bless you with a smooth death. You will taste every bit of pain as your soul leaves your body." He brought the spear away from his throat and plunged it into his thigh, twisting it deeper into his flesh.

"No!" Rose heard herself say and tried to break free, but the knife sank into her skin, but not deep enough to draw blood. Her grimaced face watched as Jack refused to express his pain, the veins in his neck throbbed out.

Baas stepped over to Rose and held her chin up, pulling her closer to his face. "Go on, heal him," he said. "Let me see this phenomenon."

"Leave her alone!" Jack bellowed from behind Baas.

Rose stared at him with loathing. She perfectly understood what he was trying to do here, but she was not going to let him use her. "I won't," she said.

Baas scrutinized her and brushed a finger on her lips. "You know your part very well. I like it. Yes, you knew that I would have doubled the injuries every time you healed him until you have no energy left. Smart girl."

"Baas!"

The Dark Leader straightened himself back and turned to his prisoner. "Don't be impatient to die, Jack. I know that you feel guilty for dragging her into this. But, you could have saved all of this pain if you had surrendered when you realized your poor position. All of your friends would be living happily now. Mark would have his Rose and she would be safe. Pitiful humans."

"You're wrong!" Rose said. "This was my fate long before I came here. My bloodline bares it."

He glared at her with his white eyes that shined in the darkness like two great moons with a speck of a black dot as a pupil. From the corners of his eyes, Baas looked at the two hooded warriors grasping Jack's chains. One of them stabbed him under his ribs with a knife and blood oozed down his torso, mixing with the rain.

Rose was screaming within herself, but she had to prevent herself from healing him. She must save her energy. All she could do was look at Jack as he crumbled on top of his bent knees, the veins in his neck popped out and his face turned paler. The muddied puddle beside him transformed into a blood pool that shone under the shadow of dawn. His body was slowly draining of blood.

"Rose!" She heard Lilly's voice from somewhere behind her. "Heal him!"

Unable to turn her head around from the knife that did not leave her throat, she casted with the corner of her eyes and saw Lilly. Her face was paler than ever and full of horror.

Baas faced her and took a few steps to where she was standing, dragging the *Ngulu* with him. "How frustrating not to be able to save your little brother."

"I'll kill you, Baas!" Lilly drew out her hands, but Anthony grabbed them down and prevented her from running into Baas.

"The rules, Lilly, the rules," Baas said and glided away. Keeping to his words, Baas pierced Jack again and again until he could no more hold himself up and fell sideways to the ground. Jack opened his bloodshot eyes and locked them with Rose's, the faintest trail of a smile lurked on his cracked lips. His face was pale, and his breathing slowed down. He closed his eyes, and Rose felt him slip away into unconsciousness.

Another spear pierced him, this time it directed right into his heart. Rose tried to shake free, but they still held her down. This was the moment she was waiting for. There was no other way to make this work. Her healing abilities would not be able to save him from this horrifying form from a distance; she must touch him in order for her plan to succeed.

She heard herself scream as Baas raised the Ngulu above his head, ready to decapitate his enemy and put an end to his only destroyer. Before the hooked blade could come down, a spear shot through the air, strengthened by a sudden wave of wind, and sliced off Baas's hands. He roared and stumbled back, the Execution sword thrown away on the ground. Two more spears soared instantly by and struck down Rose's captivators. Once she was free, she crawled over to Jack and held his head into her lap.

"Jack?" She felt for his breathing. There was none. "No!" She put her ears on his chest and listened. A faint heartbeat was still there. She cried with relief and covered the hole in his chest, arousing the Healer within.

The battle boomed around her again; the Niago Siathe was enraged at the unexpected change of events. She glimpsed Lilly and Anthony in combat with Baas, who was unable to sword fight without his hands. She searched for Zane and Mark. But, her eyes were starting to lose their focus as her energy leaked out from her to Jack.

His major wounds were partially healed, but his face was still white as a ghost. Rose concentrated on his chest, waiting for his lungs to take in deeper breaths. To her terror, he was not breathing. Her eyes widened with shock. What if she had miscalculated her plan?

"Rose!" Zane sped to her from between the increasing black smoke. He had someone held over his shoulders. "He's unconscious. Careful, he's deeply injured." Zane laid Mark down beside Rose.

She gasped. Mark had one of the hooded warrior axe jabbed between his shoulder blades. She quickly felt his breathing, keeping a hand on Jack, and sighed with relief when she felt his lungs take deep breaths. His situation was less critical.

Taking in a profound breath, Rose conjured up every ounce of energy within her and transported them to the two young men who had saved her throughout their lives. They had sacrificed a lot for her sake, and now she was paying them back. She was choosing for both of them to live. This was her choice and her plan.

The book had uncovered to her the death sentence for both of them. All she had to do was choose whom to save, and that was what she was doing. If she chose to save only one, she would not be able to live with that dark shadow of endless guilt. Jack was her choice, but Mark was her closest friend. How could she possibly let one live and the other die?

Her head spun with unusual speed, and her heartbeat pounded in her ears. She felt her veins throb as the blood rushed through her weakening body. Fighting to raise her head, she saw the shadows of hooded figures running around in chaos. She caught a glimpse of blonde hair, but was unable to identify what Heidi was doing.

Rose felt herself fall to the ground. Her energy was draining at a rapid rate. She was not sure if she was going to make it. Rose's face was drained from any color and withered under the sun's first rays.

With barely any life left inside her, the Healer within her did not cease to give energy to her most cherished persons. She had planned for this moment, and knew that this was how it would end. She waited for the memories of her life to flash in front of her, but none came. Blackness enveloped her into its pleasant silence, and she waited for the fate she had chosen.

Eighteen: Departure

Several months later...

The day was bright and cold, and the graveyard stood silent and stiff amidst the hustle of the city. She held a bouquet of white roses in her hand as she made her way towards a particular gravestone. With a deep breath, she knelt down in front of it and laid the flowers down. A soft breeze passed through her hair as she said a small prayer. This was a different battlefield, one of souls and memories.

Rose felt his arms wrap around her waist and hugged her from behind.

"She would be proud of you," Jack whispered against her ear and met her eyes.

Her smile was radiant. "We did save the world, after all."

"You saved us all."

His lips met hers in a tender kiss.

Rose, in her pink wool dress, buried herself in Jack's arms, soothed by the warmth of his overcoat. She smiled upon feeling a shudder run down his spine, his tropical body was still adjusting to London's weather. Although he was still the wild young man who once knew how to fly, his trimmed mane and clean shave brought out a different side to him. A side that Rose was still exploring. They stood in each other's arms for a while in front of Elizabeth Peterson's grave until Rose's phone rang inside her pocket.

"It's time to go," she said and walked with Jack to the taxi station. "They're all waiting for us at the restaurant."

When they got inside the car, Jack shuddered and pulled her closer. "So cold in London."

Rose grinned and held him tighter. "It's not even winter yet, Jack. Just wait until you see snow."

The car stopped and they stood out in front of the restaurant where they all agreed to meet before their paths were to part. Jack pushed the door open and they walked over to the longest table in the place. Their friends faces smiled up at them as greetings were exchanged.

"The future bride and groom are finally here," Anthony said, sitting beside Lilly who looked beautiful in her leather pants and dark jacket that matched with Anthony, both their bike helmets tucked under the table. Rose admired how they both pursued their love for the highroads and camping life.

"Did you decide on a date?" Mark asked from across the table, his arm casually wrapped around Heidi's shoulders.

"No," Rose said and sat beside Zane. "Maybe sometime next year."

"There is no rush," Jack said, meeting her eyes with a smile. "We've got all the time in the world now." Rose felt his hand hold hers from under the table.

"Cheers to that," Zane said and held up his glass. "To...?"

"Freedom." Jack finished his sentence and they all drank to the fact that they could breathe and move again without having to fear the shadows.

Her smile grew as she surveyed her friends eating and drinking with nothing to worry them except for which next flight they would board. She took in a deep breath, filling her lungs with the happiness around her. They had come a long way, and after everything, it made them stronger than before. Nara had gifted them with a magical role, and they all knew their time was up among its mystical jungles. With their glory, their powers were taken away. The necklace now stored their powers for the generations to come.

"I have a confession," Jack said, leaning into her ear. "I used to see a little girl in my dreams, standing between the trees. I kept reaching out for her, but never could get any closer to her."

Rose raised her eyebrows, surprised by his sudden memory. "I think that was me... because I saw a little boy reaching out for me from the first day I set foot in Nara."

His smile grew. "Written in the stars, it seems." He came closer and kissed her lips. "I do have one other confession." He breathed against her lips. "Rose Peterson, I can't stay away from you."

Her cheeks turned pink and she lightly pushed him away. "Jack Casper, how dare you make me blush in public." She paused and glanced behind him. "You better stop because my father is heading over here right now."

Jack straightened himself up and greeted Bill with a firm handshake.

"Good day, warriors," Bill said and seated himself at the top of the table. His eyes turned to his daughter and smiled widely. "Looking as radiant as ever, my dear. So, are you excited for your trip?"

"Of course," Rose said. "We can't wait to tour around France before settling back in London."

"Well, I want you two to enjoy it after everything you've been through. It's my gift for well, saving us all!" Bill laughed and drank his glass.

The hours passed as the Blue Water members talked and laughed, sharing their future plans. Mark and Heidi had decided to open a business together, Zane started at parkour and it was gradually turning into a profession, and the biker couple preferred life unplanned. After their stomachs and hearts were full, Mark drove Jack and Rose to the airport.

"Take care you two," Mark said, leaning against his car with half a smile on his face.

"You too, Mark," Rose said and pulled him into a tight hug. "I love you." She felt his arms tighten and his smile grew wider.

"Yeah, me too, Rose," he said and released her from his arms. "Let me know when you two are back, yeah?"

Jack nodded with a smile. "Of course, we will."

With their hands entwined, the Healer and the Leader entered the airport. Even though they no longer had their powers nor the ability to soar through the air, they were ready to embark on their next adventure and take advantage of every single day they were able to be together. After all, life was about the journey, and love was freedom.